THE TECHNOLOGY
OF REVENGE

Jason said, conversationally, "Your left arms are numb, Alecko, from the elbows down."

His security forces started forward. "Halt," she said, and they stopped. Some of them glanced at each other, nervously. "Retreat. Regroup," she said, and they did.

Alecko's father was sweating. "Don't, Captain. Please."

She glanced at him. "Do you remember when I pleaded with you, Dhimitri?

"I described to a doctor what you'd done to Bear Vouris," she continued, "and how it felt to me, while I was linked in the Net. He said you'd inflicted a condition known as 'odynacusis'—a big word which means 'painful hearing.' This is what it feels like."

Alecko screamed. . . .

THE NET

LOREN J. MacGREGOR

ACE SCIENCE FICTION BOOKS
NEW YORK

This book is an Ace Science
Fiction original edition, and
has never been previously
published.

THE NET

An Ace Science Fiction Book / published by arrangement with
the author

PRINTING HISTORY
Ace Science Fiction edition / June 1987

ISBN: 0-441-56941-2

Ace Science Fiction Books are published by The Berkley Publishing Group,
200 Madison Avenue, New York, New York 10016.
PRINTED IN THE UNITED STATES OF AMERICA

ACKNOWLEDGMENTS

Brandy Leigh and Camilla Decarnin read an earlier draft, and many of the book's current virtues I owe to their necessary and necessarily harsh criticism; Doug Faunt and Rich Dutcher both gave me access to computers, without which this book wouldn't have been written at all; Jane Hawkins provided more than moral support, when I needed it most; Dave Hartwell gave me some of the most valuable advice I've ever received from an editor: "Don't reject your own work. Let me reject it"; and special thanks to Terry Carr (obviously!), and Ginjer Buchanan, who did an amazing job of following my moebius-strip manuscript.

To Gerard Donald MacGregor
and to the memory
of Marietta Wright MacGregor

INTRODUCTION

by Terry Carr

Like all of the books in the New Ace Science Fiction Specials series, *The Net* is a first novel—but this one is a bit more "first" than that, for it's the first piece of fiction ever published by Loren J. MacGregor. All of the previous novelists in this series had published a number of science fiction short stories, and had thus begun to establish their names among the readers of sf magazines, but even if you've been a regular reader of those magazines you won't have heard of MacGregor.

All of which means you have a surprising treat in your hands.

Loren MacGregor is thirty-seven; he was born in mid-July 1950 in Seattle, Washington, of Scots, Irish, and Welsh background. His mother's family was among the early settlers in Canada; his paternal grandfather was a ship's captain in the Pacific who (1) once saved a boatload of Japanese (including some of the royal family) from capsizing in mid-ocean, and (2) once swam ashore from a burning ship, carrying a case of Panama hats.

"In my mother's lifetime she never once that I recall praised a piece of my writing," MacGregor says; "but on birthdays and at Christmas, her presents to me were reams of paper, typewriter ribbons: she supported me in a way that was subtler and stronger than praise."

MacGregor was raised in the state of Washington, and after

high school took courses hither and yon for years, "and always panicked just short of actually getting a degree." Most recently he's studied Greek, and is slowly but surely working towards his own translation of *The Iliad*. He's also worked as a carpenter and finisher in Ohio "during the storms that leveled Xenia, my first experience with tornadoes," and has done housecleaning and gardening. He was a theater projectionist, worked as an EKG technician, picked fruits and vegetables one summer ("I don't recommend it"), and acted at the Cirque Theatre and with the APT Players in Seattle for a season. He once had ambitions to be a cartoonist (a surprising number of sf writers began their creative lives that way), and later worked in hospital emergency rooms, coronary and intensive care units.

He discovered science fiction in library books by Wells and Heinlein. In grade school, he wrote his first science fiction story: "It was about alien cats who destroyed the brains of Earth's top scientists, to keep Earth from becoming any more advanced. I don't know yet whether the cats were the heroes or the villains." When he was in the ninth grade, he wrote a novel about "Johnny Sol, Son of the Sun."

In 1979, "tired of what passed for literary criticism in the Pacific Northwest," he founded with John D. Berry *The Pacific Northwest Review of Books*, a fine magazine that died of too little financing; MacGregor himself lost money on the venture. Afterward, he moved to San Francisco, where he currently works for a law firm.

You'll see some of the above experiences and interests reflected in this novel. *The Net* can perhaps most easily be classified as a "space opera," one of the oldest forms of science fiction, but MacGregor brings to the form contemporary nuances of style and characterization. His protagonist, Jason, is especially well-drawn; but so are secondary characters such as Bear, Lys, Lynch, and the antagonist, Alecko Papandreou. "Space opera" used to denote stories of heroic adventures in space, with little else to offer; in this book we not only have deeper characterization but also more awareness of the social mores of the planet and the galaxy that surrounds it. Which makes the novel a much more satisfying tale.

Enjoyment, after all, is the measure of any kind of fiction. I think you'll enjoy *The Net*, and I'm happy to present it to you.

— 1

JASON

THE LARGER MOON showed through a gap in the clouds. Jason looked up, sighed, and scowled. Water ran down her neck, inside the leather, soaking her shirt, her left waterproof boot leaked along the inseam, and each time she stepped it made a sound like an oar pulled through mud. Her pants were sticking to her thighs, her shirt to her breasts and stomach.

A beggar approached, hesitated, and for the third time retreated. This time something triggered her memory. She looked past the bad teeth and ragged beard, the shambling walk and poor posture. "Robinson. You've changed."

His clothes might have been brown; it was hard to tell. He sloshed across the road. An old knit hat was pulled low over his ears, and under the shapeless overcoat he was thin to the point of emaciation. When he spoke, his voice was curiously hesitant, as though he had to search for each word, as if each thought had to travel some distance before he could say it. He stood, hands jammed in his pockets, and bowed, as he had done years before, during the time they'd sailed together. (She'd been newly captain then, acting only, while the *Lin*'s captain had recovered from pneumonia.)

"Captain Horiuchi. I wondered if you'd recognize me. *You* haven't changed at all, though. Except for this." He quite suddenly ran the ball of his thumb down her jaw, from the corner of her right eye to her chin. As suddenly he stepped back again.

"I've got a scar like that, on my thigh." Robinson patted his leg. "Mine came from a broken bottle." He sat down on the wet pavement, his back against a store window. "I forgot how much you liked to walk, Captain. If I'd'a remembered, I might not have been up there waiting for you."

Jason hunkered down on the heels of her solid black boots, setting her back pack carefully to one side. "Why were you?" A transit bus glided by, silent on its cushion of air. Behind them, light from a hologrammatic display in a clothing store window splashed onto the wet pavement and rippled in hypnotic coils.

Robinson scrabbled in his pocket and found a cigarette and a soggy cardboard folder. "Thinking about old times, maybe. Good times, not like now. I haven't had the breaks, Captain, not like you." He pulled a match from the folder and tried to light it. The cardboard gave way instead. "Shit." He threw the match and matchbook into the street and watched as they floated away. "I heard you were coming in, from some kid in a bar." His lips stretched back from his teeth. "He extorts money from me, when I've got it. Sometimes he even gives me some. It makes him feel big, I guess."

"You let him steal from you?"

"It's not worth a fight, Captain," She thought for a moment that he'd gone to sleep, but he started to recite in the oratical style he'd played bit parts in the *Mya Lin*'s theatrical productions. "'Visit Moulinos, garden spot of New Crete. Moulinos has mild winters and hot, dry summers. The rainy season typically lasts thirty days, leaving four hundred thirty sunny days each year.' That's from a brochure. Sometimes I get drachmas from tourists because I can quote the damn thing.

"Anyway. Tonight the man, he says, 'That woman you're always bragging about? Your ex-captain—if you're not lying. She's downporting tonight. You know her so well, you ask her on out so we can meet her.' Then he laughed, you know, like he'd said something funny. But I checked with Port and he was right, so I watched your landing, and waited. That's a pretty ship you've got, Captain; better than the *Lin*."

"The *Lin* wasn't mine. I designed every inch of the *Argo*."

Robinson had pulled a flat bottle from his overcoat. He offered it to Jason. She shook her head. "That's right, you never did drink much." He twisted the cap and took a sip and, immediately, a deeper swallow. For a moment he shut his eyes. He shivered, shook his head, held the bottle up to the light, replaced the cap, and slid the bottle out of sight, back into a deep pocket. "It sure keeps you warm on a night like this. You here to see your brother?"

"Michael? Yes. Jaime and Jessie, too. His sons. They weren't born yet when Michael moved here. I haven't seen Jaime in person since he was four, and I haven't met Jessie at all."

"Hard to believe he's your brother. That red hair he's got could stop traffic throughout the Core. And that cut on your face makes you look more like a samurai than ever." Robinson rested his hands on one soggy pants-covered knee. "He doesn't look any older, either, Captain. You know what? I think it's that thing you got in your neck, back here." He pressed the palm of one hand against the base of his skull.

"It may have helped some," she said. "That and good genes." She eased back onto her heels. "Michael's my quad-brother. He's collaterally linked, but there's no straight blood tie. If we both age well, it's more or less an accident." She looked at her watch. "I have to leave soon. I've got an appointment tonight."

"I remember a couple of things about you, Captain," Robinson said, "from when we sailed together. One's that you like to be warm and dry. Must have taken something pretty important to get you out on a night like this."

"It wasn't raining when I started. But you're right; I'm meeting someone tonight, and it *is* important. Do you know Alecko Papandreou?"

"Know *him*? He wouldn't exactly take high tea with me, Captain. I 'met' him once. He ignored me." Robinson stopped to consider. "No, it was more like I wasn't there for him at all, until I grabbed his arm. He noticed me then, by God! It was a hot day and he must have built up a hell of a static charge, because I got a shock that nearly knocked me flat on my ass. He *owns* this city, Captain; his father does, anyway. I thought, shit, I'm going to be thrown in the can; but he just stood there rubbing one arm with the other three, and after a while he said, 'I'll remember you. Don't ever do that again,' and walked off. That's it: my big encounter with fame and fortune."

"You still know more about him directly than I do," Jason

said. "I've met Dhimitri Papandreou, but not Alecko. All our business has been done by hologram transmission."

Robinson was very drunk. It took him a minute to stand but he managed. "I've got to go, Captain. I live in a rooming house. They'll close the doors on me if I'm not back by curfew. Good night."

Jason picked up her pack and shouldered it. "I'll only be in port for a few days. Come up to the ship and see me. Bear's there, too."

"I will. And . . . Captain?" She had started to walk away; now she turned. He had his hand out. "Spare change?"

"No," she said. "You should get home, not to another bar. Good night, Robinson."

"I should," he said, and laughed. "But I won't."

Listing, he left. Jason rubbed her neck. The cold weather pulled the skin tight around the spinal socket, and even the scar down the side of her face hurt. The fold of her eye itched, too. Damn. She hated being cold. Why the hell had she agreed to meet Papandreou tonight, of all nights?

The answer was simple: she controlled Horiuchi, Pte. (pronounced, when she was in a fey mood, *pity*), the largest privately owned group of companies in the web of civilization that spread out from the Core at Metacenter. And Papandreou et Cie was Horiuchi's closest rival, in nearly everything from heavy metals to housewares. In many cases it was an amicable rivalry, but in some areas the competition was intense and bitter.

Yet Dhimitri Papandreou ran the company, and it was his son Alecko who'd set up tonight's meeting. It might mean nothing; it might mean Alecko was angling to take control from his father.

So she'd agreed to the meeting. Hell, why not? She hadn't increased her fortune by avoiding risks! And so Jason Horiuchi, chief executive officer of Horiuchi, Pte., had set out from the *Argo*—her flagship and part-time trading vessel—into the tropical night of Moulinos. And then it had started to rain.

It couldn't be helped now; she couldn't get any wetter. She pulled out her map. A slight phosphorescent pulse elongated and became a tracery snaking through the streets. In a moment there were two pulses connected by a line of green light: her location and that of Papandreou's bar. With a shrug, she loosened the straps of her pack and drew forth a thin wire tipped

with a silver probe. Pushing aside her club of black hair, she
slipped the probe into the socket at the base of her skull. With
a quick hunch of her shoulders she snapped the connection
into place. The action sent a message to the ship: Vector, on
duty, echoed back a terse «Yes, Captain?»

«I'm almost there, Lys. Who's on watch?»

«Denny's available if you need her, Jason. Kenot's said he
expects to be out tonight, and I assume M'orru will go with
him.» Lys hesitated. «That's about it. I can notify Kenot and
M'orru to stand by, if you insist.»

Jason grinned. She knew how reluctant Lys was to talk to
either of them. It caused friction on board, but sometimes
Jason *liked* friction; it made things more interesting. To Lys
she said, «Not necessary, although you might ask them to
leave word where they can be found. I don't even think I'll
need Denny, but I'd feel more comfortable if I had someone
within hailing distance.»

It was hard to get much emotion through the mandibular
microphone, which tended to strip any nuance from a transmission, but Lys managed. «If you hadn't fired our Sight, our
Sound wouldn't have quit; and you'd have your backup with
some to spare.»

«If I hadn't fired Klaus I wouldn't need a backup; I
wouldn't have a ship. He's already sold everything that wasn't
tied down. He would have sold the *Argo* if he could have
managed it. From now on the only drugs on board will be
those Kenot cooks up in his lab!»

«Nice trick if you can do it, Jason. Do we start with your
bottle of Blue Ice? I'll send Denny. Lys out.»

The Beehive ended abruptly as though someone had drawn
a line and said, "Beyond this point financiers shall not pass."
Jason walked through alleys where milk-colored walls alter-
nated with light pastels, mostly eggshell blue or rose. Occasionally the lights of streets and stars were cut off as she
passed under a low bridge between two houses.

Kenicki's was housed in a large building garishly painted in
bright greens, reds, and oranges. A sign in a facing window
claimed it was a "Cafe and Bar"; bright neon signs in several
colors advertised various brands of alcohol, most of which
were unfamiliar. Inside, crowded tables—some on force plat-
forms, some more sensibly resting on the barroom floor—
were steeped in a haze of smoke and sound. On one wall were

the heads of three large horned animals; on each horn of each head hung hats of varying ages and disreputability. Street signs in various languages pointed the way to odd corners of the bar. With delight Jason saw a sign pointing to Beaver Street; she'd lived on Beaver Street when she was young, before the rising tide had buried San Francisco.

She stepped aside to avoid an unsteady woman who was heading with determination but little skill toward the door. At the rear of the bar a short flight of stairs led down to a tiny dance floor with small wooden tables scattered around, while a longer flight led to a darkened alcove, inconspicuous, from which it was possible to keep the rest of the bar in view. That seemed promising, so she made her way patiently through the throng of people and on up the stairs.

Although there were a few tables and chairs scattered around, the balcony was deserted. She took the largest of three tables and settled into place. Almost immediately a bar tray flew up and hovered discreetly. Jason took out a credit card and nudged it into the slightly recessed slot on the tray, held her hand over its scanner, and waited while information was relayed to the bar computer. After a moment the tray said, "Thank you. Please take your card. Your credit limit is . . ." and there was another pause, followed by a reverent " . . . unlimited." As it damn well should be, she thought, and ordered Blue Ice. She felt mildly guilty, but what the hell; it was only *slightly* narcotic—nothing like the cocktails Klaus had cooked up for himself—and it looked beautiful in a glass, like a summer sky on Earth.

Thinking of Lys reminded her. She triggered the cervical transmitter and called the ship once again.

«Lys? I want to review Alecko's file again before he arrives. Not the whole thing; just the highlights I've marked.»

She slumped in the chair with her black boots stretched out before her, her hands jammed into the pockets of her black denims. Papandreou. She hoped to hell they wouldn't fight again. But Alecko Papandreou was too pretty, too arrogant, and too ambitious to negotiate reasonably.

Lys interrupted. «I'm still editing the file, Jason, but while you were waiting I thought you might appreciate a chance to orient yourself.» Without waiting for an answer, Lys began to build a three-dimensional model of *Kenicki*'s at her terminal on the *Argo*. Jason chuckled. Lys seized upon any excuse to build her models; she was fascinated by the architecture of cities, and Jason knew that by the time they shipped out Lys would have plans drawn for most of the city. Still, she closed her eyes and concentrated on the building schema because, no matter what reasons Lys might have for creating them, they were invaluable guides. Lys had never been content to simply draw the buildings themselves but, using her extensive knowledge of computers and her own experiences in cargo lading, often was able to pinpoint with startling accuracy not only the structure of warehouses and storage bins, but the amount of material they contained and where it was stored. It had helped Jason more than once when she'd had to get out of a tight spot quickly.

As her model grew, Lys explained. «You're the blinking blue light. Customers are bright yellow, human staff amber. Denny's there now; when I locate her the light should change from yellow to blinking green. That's got it.» Two steady yellow lights suddenly turned green and started to blink; but a third green light formed outside the confines of the model; each blink brought it a tiny bit closer to the entrance to the bar.

«Three?» Jason asked. «Denny must be here; who else?»

Lys laughed. «Denny's brought someone she wants you to meet; she wants you to hire him. The third one's a surprise I've been saving for you.»

Jason nodded. She studied the bar, reconciling what she saw with Lys's model, rapidly nearing completion. From where she was sitting she could see a door off the right side of a small stage. Apparently it led out through a warehouse and into an open-ended alley. That was good. She liked to be able to leave a place fast if she chose. If trouble erupted she'd be able to vault down from the balcony and onto the stage, and be out the door before anyone noticed.

«You're assuming I'm going to hire Denny's friend?»

«Don't you always? Of course, they always work out well, for a while. Trouble is, they never stay for more than a trip or two. Remember the one before last, who got arrested for stealing the yacht?»

Jason laughed. «*But I only meant to borrow it for a while; I din't mean to steal it, honest I din't. But it was a lot easier takin' it out then it was bringin' it back. So I just headed for the harbor and tried to hit somepin soft.*» He was a good crew member, though; good time sense. Too bad he was arrested.» She sighed and added, «I hope this one's a Sight; otherwise we'll be flying blind. Okay, that's two. What's my surprise, then?»

«Don't be impatient. First, Alecko's file. This is the first chance I've had to look through it. He's quite the boy, isn't he?» Jason agreed. Papandreou was in his middle thirties now, standard calendar, but at thirteen he'd slipped away from school and used some of the Papandreou fortune to check himself into a modification clinic, where he'd gotten himself two extra arms. «I bet he's got one hell of a tailor's bill,» Lys commented. «Can you imagine the stress factors for the lower arm seams?»

Lys transmitted the file; Jason closed her eyes to aid the visual imprint and flipped through it quickly, stopping at a picture of a young, handsome Alecko Papandreou standing in front of an impressive marble facade. He was dressed in tie and tails, starched shirt cut across with a brilliant scarlet sash; opening night at the opera or symphony. Lys's voice was dry as she said, «When you're done with him, save something for me.»

Jason skipped the CDC's psyche profile; it was probably no more accurate than her own. CDC sent out its ubiquitous 3Vs to every event likely to draw people of interest and recorded everyone with any degree of notoriety, under the theory that if any public person was watched long enough, a private persona would show through and the profile would, eventually, come close to accuracy. She pulled her own file periodically, for amusement.

There was nothing particularly helpful; she hadn't expected there would be. Lys replaced the file and said, «Now. Look toward the entrance.» Jason tilted her chair back for a clear view and saw a tall, stocky woman below, her back, shoulders, and arms covered with a thick brown pelt, now shedding water on the barroom floor. Bear! Her clothes were sodden with rain (Jason felt her own wet denim ruefully), and as soon as she entered she bellowed in a deep bass which carried with remarkable clarity throughout the bar. "I'm *wet!* I'm shedding *all over* your goddamn floor! Get me a towel, quick!"

Jason was still out of sight in the shadows, and she leaned against the wall, arms crossed, watching. Bear was always worth watching. Now she was wearing bright yellow pantaloons that normally would bloom out in jaunty bags from the tight fabric at her thighs to the string closure at her ankles, but now the fabric draped sullenly. A brown leather vest, covered with a filigree of fine red, yellow, and white beadwork, was laced loosely and through its gaps it was possible to see where her pelt gave way to bare skin on her breasts and abdomen, leaving a curiously piebald effect. She shook herself like a dog and a shower of water sprayed everyone nearby.

The bartender left a series of drinks floating in midair to find an incongruous bar rag, a fluffy white towel the size of a beach blanket, which she tossed to the woman. Bear removed her vest and began vigorously to dry her wet fur; several people in the crowd, interested, looked as though they'd like to help.

Jason could make herself heard when she needed to, though she didn't have Bear's ability to project. She moved down two steps until she was framed in the light and shouted, "Hey, lady? Buy a sailor a drink?" Bear looked up, waved, gestured to the people around her, shrugged, smiled, and pushed her way across the crowded floor. She cleared the steps three at a time, whooped when she reached the platform, pulled Jason up for a crushing hug, released her, frowned, reached for a chair, and sat down.

"Christ, Jason, it's good to see you! I called the ship and Lys said you were here. You need someone to Sound?" Exuberantly, she spread her arms wide, tapped a serving tray, looked back to see what she'd hit, laughed, and said, "Vodka." The tray skittered away. "Well, I'm your woman. I've just spent three years kicking ass on Calyx, and I'm in the mood for a change." She looked after the serving tray. "Those things are convenient, I suppose, but they've got the best bartender I've ever seen below. She's terrific—telekinetic! Did you see her when I came in? Mixing a row of drinks in midair, bottles and everything! I came in once and she had a display lined up all along the bar: whiskey in spheres, baby drinks like Tequila Sunrises in cylinders; she even had one drink floating in a square. I wonder what the hell it was," she mused.

Jason thought: I put up with this for several years when she was younger. I wonder how I did it? "Don't you *ever* slow down? Damn it, Bear, I never know where you're going to turn up next. What the hell were you doing on Calyx, anyway?"

Bear quieted. Slightly. "Fighting," she said simply. Bear

hunched forward in her chair, holding her glass in two hands between her knees. "I was a mercenary for the Niarin during their war with Hasiq. Both the Hasiqi and the Niarin had exhausted their own troops, but they kept hiring soldiers on a contingency basis long after anyone else would have given up."

"They had a lot to fight for, Bear. You know I tried to acquire the mining rights on Calyx? I didn't get them, but it would have been worth it if I had—and well worth fighting for."

"We're going to disagree on that until we die, Jason. Fighting to save lives I can understand; fighting to save mineral rights strikes me as horrible. I'll do it, and do it well, because that's what they pay me for; but I don't have to like it.

"And I knew it was time to get out when the Niarin captured some kids, half of them under thirteen, the rest not much older. They were the remains of a local fighting force, privately trained—if you could call it training. The Hasiqi refused to ransom them, claiming they should have fought to the death, so the Niarin turned them loose. No food, no supplies. The Niarin kept their kits—'spoils of war.' I tried to help them; so did a few others. But we were ordered to stop.

"As to why Johnny went for soldier in the *first* place . . ." Her mood changed abruptly and she grinned. She wasn't conventionally attractive—her face was too broad, and her nose, what there was of it, had been broken more than once—yet her moon face was so obviously informed by good humor that people were carried away by her exuberance. She kept her brown hair short and shaggy, except where she'd tried to blend it with the fur on her back. The texture of the two was completely different, and the experiment was pretty much a failure; but she liked it, and clung to the effect stubbornly. She'd evidently had her hair in a military brush cut, which only now was beginning to grow back, and now it curled in disarray around her ears.

"Well, the Net's changing, and I thought it was a good time to learn some new things. The army's a good place to do it; I have someone to wake me up, tell me to sleep, and tell me to learn what I have to learn or get slapped in brig. Discipline, that's what *I* need." Her laugh was loud and boisterous. "And if someone's throwing a Net, I want to be part of the toss, not part of the catch. Besides"—defensively— "I *like* Sound.

Which reminds me: what are *you* doing here? It's not your kind of place. *I* like it." She looked around with obvious approval.

Jason hesitated a moment. "I'm being tested again, Bear. 'Does she have the stamina for the job?' You'd think after four decades people'd accept the fact that I'm not going to run Horiuchi into the ground. Wouldn't you?"

On the dance floor, two young men, arms around each other's waists, were facing a color wheel. One held a coin; the other kept shaking his head. Another tray floated by. Bear finished her drink and ordered another before she answered. "They did the same to your father, Jason. Wishful thinking. That's a big hunk of business you've got, bigger than most countries; more profitable than many planets. A lot of people would like to see you fail."

Jason sighed. "True. And they're probably convinced it will fail now because of the way I run it. Damn it, I *can't* sit in an office like Osamu did! I have to get out, check on my holdings. That's why I bought the *Argo,* and the ships before her." Momentarily, she closed her eyes. "Osamu never agreed with me on the need. I had to buy my first ship with my own money. After that he let me do what I wanted—not that it would have made much difference if he'd objected. He didn't give me the business. I took it."

"As I'm going to take my father's." He was more handsome in person, and self-assured: Alecko Papandreou stepped up from the stairway onto the balcony, and used two of his four hands to correct the perfect line of his jacket. His thin, almost triangular face was the color of an olive not yet ripe, and his aquiline nose was framed between two high cheekbones and broad black eyebrows. His black curly hair was so glossy it seemed oiled. He was carrying a lemon-colored linen jacket and wore a well-tailored, flowing white shirt, tight at the shoulders and down the four arms, widening into puffed, pleated sleeves and caught at each wrist by four filigreed silver buttons. Oddly, in a man with such dark hair, he had no discernible beard; his chest, visible through the wide v-neck of his shirt, was smooth and hairless.

They were reacting to each other like cats. Papandreou was stiff and hostile; Jason seemed relaxed, but Bear noticed the ball of her thumb rubbing casually down the line of her jaw, and recognized an old sign of inner tension. Her hazel eyes were alert. "We've had no success dealing before," she said abruptly. "What's different now?"

He looked at Bear. "I asked you to meet me alone, Captain Horiuchi. I am *not* pleased."

Jason shrugged. "I didn't ask Bear, but she's here now and I won't ask her to leave." With the trace of a smile (which seemed to irritate Papandreou even further), she said, "For that matter I prefer to have witnesses when I talk with you."

Alecko had ordered, and a bar tray floated by bearing a silver coffee service. Papandreou took a cup and poured coffee with one hand, spooned sugar with a second (from a silver cup held in his fourth hand), and cream with a third. He set down the coffee, sugar, spoon, and creamer and drank. It was an impressive performance, and despite her hostility Jason wondered what *else* he could do with those hands.

He set down his coffee, looked up, and grinned boyishly. "Quite a lot, actually."

Jason flushed, and Bear looked back and forth between the two of them. "Now what the hell is *that* all about?" she asked curiously.

Jason replied carefully, "There is a persistent rumor that Dhimitri Papandreou's son is a telepath. Now he's trying to prove it."

Alecko brushed two hands through curly tangled black hair. "Sorry . . . Bear?"

Bear grinned wolfishly and nodded. "But you can call me Kyria Vouris."

He bowed. "Kyria Vouris. *Hehro poli.* But if I'm rude, you must excuse me. I dislike talking in public. Rumors spread in a city like this. If I were to whisper now that I like young boys, in three days the mayor would ask me how young, and don't I know there're laws against that sort of thing?"

Bear muttered, "Oh, good Christ," in a voice that conveyed a world of disgust. She jabbed a stubby forefinger in Papandreou's face. "You. Have you got something to say? Because I've got better things to do than sit here and listen to you hypnotize yourself with the sound of your own voice." She crossed one leg over the other, folded her arms across her chest, and tilted her chair back, daring him to answer.

Jason thought, Good for you, Bear.

Papandreou's reaction was predictably hostile. He glared at

them both, and Jason suspected that he was sipping his coffee because he was too angry to speak. But now he said, "I don't like you, Captain. I think my father has been too soft on you, and if I were running the Papandreou we would not be in competition. I would drive you into bankruptcy if I could. I am also a businessman, though; and I am a sportsman, too—sometimes. So I have a sporting proposition for you." He steepled the fingers of two hands, holding his coffee cup in one hand, his saucer in the other. "I have been following your history, Captain, and I now know a great deal about you. Your Second is very efficient, but if one has money it is easy to manipulate the CDC for information." Papandreou set his cup and saucer delicately on the table and leaned forward. "You're a thief," he said bluntly. "Certainly not a common thief; certainly a successful one. If Metacenter ever thought to correlate all of its information, as I have, they would find out where many famous gems may now be found. It's fortunate for you that the CDC is simply a depository of knowledge and not a police service. I think you wouldn't last long as chief executive of Horiuchi if all this were generally known."

Jason said, "Come to the point." She might have been asking an opinion on the weather.

Papandreou raised an eyebrow. "Am I boring you? I'm sorry." He reached into the pocket of his linen jacket and brought out a chased silver case, pausing with conscious drama while he went through the ritual of lighting a cigarette. "My proposal is simple. You know the Museion ton Papandreou. Your brother has exhibited there, I understand?" She nodded reluctantly. He smiled. "And you also know my father collects gemstones for their histories. It's an obsession you two share and I do not. I think it's absurd to waste your time on jewelry when you can make a better emerald or diamond in any competent laboratory."

He paused again. "*I* designed the security for the Papandreou. I know there's one stone in the museum you want desperately, God knows why. You may have heard about it: in 1796 standard calendar, Catherine II of a country known as Russia died, and much of her estate disappeared. Among the missing items was a ruby, given to Catherine by Gustavus III, a Swedish king. It's about the size of a large bird's egg, clear red throughout, and flawless. My father found it and had it authenticated. If you come to the museum, I can show it to you." Jason had never seen an artificial stone to compare with the natural rubies she'd owned over the years. And this one had a bloody history to go with it: perfect! Papandreou looked up at her and his eyes were challenging. "If you can steal it you can have it; and I'll agree to withdraw from any businesses we hold in common between our companies."

Jason said, *"If* you can withdraw without creating havoc and thereby interfering with the value of the business left to me."

"If I can withdraw without havoc, yes. We can work out details later that will be satisfactory."

Jason sipped her Blue Ice and decided not to have another. The first had made her tipsy, and the effect would wear off soon; but she didn't want to be even slightly intoxicated during this conversation. "There's no way we can memorialize this agreement. You realize that."

He nodded. "I realize that. But, as I've said, I read up on you. I believe I can trust your word." He was very near to laughing at her, Jason realized, and wondered where his level of secret amusement was coming from. "And I suppose you'll just have to trust me as well."

Jason tried to recall the levels of competition between Horiuchi and Papandreou, and to work out the potential increases in profits if Horiuchi had a clear field in any of them. The mathematics were too complicated, though, and she gave up. "That's what I'll get if I win; what happens if I fail?"

He said, wonderingly, "You aren't even outraged that I've called you a thief. My father would have anyone who suggested such a thing publicly whipped." He shrugged. "It makes no difference. If you fail we make the same deal, only you withdraw and my family has free reign—with the understanding that if you don't pull out within what I consider to be a reasonable time, I'll release all the data I've assembled to the media. Including the story of your arrest following your unsuccessful burglary of my family's museum."

Jason laughed then. "You're too goddamn sure of yourself, Papandreou."

He was eager: "Does that mean you'll do it?"

She laughed again. "You won't know until I leave New Crete, with or without the ruby." And then, because she had her own level of arrogance, she added, "There's not a security system made anywhere that I can't outmaneuver."

They talked a very short while longer, but it was evident to them both that everything they needed to say had been said, and that they'd only irritate each other if they continued to talk. But Jason, curious, finally couldn't resist asking. "I've dealt with your father for years, since your grandmother died and he bought into the business. I've always found him ruthless but charming. Why do you dislike him so much?"

He said, "Those calluses disfigure your hand. They're ugly. You really should see a dermatologist."

She looked at the fingers of her left hand, curled around her drink. Through the clear blue liquid the callus pads were distorted, enlarged. Jason didn't think they were ugly. She'd worked hard to get them. She shrugged. "I play guitar. It's a price I pay. I asked you a question."

The angles cut by the tip of his ear, the edge of his cheek-bone, the point of his jaw formed a triangle which now seemed flat and hard. "I am thirty-five years old—your years, *kyria*. My father is over seventy. He is . . . difficult. If you wish, I'll show you a bit of what he's like. Both of you: hold onto my hands for a moment."

Bear looked at Jason. Jason shrugged and reached forward. She felt her hand slip into Papandreou's, and then she was . . . somewhere else, where sun blazed down on a wide, shady veranda. An empty glass sat beside her on a low ceramic table, white, with an inlay of blue and yellow flowers, and her tongue tasted the smoky flavor of a strongly resinated wine. Across the table sat an aging man whose leathery skin was bleached to the shade of old red brick. His nappy hair, gray-ing, framed a square, solid face with incongruous azure eyes. When he stood, she saw a pendulous belly. "The rest of the field is ready, *kyrie*. Shall we race?"

She took her time answering. The sun was warm on her skin, and she was enjoying the slight breeze from the ocean. "You're too impatient, Yiorgio," she said in a pleasant bari-tone. "The race can wait a few moments. Enjoy the sun! Have Irena fetch you another drink." She followed her own sugges-tion and pressed a small button inset in the edge of the table. A young woman walked out through the terrace door, her low heels clicking against the terra-cotta tiles. Jason watched her as she stood, blinking in the strong afternoon light. The woman was wearing a light, almost transparent cotton dress, and Jason felt an agreeable stirring in her genitals as she stared at the woman's prominent nipples in their wide aureolae and at the dark triangle of her groin. She reached down and adjusted her penis before settling back comfortably in her chair.

The woman had a voice like the wine, filled with smoke. "Yes, Dhimitri?"

"I'll have another drink, Irena, and fetch one for Yiorgio as well." From under narrowed lids Jason watched Yiorgio's left hand slowly clasp and unclasp, and she watched him blink slowly, like a lizard.

"I'm partial to raki," Yiorgio said finally. "My family drank it years ago, back home." He patted his stomach. "Of course, my health is not what it was when we were both younger, so I cannot have as much as I'd like. But today— yes. I'll have raki. *Tesekkür ederim!*"

Jason recognized Yiorgio's use of Turkish as an attempt to provoke a response, but she only continued to smile lazily, and didn't stir from her chair. Irena nodded and returned to the house.

Yiorgio stood to look out over the porch railing toward the celadon water. "The view from this terrace is good. I wish my own home were so well situated."

The young woman returned with two tall glasses. As she set them down, Jason reached out and cupped her right breast, rolling the nipple between thumb and forefinger. Even then the woman didn't look up, but waited until Jason released her breast. Then she bowed, eyes averted, and left the patio.

"You say the horses are ready?" Yiorgio nodded. "Good. Begin." She set her drink on the small table and closed her eyes. The comfortable lounge chair, the warmth of the sun, the scent of the ocean faded. One small part of her mind remained aware that she was sitting in the sun, warm and relaxed, but she let that controlling voice slip away. She was simply a frightened horse, shuddering in its stall.

It was delicious. The muscles of her flanks heaved. Nervously, she kicked at the dusty, hard-packed ground with one hoof. Her body bulked large within a small enclosure, and as she moved restlessly her shoulders and sides scraped against wooden slats. There was a barrier before her, and beyond it was a clear path. Then the gate swung open and she was running, surrounded on both sides by other running horses. Their smell, acrid with fear, caused her to run more wildly still. Occasionally one stumbled, and she would jerk aside to avoid a collision.

She passed the same horse twice as she swung around the wide oval of the track. The first time the mare was injured, leaning against the rail and panting. The second time it was dead, half her skull flattened by a hoof and the edge of a rib sticking through an open wound in her chest.

There was none of the pacing of an ordinary race here, no hanging back. Each horse ran at top speed, or died. Some died anyway. Her vision blurred. She ran.

Sweat slathered her sides and rolled into her eyes; she tossed her head, but her vision barely cleared. She could no longer see other horses around her. She moved mechanically, like a piston in its sleeve. She stepped on another fallen horse and stumbled. The track ahead was clear, but her gallop became uneven, ragged, and irregular. She slowed and stopped. She took a shuddering breath, not enough—not nearly enough—to ease her pain.

She died.

She opened her eyes. "Splendid!" Jason pressed the call bell again and Irena came out of the house, shading her eyes from the sun. "Yiorgio's arranged a marvelous treat for me; I've won! Be a good girl and claim the carcass for me; the kitchen will have it cleaned and dressed." She reached across the table to tap Yiorgio's fleshy arm. "You come, too; bring your wife and another couple if you wish. I haven't had a horse roast in a great long while, and my cook does wonders. You'd think lactic acidosis would make the flesh bitter, but she's gotten up some recipes that you'll find hard to believe." She sat back in the deck chair and stretched out her long legs, lacing her hands over her flat belly.

Alecko looked ill. A sheen of sweat covered his face. "That was my father, racing horses. They run until they die, and the last survivor wins." He let go of their hands and flexed his fingers. "That's the way he runs his business, too." When he stood he swayed slightly, and his face paled. Apparently his blood pressure dropped dangerously when he went into rapport with anyone, she thought, which might be useful to know. He was also vain enough to try to hide any weakness; when he leaned forward to offer a hand, he kept his left lower arm braced on the back of the chair in a manner that was almost furtive. "I think you'll do it, *kyria*," he said. "You'll like the challenge." When she didn't take his hand a little color returned to his cheeks but he said nothing. He bowed, to Jason first and then to Bear, said, "Thank you for your time," and walked slowly down the stairs.

Bear watched him go, thoughtfully, but Jason's back was to the staircase and she didn't bother to turn. "The crowd here must know him fairly well," Bear commented. "People are moving out of his way before he gets to them. Even I had trouble pushing my way through." She watched him until he was out of sight. "He moves like a dancer."

Jason rubbed a finger around the rim of her empty glass. (Bear, pleased, said, "C sharp!" and grinned. "Perfect pitch!") She rubbed her eyes with the balls of her hands. She was stiff with fatigue and she wanted nothing more now than a hot shower and a warm bed.

Bear hooked her thumbs through the first two belt loops of her denims. "Your birthstone's ruby, isn't it."

Banks could learn a lot about security from museums, Jason thought, and answered: "Yes."

Bear stretched her legs, arching her toes in her wide black boots. "It looks like Papandreou's done his research, doesn't it?"

On the other hand, she had Lys and Lys had her computer. "It does look that way, yes."

"You're going to try for it, aren't you?"

And Jason's smile was wide and brilliant, showing her even white teeth. "Yes!"

Bear saw her vacant look, asked, "Lys?" and Jason nodded.

"You remember Denny? She was sitting at the bar when you came in. She's found a new lover and he's anxious to show her the town. Also, my brother wants me to stop by tonight." She frowned.

Bear laughed. "You know damn well you'd use any excuse to see Michael and his kids, so you won't make much of an impression on me that way. Let's go down and see Denny. If her friend's town is more interesting than the places I know, maybe I'll join them."

Jason reached up and ruffled Bear's short, shaggy hair. "Just don't break your nose again, hear? I wouldn't want it any flatter and it's off-center as it is." She stepped back and tilted her head to one side critically. "No, it's just fine the way it is. No fights. Promise me, and I'll find you a noisy bar someplace." She didn't look to see if Bear was following, but started down the stairs. In one corner of the large room was a long wooden bar, stained an improbable pink, and at the far corner of the bar, near the door, Denny sat with her arm around a tall thin figure. Jason worked her way through the tangle of bodies singlemindedly.

Bear followed. "You've known me how many years? And you've only had to pull me out of one fight. The way you talk, anybody'd think it happened daily."

But Denny had already looked up and seen her coming. "Captain," she said, her voice breathless, "this is Capella. Did Lys tell you? He calls himself that because he's a singer and he thought it would be a good name, like me calling myself Dendrite because I'm like a nerve cell in the Net, you know?"

Bear, rumbling up behind Jason, laughed at the last of Denny's speech. "Now who the hell ever calls you Dendrite besides yourself? That's a silly name for anyone, and you know it." She reached out a hamlike hand. "Capella? I'm Bear Vouris. You're a singer?" He nodded. "You'll have to talk some about that. I used to sing a little, too; I like talking to musicians."

Capella smiled shyly, and seemed about to say something when Jason interrupted. "We'll get to know each other later. Do you have a place to stay here? If not, spend the night on the ship. There's room." Then, as he stood up, she looked at him speculatively and amended it: "Well, there's room if you fold up. I don't think we've got a cot your size."

He raised an eyebrow, like a blond caret against his dark skin. "Nobody ever does. I'm used to it."

She nodded. "Good. In the morning we'll talk about a job. Bear, you're still planning on going out?" Bear nodded. Jason glanced at her watch. "Lys'll find a place for you. I'll walk with you so I'll know where to find you later, but then I'm heading out. I promised Michael I'd see him tonight, and it's getting late. Maybe that's best, anyway. The twins will be in bed, and we can talk." She nodded. "Yes. But now let's go to whatever den of iniquity Lys's found for you."

* * *

The lurid sodium streetlights came and went as they walked. Jason hung back slightly, watching reflections shatter on puddles of water and listening to Bear talk about Rat, her old shipmate. She smiled. Apparently Denny hadn't yet told her she'd be shipping with the Rat, who'd found a berth on the *Argo* on her last pass through Metacenter.

He'd been in somewhat of a hurry to get out, too. He usually was.

Bear was winding up her story of the Rat and Duclos the pastry chef. Jason edged closer. She'd heard the story before, but she liked to catch the reaction of those who hadn't.

". . . And then, just before she reached the dock, the entire spun-sugar confectionery boat lurched to one side, belched a huge bubble of air out the other side, and dropped under." Bear's face was red with the exertion of telling her story, and she had a wide grin splitting her flat, ugly face. "Only the tips of the masts and a little bit of sail showed through." She slapped her thigh for emphasis. "And that, my children, was the Rat sinking a dessert ship."

Capella said, "That was awful."

Bear looked pleased. "It was, wasn't it?" She looked up. "Is this it? It doesn't look like much."

They were standing before a dark alley, slightly drier than the surrounding pavement because of a network of overhanging buildings. Three people sat in the alley, caught in the act of passing a bottle between them. Two were men, at first sight; it was difficult to tell with the third, but Jason thought it was a woman. She knew one of them.

"I thought I told you to go home," she said.

"That you did, Captain. I didn't say I would." Robinson shaded his eyes against the glare from the streetlight. "Hello, Bear. Want a taste?"

Bear squatted on her haunches and reached for the bottle. "Thanks. You look terrible. Anyone ever told you you'd be dead in five years?" She handed the bottle back.

"More than one, Sergeant Vouris, more than one. But I was told that more than five years ago, so I didn't listen." He took a swallow, and pulled his legs back as Jason and the rest tried to maneuver by.

One of the other two jumped up then, a skinny, ragged man in a coat several sizes too large. "You going into Fibi's? You got money then. Just a drachma? You've got a drachma. Look at that coat you're wearing! That leather's expensive, you got to have money if you treat it so badly. Only a drachma, that's all—"

Jason pushed the beggar away, not roughly; but she was prepared to be more rough if he persisted.

Bear walked beside her and said in a voice intended only for Jason to hear, "Are you always so rude to your old crew members?"

"Robinson? We talked earlier. That was just the tail end of a conversation."

Bear shook her head. "Not Robinson. The Rat. The short one who wanted money."

Jason looked back. "That's the Rat? Really." She was amused. "He told me I'd meet him one day and I wouldn't know him. 'Like Peter denying the Lord,' I think he said. Hold on." She walked back. "Here," she said and handed Robinson several small-denomination bills. "This is for old times. Of course, it'll have to come out of the budget somewhere, I may have to cut someone's salary, and I think I know who. Good night."

"Evharisto, kyria," Robinson said.

"Kalos ilthes," she said. "You're very welcome."

They were standing in front of a plain wooden door. A brass plate, almost invisible now that they were out of the direct glare of the streetlights, was inset on the right-hand side of the door. Bear held the map close to the door so that its phosphorescent light was cast against the brass. "I *guess* it says Fibi." She shrugged. "It's worth a try, anyway." She pushed open the door.

A physical wave of sound came blasting into the alley, intimidating in its intensity.

Bear hastily closed the door. It apparently contained a sound shield of some sort, because the resulting silence was abrupt and complete; they heard nothing now but the background sounds of the city around them. "Wow," Bear said. It was an understatement. "That's terrific. Just what I want! Jason, you're sure you won't come with us?" Smiling, Jason shook her head. "Well, then." She opened the door and shouted. "We'll see you later. Denny? Capella?" Bear put an arm around the shoulder of each and walked in.

*   *   *

It was raining again in the alley, but with a clearing smell. Jason tucked her hair inside her jacket and flipped the collar up to cover her neck. Off in the distance a siren sounded, coming closer. The alley was green, a combination of the sodium vapor leaking in from the street and the light blue walls. The dark red brick showed up black in the light.

A dog came by, edging past her apologetically. She squatted down and snapped her fingers. His expression became anxious; he flattened himself against the opposite wall and oozed past her, making as small a target as possible. She watched him wistfully as he walked away. She liked dogs, but they never cared much for her. On the other hand, she couldn't pass a cat without it wanting to walk along, twining between her legs.

The sirens were louder now, and there were spools of harsh blue light unraveling somewhere near. She took a turn from the alleyway into a broad boulevard and blinked. Somehow she'd managed to circumnavigate, and had made her way back to the storefront where she'd met with Robinson. Now the window lay smashed, and the mannequin lay, half smile enigmatic, under a young man, bloody, who was trying to push himself to his feet amid shards and slivers of broken glass. One siren she heard she now identified; it was a burglar alarm, not a characteristic bell but a shrill ululation that, now that she was under it, nearly deafened her. Some of the ribbons of light were broken holograms from the display, which projections now danced and yawed on the walls and on the bodies of a small, silent crowd of people who neither helped nor hindered the man in the window. They simply watched, as they watched the even younger man standing dazed on the sidewalk, blinking owlishly in the vibrant but unsteady light. He wasn't very tall, just a few inches over five feet, and wiry. Describing him in general, Jason would have said "unkempt"; his clothes were old and well-worn, his canvas shoes were shabby, and his hair stuck up in irregular patches, like a hedgehog with mange.

"My glasses," he said. "Someone—please find my glasses."

She watched the people watch the boy and then, as more sirens joined the shrill alarm and blue and red lights flared, she saw half the people present—including the mannequin's inadvertent lover, who raised himself, brushed off glistening glass—leave, quickly and silently.

Of those remaining, one offered the boy crushed gold frames, another a broken lens, and then they, too, left.

She watched.

Lights flared and flickered. The boy took one hesitant step; another. She realized suddenly that it wasn't affectation, that he really couldn't see without his shattered spectacles. But surgery could correct any visual defect, and even where there was an organic problem surgeons could simply grow a new set of eyes. Why didn't he get his eyes replaced?

The sirens, still sounding, suddenly stopped. Two police officers came out of the car; the shorter one reached out to touch the boy's shoulder.

The touch was galvanic, like probing a muscle with current. The boy nodded, shook his head, reached to brush his eyes, lowered his hand, and, hand half lowered, shuddered convulsively; and was suddenly running, without warning, down the center of the broad street.

The older cop, brawny, taller of the two, was running almost as quickly; the shorter woman turned to Jason, who realized then that she was the only one still watching. *"Dhespoinis?* Did you see what happened? Who are you? What are you doing here?"

She asked the second and third question before Jason had a chance to answer the first. Jason shrugged. "No. I was just out for a walk and I heard the alarm. I saw the boy your partner's chasing standing, looking blind. The other was lying in the window display. He couldn't have been badly hurt. He got up and walked away by himself." As an afterthought she said, "I didn't see who started it." Then she paused. Should she give her real name? She decided it was unlikely Moulinos would harbor a host of short Oriental women in black leather. "Horiuchi. Jason Horiuchi. I'm captain of the *Argo,* San Martin registry. I'm staying at the port if you need me." She glanced over and saw the woman trying to transliterate her name into Greek. She grinned. "Good luck."

The woman snapped shut the metal cover of her notebook. Her plain uniform—brown jacket and slacks with a white shirt and black tie—wasn't flattering, but she wore it with a certain grace, even though the pants were about an inch too long and she had to keep hitching up her belt to keep them from dragging. It was a largely unconscious gesture, but she looked up once after doing so yet again, caught Jason's amused expression, and grinned. "General issue. I'm supposed to be taller, I guess; but I just got them and I haven't had time to hem them yet." She held out her arms; the jacket cuffs came to her knuckles on both hands. "The tyranny of the average, and I'm too damn short. If you're a visitor I don't suppose you recognized any of the other people here?" Jason shook her head. The woman sighed. "Right. No one ever does, even when they do. Well, thanks for your help. I'd best go and see how my partner's making out."

Jason nodded in the direction where the two had disappeared. "Should you be letting her chase after him alone like that? Not that I think that boy's any threat to anyone but himself."

The cop shrugged expressively. "You saw her run after him? She wants glory. She can have it, too. She wants everyone to know how tough she is." She smiled wearily. "I'm not going to help *her;* I'm going to help him. Good night."

Jason watched her walk away, troubled. She wondered how that scrawny little kid had decked someone a foot taller and fifty pounds heavier than he was. She wondered what was wrong with his eyes.

Niko. *He'd* know. Niko had trained Lys, and he was still one of the best information sources she knew. He'd been Jason's first Gestalt, her first Vector. Now that he'd retired from sailing she saw him only occasionally, but he kept up his connections. It would only take a phone call.

She turned her head slightly to her left and moved her jaw sideways, an uncomfortable movement that grated the mandible against the zygomatic but which completed the cellular circuit tying into the nearest telephone system. She didn't use the mandibular phone much because of the discomfort, but the connection was so set up that it was nearly impossible to trigger it accidentally, even while chewing—and it came in handy during emergencies. She waited for a dial tone and subvocalized Niko's number from memory. A pause—relays opening or closing; a computer somewhere evaluating, translating and transferring her call—and a sudden, cheery voice by her left ear: *"Yia sou?"*

She grinned. *"Yia sou,* Niko. Jason. I need a fix; a young boy, maybe seventeen, just picked up on . . . make it D and D,

possible felony assault. Probably resisting arrest, too; he ran
away. They may not even have completed the arrest yet; the
squad car's still in sight by Piecemeal Road in the Beehive. So
it may take a while to clear through your terminal." She listened to his protests for a moment while she wiped the back of
one hand against her forehead, but interrupted eventually.
"This is supposed to be a sunny climate, but I'm soaked and I
don't like it. I'll see you after I've taken care of some business. Give me a name then, and when I come by tomorrow I'll
have time to talk. *Audhio sas."* Jawline straightened, head up,
she heard the click of disconnect.

She stepped away from deep shadow to the muddy demar-
cation where "roadside" became "roadway." Light flicked
water, oil, shattered glass. One black boot scattered shards.
Bilious orange globes, high up, shed brilliant pools on each
corner; the lapping waves didn't reach the center where she
stood.

A glass shard screed beneath her boot. The alarm mind-
lessly shrilled on. Thoughtfully she reached in and selected a
watch, a ring, and three small hologrammatic pendants for
Lys. Nothing else attracted her attention. She slipped them
into her knapsack and walked away.

Her brother's small house had changed little in four years.
It was one of the ways they differed. Jason liked space and
tended to sprawl to the limits of any place in which she found
herself. Michael Galwyn was more self-contained, and the
neat living room with its walls of books and comfortable
wood-burning fireplace reflected a serenity she envied.

The house was quiet with the boys sleeping. Michael often
said that he'd be happier without them; then they'd go away,
to visit with friends or to see their mother, and he'd moon
around until they came back. Now, missing them, he sighed,
then looked up to catch Jason's eye.

Creases around her eyes deepened as Jason smiled. One
corner of her mouth lifted, lines of laughter forming unexpectedly. She leaned back in her chair, one slim leg crossed over
the other. "I'm afraid I've painted you as a black, evil villain
again, Michael," she said. "I told everyone you insisted on
seeing me, even though I'm bone-weary and haven't slept for
a week."

He ran his hand through spiky copper hair in exasperation.

"And why did I insist on seeing you?" He leaned back in his own matching rattan chair, the color of his slacks matching the cream of the cushion. Watching the two of them together, it was possible to see the resemblance between them. It lay not in physical details, for Michael's round ruddy face with its galaxy of freckles was the antithesis of Jason's triangular ivory mask, but rather in the posture of each, in the way they gestured, in the way they talked. It was like looking in a funhouse mirror, seeing them sitting on opposite sides of the room, in identical chairs, identically slouched, his hands balled into fists and jammed into the pockets of his cream cotton slacks, her own fists tenting the pockets of a thick velour robe. (Michael had taken one look at her and insisted on throwing her wet clothes in his dryer. "Lys already thinks I neglect you," he'd said. "I don't want her claiming I gave you pneumonia as well.")

Jason leaned back until she was staring at the rough, unfinished oak beams, four-by-fours, that marked the ceiling with crossed shadows. "I've taken up a dare, and Lys won't approve of the way I'm going about it. She'll want me to play it safe."

Michael shrugged. "That's generally good advice."

She stopped contemplating the rafters and looked at him, and grinned. "Certainly it's good advice. That's what I pay her for. But that doesn't mean it's appropriate here." She leaned forward, elbows on her knees. "We'll talk about the trust instrument, too, but later. It won't take long. Wolde had some changes to suggest. I hope they'll be final. I *hope* they'll be final. We've spent six standard years haggling over details."

Michael's smile was forced. "You've done most of the haggling, Jason."

"You know damn well it was necessary, Michael! When I took over as trustee, the value of the trust had declined by twenty percent—twenty percent!—and there was no provision at all for independent decision on the part of any of the beneficiaries. All I've done was for the benefit of the trust and the family."

Michael said mildly, "A twenty percent decline on a balance of over a hundred billion still leaves a substantial amount, Jason. You know damn well I'd prefer we endow some sort of charitable foundation, and each take less as personal income."

Jason stood up, stretched, and started to pace back and forth in the small living room. "You're an exception, and it's one of the reasons I like you, I think. But I have to think of the rest of the family, and hammering out a compromise that leaves them all thinking they've put something over on me wasn't easy. I don't know. Maybe they have. But I'd stack Wolde Dawit and Kin N'Lopez against their lawyers and accountants any day; maybe even give them cards and spades." She stopped pacing. "Anyway, if you're so damn altruistic, you're not going to like what I'm planning to do, because it'll increase the family finances even more, and pump even more value into Horiuchi stock."

Michael clasped his hands behind his neck and looked up at her. "You know, you really look ridiculous in that robe. If you plan on going swimming before you get here, next time let me know and I'll get a robe that fits. Tell me why I won't like what you're doing."

She didn't answer him directly. She didn't answer him at all at first, but kept walking. Finally she went back to her chair and sat, gathering the extensive folds of cloth around her. "It was pointed out to me tonight that you've got some of your pictures hanging at the Musieon ton Papandreou. I want to know about it." She leaned forward eagerly. "How big is it? How is it arranged? How many storage rooms are there? Where's the generator room? Who handles the security? Who's their acquisitions manager? How often are the exhibits changed? And anything else you can think of."

He blinked. "Gosh, I'm sorry. I had the plans last week, but they were getting dusty so I sent them back." He braced his hands on his knees and stood. "You come out here and tell me what's going on while I fix us something to eat."

His kitchen was small but efficient; he'd learned to cook aboard an actual sailing ship which, unlike the *Argo*, placed a premium on size. It was amazing how many things you could fit into a small space if you tried. She followed him, but it seemed that everything he wanted was directly behind her, and she finally moved back to the doorway, blocking it. She told him about meeting Papandreou, and what he'd proposed.

"Alecko Papandreou." As he talked he broke a half-dozen eggs into a bowl and began to stir. "I've never met him. But my lawyer has to deal with him. He says, 'If you ordered a carload of sons of bitches, delivery of him alone would constitute substantial performance.' "

"Do you agree?"

"Yes. You know about my three-dimensional study, the one Dhimitri Papandreou bought?"

"That's the one that looks different from every angle; you used some sort of prismatic paint?"

Michael looked pained. "No. I sculpted it with lasers, with the use of waldoes and a micrograph. Never mind. It was an experiment, and it didn't work out well, frankly. When Dhimitri bought it, I was surprised; when he donated it to the museum I was even more surprised. But Alecko Papandreou hates the picture, and is still angry that it's hanging on display.

"But he didn't react to the painting, not directly at least. He came to my studio and said he'd learned of me from Dhimitri and was interested in my work. I'm as susceptible to flattery as anyone else, so I spent the better part of the day showing him around. We visited my workrooms, and he watched while I added to one of my canvases. He made suggestions, too, which were knowledgeable and appropriate, one of which I acted on. And then he asked me which painting was my personal favorite. He can be charming; I told him. He bought it. Later he destroyed it, and sent me a holo of the destruction. Attached to it was a note which said, essentially, 'Why not become a plumber?' "

Michael poured the batter carefully, waited until it began to set, and added filling and more batter. "So you're going to steal another jewel, dripping with history. I'd seriously suggest you resist it." Preparations done, he set a timer; but he didn't leave the kitchen because he trusted his own instincts more than he did the clock. "But I know you won't. Let's see." Michael closed his eyes for a moment, thinking. "The museum is on the far end of Mykonos, on the northeast slope of a mountain, overlooking a bay. You've been here before, and you've seen the island from the air, so you know it's about five times as long as it is wide, and rocky." He folded. "The museum's on one of the thinner sections, where the island grew up instead of out. It's open to the public, but you have to make an appointment, and you have to call in advance to let them know what kind of car you'll be driving and your license number, because otherwise they won't let you stop, they'll just direct you back on down the road."

"There won't be any trouble getting admission. What else?"

"It sprawls, Jason. That museum covers several hundred acres, and is scalloped all up and down the hillsides. It's magnificent. You won't stand a chance."

"There's always a chance. You don't have my crew. Go on, Michael."

"I don't really know where to begin. The first few rooms are dedicated to Old Greek art and sculpture. The lighting is natural light, or seems to be; but it's indirect, and whether you go there in the morning or at night the light's the same. Each room is a huge square that seems somehow intimate. Designed by Leung; that's her trademark. The walls separating each room are thick. I suppose there are maintenance corridors between the rooms, I don't know. But you can't get within five feet of any of the paintings, and all except the biggest of the statues are protected by touch-me-nots. If you break the sealed beams surrounding the art you'll get a slight nerve tingle; the closer you get, the stronger the shock. If you get close enough to touch something the shock can knock you out, but by that time there's usually a guard at your elbow warning you to stay back.

"That's in the public rooms. The private rooms have progressively more security, and in some of the rooms you can only see the art from behind a glass wall. If you want to look at anything any closer you have to go to the video displays. All the statues and books are copied in 3V in incredible detail. I wondered once how closely I could examine something; the video stopped just short of microscopic."

Michael checked the oven seconds before the alarm went off. Satisfied, he set the pan on the counter to cool and put bread in the toaster. As the smell of the bread began to spread through the kitchen he divided the omelette, flipping half deftly onto a plate and handing it to Jason; then he reached into the cooler for some juice and poured them each a glass.

"The periphery of the museum is all the popular material. Valuable, certainly, but it's mostly for the tourists. The next level in, roughly, has the beginnings of the historically important pieces, the marble torso studies and the beginnings of what became the Greek style. The deeper you go, the more obscure the art grows. There are some levels I haven't seen because you have to have a student card or a teaching credential before they'll let you in the door. And, frankly, I'm not all that interested."

She carried her plate back to the living room and set it down on the low table. "What about Dhimitri's gemstones? How are they protected?"

Michael carried his plate, the platter of toast, and a carousel of jams and jellies balanced on his arm like a professional waiter. He set them all down on the table and pulled his own chair close. "They're in an inner chamber. I don't see that they're guarded any more or any less than the rest of the exhibits, but you have to go through several rooms to get to them, which means you have to go through several rooms to get out again. Oh, and there's some sort of sonic system in the gem rooms; but I've only been in them once or twice. I'm not as interested in jewelry as you are."

"Most people aren't. I'll admit it's an obsession. How are they arranged? Glass cases? Vaults?" Jason's voice was muffled as she ate her omelette. "You're as good a cook as ever, Michael. Do you want a job on the *Argo?*"

Michael yawned. "No. Eggs are the only things I know how to fix. Neither of the boys will eat them anymore." He rubbed his eyes. "How are they arranged? Glass cases, as far as I know. It looks like glass. There's no reason why it shouldn't be." He yawned again.

Jason yawned too. She ate some toast, looked at the remainder of the omelette regretfully, set her plate on the floor, and stood. "That should be enough for tonight. I really didn't expect you to give me a guided tour, but you've been a help."

Michael said, sadly, "You're not going to stay to see the boys, are you?"

"I can't Michael," she said.

But he turned away. "I think your clothes should be dry," he said, his voice carefully neutral. "Let me check."

She watched him walk away with mixed feelings. She loved Michael's children, but she avoided seeing them for her own reasons. She couldn't see them as often as she wished, and she didn't think it was fair to them to let them form an attachment she couldn't reciprocate. At times she compared herself to her father, and his treatment of her as a child; but she had convinced herself that this was different.

Michael came back with an armload of clothes, still warm. Jason put them on gratefully, then stretched and stooped to pick up her pack. She took out a bulky vellum package. "Here's the new trust instrument." She tapped the document on the table, squaring the edges, and handed it to him. "I've highlighted the changes for you. There's a few changes in the tax structure because of the new Metacenter multiplanet inheritance regulations. I don't have any control over those, so don't call me about it. Call Kin N'Lopez." She grimaced. "We'll both call him. He managed to track me down here, so I've got to see him."

Michael took the stack of paper from her and crossed to his "office," a small sun room at the front of the house. He flipped through the pages rapidly and put them in a drawer without reading them. "I'll go over them tomorrow." He closed the drawer quietly. "Maybe." Then he ran a hand through his brass-wire hair and grinned. "It's nice to see you again, Jason. I'm glad you could drop in for a visit." He pointed to the back of the house, where his twin boys were sleeping. "Come back again when the boys are awake. They'd like to see you."

She nodded. "I will. And—Michael? Thanks for not asking questions. Friends?" She held out her hand.

He seemed to consider it for a minute; then his uneven white teeth flashed in a boyish grin and he held out his own hand.

Jason tossed back her wet hair. The rain had begun again, not seriously, but with a dreary persistence. The alley in front of Fibi's was several inches deep in muddy water.

"Is she still upright?"

Denny said, "Well, yeah. But she's swearing at the machines, and she sounds like she means it. She said she wasn't going to leave until she beat the fuckin' thing. I'm not sure whether she meant winning or taking it apart piece by piece."

Jason pushed past Denny and looked around. The place was a maze, with machines jammed haphazardly back to back and side to side. In addition, benches and tiny stone tables were packed in wherever there weren't any machines. There was a greasy spoon in back, and the tables were for the few people polite enough to eat and drink away from the games.

Jason took out her silvertip and reconnected, motioning to

Denny to do the same. Denny nodded and used one hand to open her pack and reach for her probe while she used the other to hold aside her straight brown hair. She located the probe, brushed it ineffectually on the rough wool of her sweater, and slipped it into place, waiting to hear from Lys; without Lys's patch circuit she could hear Lys but not Jason. It was a little like listening to the dispatcher over the radio of a taxi.

Jason spotted Capella and Bear at the same time. Bear was staring intently at the video terminal and growling. Jason pointed to Capella with one finger and used the same finger to tap the back of her neck. He nodded and reached for his own probe.

Jason said, «Lys? You awake yet?»

A sleepy voice said, «Barely. When you say two hours, you mean it, don't you?»

She permitted herself a dry chuckle. «Usually, yes. This time, no. It's almost three o'clock local time. And we've got a crisis.»

Bear, after one brief disinterested look in her direction, had turned back to her terminal. Her pupils were pinpricks. She kicked the machine savagely, and automatically moved to another before it had a chance to shut itself off. She dropped in two coins and started to punch them up. Jason reached into her pocket for a token and flipped it up on the glass. "Mind if I join you?"

Bear looked at her through red-rimmed eyes. "Does it make a difference if I do?"

"I suppose not." But Jason reached up and took the brass coin back. "I just noticed you'd put up two players and thought you might have room for me."

"I *always* play a two-person game, Captain. I'm superstitious. I don't like to play alone." She reached down to start a game, hesitated, and said slyly, "I'll let *you* play with me *any*time." She punched up the second player and began explaining the game while the screen reset itself. Her voice was slightly slurred, but otherwise she seemed fine. "'Sa simple game. Gray ships're neutral, blue defense, red attack. You c'n take out gray and red ships with the laser, but not blues. Defensive, see? Shielded; reflects your fire back. That'll put you out of the game. Costs points, too. If you *don't* attack the red ships they'll blow you away. Gray ships're gonna turn, red or blue, and you won't know which. So blow them away. But you won't get any points if you do."

She took a deep breath. "If a ship goes into warp, it'll come back somewhere else." She turned to wave a finger drunkenly in Jason's face. "Don' let it. Whoops." She'd almost lost a ship, but went inertial and dropped through a couple levels of the playing field. Her score dropped as she fell. "Son of a bitch. I forgot. This thing subtracts points, too. That's not fair. Do you think that's fair? Hah!" She'd maneuvered an enemy flyer into an orbiting rock. The resulting explosion was colorful and satisfying. "I mean, if I *get* the points, I should be able to keep 'em, shouldn't I?"

Scrap from the explosion holed her ship. Bear looked dismayed as the machine said high and shrill with excitement, "Explosive decompression has occurred in your hold. You have five seconds to decide which of the following is the correct maneuver." In a more natural voice, it added, "Better get it right or you'll loose your ship." A series of choices scrolled across the screen. Bear scowled at the list, gave up, and chose one blindly. Her ship imploded. She stared at the screen. "Damn."

Jason said, «Get ready, Lys. Have Capella and Denny ready to link.» She stepped up to the machine. "Out of the way, Bear. Let a pro handle this." The machine flickered. Behind her, Denny and Capella were sitting at a bench, heads together, looking as though they were deep in conversation. She hoped Bear wouldn't try to talk with them. She felt their presence, comfortably, at the edge of her mind, and noted with satisfaction that Capella had managed the transition without any trouble. For a moment their personalities were separate within her; and then, easily, they merged.

She felt, suddenly, the texture of the clothes she wore. The cotton socks she wore formed a comfortable ridge against the inside of her boots. Along her instep flannel had bunched so that cool leather pressed against the knuckle of her foot. She was uncomfortably aware of her wet shirt as it clung to her breasts with each breath. With her right hand she touched the three controls for weaponry (scored and nicked; someone had taken a knife to it once; someone else had tried to file it smooth; the marks of both were still palpable), attitude (surface slightly melted, as though someone had held a cigarette to the button), and thrust (new, smooth: it had been replaced, with a plastic different than that used on the other controls); with her left she gripped the stick controlling trajectory (hard plastic with an emerylike surface) with its three thumb buttons for warp field, force field, and inertial shift. (Denny: a sponge for physical sensation; when she was not in the Net she touched and felt everything she could.) The screen shifted and a gray ship appeared above her, to her left, slightly behind her own ship. A clock began ticking. (Duration: Capella's delicate sense of time was counting, evaluating.) The ship flickered and turned blue. She could ignore it, and did. (Next time a gray ship appeared, he would warn her before the shift.)

She fired missiles experimentally. She measured their speed; she gauged their distance; she felt their impact when each struck. She lost a ship, her first, and her heightened senses filed the information, to be used on her next pass through.

Bear, suddenly cheerful, said, "I thought you were going to show me how to play this sucker, Jason." She laughed uproariously and took another huge swallow from her mug of beer.

One of the problems with using the Net dirtside, she discovered, was that it was too distracting. There was so much going on, so much that she never noticed when she was unlinked. A roach ran across the floor and she found herself compelled to time its flight, and to estimate how long it would take to get across the room. She stepped on something uneven when she stepped back from the machine and tried to identify it by feel alone through the sole of her boot. Everything was equally attractive to her and she felt as though she'd taken AdaMax. There was the same feeling of well-being, as though everyone around was potentially friendly, as though they'd all help her if they could.

It felt dangerous.

Bear stepped up to the machine and Jason began automatically to analyze her play. Even without the benefit of the Net, Bear was handicapped. She was a creature of sound and the machine used sound to distract. Its pattern of rising and falling noises bore little resemblance to what was happening on the playing field, and Jason felt as though broadcast subsonics were in use. That would account for some of Bear's irritability. The voices were also deliberately distractive. The machines tried to provoke verbal responses, and were programmed to analyze the speech patterns of players. Once they had enough information to act upon they started insulting whoever was at the keyboard in his or her own idiom. Whenever Bear started arguing with the machine, she paid less attention to what she was doing.

From the point of view of the designer, of course, the more people who enjoyed arguing with the machines, the greater the profits. There was obviously a delicate balance to be struck between distracting a player and enraging him to the point of violence.

She wondered how often the machines got trashed.

When she felt herself moving her arms so she could feel the material of her shirt slide across her skin, she called Lys. «Is there any way to lower the threshold of feeling? This is so intense it's distracting. It's not like this in space,» she complained. But Lys had joined Capella and Denny, contributing another level to Jason's awareness, allowing her to effortlessly measure the direction and magnitude of the forces portrayed on the screen.

Bear, grumbling, had lost another ship. Jason ordered her another beer and stepped in to play, her head buzzing with heightened awareness. She seldom tried the Net dirtside because it was too seductive. Were Denny's feelings always this intense? Did Capella time everything he heard?

She was playing the game well, with half her attention. Capella's time sense told her when to fire; Denny's touch told her which control to use; Lys's geometry computed the angles. (Firing wildly cost points and wasted fuel. If you ran out of fuel, you lost. If you wasted a torpedo, you lost points. If you warped unnecessarily, or went inertial in relation to the rest of the playing field, you lost points. There wasn't much to do to gain points, except hit everything you aimed at and make sure everything you aimed at was an adversary.) Jason reacted to each object without conscious effort, dodging those that were no threat, firing on those that were, and weaving through the various levels of the playing field. The digital readout of her score was a constantly accelerating spiral.

She was having a wonderful time. Partially it was because she was cheating and no one but Lys, Capella, and Denny knew. Partially it was because, she found, she *liked* watching ships explode in such a realistic fashion. In the background, she realized, she'd gotten herself a coterie of admirers who

were making comments on her skill. She was pleased to hear
Bear's booming voice explaining proudly that Jason was *her*
captain, the best damn captain around, and if anyone wanted
to deny it, well, she was ready, goddamn it, to take them on,
singly or all at once.

That was one problem out of the way. She'd successfully
diverted Bear's rage. Now if only she could finish up this
game and get her back to the ship before she passed out; Jason
was uncomfortably aware that Bear was still drinking while
singing her praises, and while her capacity was immense it
wasn't limitless.

She took out another ship, a drone, and realized with Capella's awareness that meant another ship was nearby, invisible but present. She felt its proximity—another contribution
from Denny. It emerged, firing. She took out its two torpedos,
scoring points, and executed a deliberately clumsy maneuver,
not quite evading laser fire. The resulting hit took out a right
distal lateral support strut. Out of balance, her ship rotated
into an asteroid and erupted in a blaze of light. She was satisfied; it had looked accidental. Bear would play her final ship,
Jason would play her own, and then they could go home. It
was—Capella again; she wondered if he even bothered to
wear a watch—almost 4:30.

Bear stepped up to the screen and Jason stepped away,
listening with pleasure to a string of compliments. One young
kid, his face roseate with some form of skin disease, said,
"You shouldn't'a been taken out like that. You gotta pay attention. If you'd stayed on another coupla minutes, you
would've beat the high score."

She grinned at him. "I've got one more ship, don't I? I'll
get it." It was odd, functioning with half her senses hypertro-
phied and half nonexistent. She couldn't Hear; she couldn't
Smell; she couldn't Taste. She could See, because earlier in
her career she'd run as crew and that had been her function,
but even her Sight was fuzzy, out of focus, in comparison to
the sharp, preternaturally clear reports she was receiving from
Denny, Capella, and Lys.

Bear lost her last ship, but accepted the loss cheerfully.
"All right, *kyria mou*. Show these little bastards what a real
pro can do."

She played the final round quickly. The spiral of numbers
met and passed the high score displayed in the upper left-hand

corner of the screen. She played on, reasonably, until the chance arose to lose and make it look accidental. She took it: her ship collided with another, and they both exploded in a welter of gas and metal. She grinned, satisfied, and arched her neck as if to stretch kinked muscles. The relay in her jaw tripped, and the connection to the ship was broken.

Behind her, Capella yawned and Denny, standing, reached up and bowed her spine till the bones cracked. "I never realized it was so hard, just sitting," she said disingenuously. "I'm tired. I think I'll go back to the ship."

Capella stood and wrapped his arm around Denny protectively and said it sounded like a good idea.

Jason looked at Bear. "How about it, sport? Are you ready to turn in yet?"

Bear squinted at Jason, one eye closing in a deliberate wink. "After a performance like that? What can I do to top it?" She laughed, a rumble of mirth that seemed to come from her shoes. "Legends are made of this! In years to come, they'll tell the tale of Starcaptain Jason, pilot of the *Argo*, who took all that Arcadia had to offer and gave it back, cards and spades." She laughed again and drained her beer. "I'm ready to go, Captain, ma'am; lay on. Did I hear a lay? Let's sing!" She broke, surprisingly, into a fragment of *Pagliacci*. After a moment Capella joined her while Denny looked on in proprietary amusement, as though she'd invented them both.

Bear tapped Jason's arm and pointed. "Oh, my captain, look there. She's back again."

Jason looked around but saw no one she recognized. Reasonably, she asked, "Who?"

"The 3V lady! See that tripod? She's been setting it up here and there all night, taking pictures of giddy boys 'n' girls on their first date." The tiny woman was staggering under the weight of the bulky unit. The camera itself was quite small, but the spinal column had to be taller than any of its subjects, and some of the people she photographed—Gethnians, for example, or natives of San Martin—were extraordinarily tall.

She collapsed on the stone bench and sat, wheezing. "Whew. I've *got* to get an easier job. But I like to give the kids mementos. I like to think they'll thank me, when they get to my age." She pulled back the sleeve of her ragged blue coat, revealing the unraveling ends of at least two sweaters beneath it and the surprising gleam of an expensive gold watch. "Getting late." She patted the 3V, making sure that it was stable on the bench, pulled her woolen cap down over her spiky white hair, and looked up to catch Bear's eye. "How about you?" She reached over and plucked at the soft brown fur on Bear's arm. "I've never taken a picture of an animated fur coat before. That'll be interesting."

Jason hesitated. But the old woman was assembling her rig, deploying the tripod legs and the spine so that the whole unit listed slightly aft. The woman prodded Bear into place, then did the same to Jason. "You, young lady, you stand next to her. Yes. Like so. But for God's sake look like you're enjoying yourself!" When both of them were satisfactorily placed, the old woman backed away. "Now don't jump. I'm going to trigger the guide wire, which will come out in a spiral from the top of my machine. As soon as it's locked into place at the bottom, the camera will follow it, so when you hear the wire click into place, smile and try to stay still while the camera tracks."

She started the machine; the brass guide wire whipped around them like a broken watch mainspring, and looked as though it could slice through them easily if just once it should slip from its mooring. But it snapped into place at the bottom of its spiral, and while they were still reacting the camera spun around them, chuckling steadily as its multiple lenses recorded their serial images. As it finished its arc the brass wire snapped from its socket and recoiled into the apex. A few moments later the woman handed Jason a six-inch hologram, displayed on a tiny rotating pedestal. "There, now," she said. "Wasn't that worth the wait?"

Jason turned the statue in the light, looking at it from several angles, concentrating. Bear said, "Jason?" and Jason looked up. "It was worth it. Yes." She got out her wallet, got out a bill. "Thank you very much!"

Bear's deep rumble held an element of surprise. "That's way too much, Jason."

A triad of tiny lines formed at the corner of each eye; Jason smiled. "Not for what I got, Bear. Come on, let's go home."

Bear reached over for the plaque. "I don't like that smile you're wearing here. You look like you're planning something."

"I was smiling because she called me young. I like that. I'll bet you your first week's wages I'm older than she is."

But then Denny came on one side, Capella on the other, and they began to steer Bear steadily toward the door. Jason stood back and watched the trio making its way (with only slight difficulty) through the arcade. Eventually Bear had one arm around Denny's shoulder, one arm around Capella's. As Capella was nearly a foot and a half taller than Denny, Bear was of necessity walking in a somewhat skewed fashion, and all three of them were giggling uncontrollably.

Jason said, "If you can't act with a little more dignity, I'm not sure I want *any* of you on my ship."

Bear said, affronted, *"Dignity* she wants. Oh, yes. Dignity. Let's be dignified." She let loose of Capella and Denny and walked forward, shoulders back, stomach in, chest out, striding like a self-important general. Denny and Capella flanked her, the general's aides.

Within a few steps she was humming, then whistling, then singing under her breath. "De-*die.* Dah dee *dah.* Guarda 'mor mio, che nettare di vino t'appor - ta - i! Ah!" As she walked her voice grew louder and more assured.

"Guarda, Amor Mio" from *Pagliacci* is that kind of song: elegant and mischievous, and at first Capella simply listened, his head nodding in time, watching her, pleased. But when she sang the gavotte through a second time, singing both Harlequin and Columbine, Capella insinuated a lush high tenor, playing an arch, coy Columbine offering food to a lascivious Harlequin, who himself offered wine. They sang, and the crowds surrounding the video machines gave way to the lunatics passing through, singing "Amabile beone!" and "Colombina!" to each other at exaggerated volumes.

Encouraged by their audience, Bear threw back her head and howled, and shouted a laugh, and sang. "E allor perchè di', tu m'hai stregato se vuoi lasciarmi senza pietà?"—"Can you deny me, all that I ask thee? Cannot your heart persuade you to stay?" She sang the baritone role with authority, more naturally than she sang tenor.

Jason waited through the opening bars, eager to see if Capella knew the soprano role. Bear hesitated slightly, prepared to continue both roles if necessary, but Capella, obviously enjoying himself, swept into the duet easily, pushing the tempo a bit more than it was written, crying "Do I remember you? How could I forget?" When he sang "viver voglio a te avvinta, affascinata," he might have been saying "Beat me, kick me, bind me in chains; you fascinate me, I love you."

Jason heard Bear whisper to Capella, "Nice job, son; but watch me *really* lay them on their ass." She began, easily at first, then angrily, Canio's aria from *Pagliacci*. When she reached the lines, "Why not be a man? You're just Pagliaccio," she winked at Jason with her upstage eye. But she sang the *vesti la giubba* sincerely, without bathos, with dignity. The final words of the aria were bitter and poisonous and powerful; and the room, miraculously, was momentarily quiet. Bear stood with her head bowed, listening as applause splattered throughout the room, louder (a little) than the sounds from the machines. Then she looked up. "That was nice," she said in understatement. She was panting with exertion. "We can go home now, Jason."

At the door Bear said, "I've got my bus nearby. Come on and I'll take you back to the ship."

Jason watched the slight sailor's roll in Bear's walk with well-founded suspicion. Bear led the way to a beaten old touring car whose surface was cratered with the results of many minor collisions. She made a few vrooming noises, as though revving up, and made a production of turning the key.

Nothing happened. She turned it again. "Hey, what the hell," Bear said. "I just had this thing tuned up. It can't be on the fritz already."

The car coughed apologetically. "I'm sorry, Bear. I can't let you drive."

Bear snorted. "Why not?"

"Because you're drunk. Why not wait an hour or so and try again? Your BMR is high enough that you should metabolize a fair amount of alcohol by then."

Bear said, "I want to go home *now*." She turned the key again. "Start up, damn you."

"I'm just trying to protect your interests," it said. "You don't want to get picked up for drunk driving in Moulinos."

Denny leaned forward from the backseat. "Why not?"

"Drunk driving is considered a felony, and a felony conviction carries an automatic sentence of public flagellation. And the word of the arresting officer is considered sufficient evidence." It paused. "If we were on a world with broadcast power I could take you home. Perhaps one of you other gentlemen or ladies could drive?" The suggestion was made hope-fully.

Jason turned sideways in her seat, one arm hooked over the seat back. "The car's probably right, Bear. I had some wine earlier, but not much else. Why not let me drive?"

Bear clenched her teeth and snarled. "I spent all goddamn night losing to goddamn video games. I'm not going to let any goddamn car tell me I'm too goddamn drunk to drive. It's a goddamn machine. It's *not* going to tell me what I can or cannot do."

Three of them enjoyed the walk back to the ship.

— 2

LYS

LYS BACKED AWAY from the console, coaxing the wheels of her chair over the edge of the plastic matting and onto the close-napped rug. She noted that the nap was wearing thin and reminded herself again, as she did each time she passed the spot, to find a replacement. She ran a hand through the stubble of her fine dark hair and thought about Jason. She'd take Alecko's bait, Lys knew. Because it was a challenge. Because Jason didn't believe anyone could outguess or outmaneuver her. Because Alecko had made it personal; that was something Jason couldn't resist.

Lys wondered why Alecko was so hostile, personally, to Jason. Dhimitri Papandreou and Jason Horiuchi had been rivals for years, true—but their rivalry was professional; it didn't seem to leak into their private lives. Jason and Dhimitri respected each other's abilities, and liked each other as well. Alecko, on the other hand, seemed unreservedly hostile to them both.

Lys knew it would be a while before Jason returned, with Bear and Denny and Denny's new find. (Lys searched through the mental debris of the last hour and located the boy's name, buried in a half-dozen conversations she'd partially overheard and stored away from the babble at *Kenicki's*. Capella. She twisted the name in her mind, looking at it from all angles. She decided she liked it. Satisfied, she tossed it back into the clutter of her brain, to sort out later at her leisure.) By then

Jason would expect Lys to know the size of the museum and the nature of its security systems. If Lys could suggest plans of attack, so much the better.

She grabbed the ramp railing and swung the chair around and down. Blueprints, she knew, would be on file at Moulinos's civic center. There was no guarantee they'd be correct, though, and a lot to suggest they wouldn't. With or without the cooperation of the authorities—who were mostly members of the same five families, the aristocracy of this newly settled planet—the Papandreou museum would have arranged to file mistaken or misleading documents.

At the bottom of the ramp she grabbed the rail again and swung in an arc in the direction of the galley. She liked it when she had the ship to herself; there was no need to look out for clumsier crewmates. She popped the front wheels up to avoid the slight lip of the doorway and rolled up to the terminal. It was Denny's turn to fix dinner, but it was already late and even if she remembered (which was unlikely), any food she cooked wouldn't be anything to write home about. Lys asked the terminal for a list of possible meals with the materials on hand, and drummed her fingers lightly on the keyboard while the information spooled.

She could always check the file blueprints against the allocation of materials, find out how much would be required to build the museum as planned, and then compare it to the raw material actually used. Most contractors' records were computerized. If the information was still on file she would find it. The assessor's office would show the approximate footage of the museum for tax purposes, and a set of satellite pictures would offer another useful check, especially if the satellite were set up to transmit false-color photographs.

The terminal screen stopped flickering and Lys looked up to check the result. Out of a list of four reasonable suggestions, she picked Tuscan Chicken. The "chicken" was a native game bird, and the wine a resinated Fileri from Arcadia, but she'd picked the brandy herself on a trading run to St. Augustin, and the computer assured her that even with the substitutions the meal would be edible. Well, it wouldn't be as wild as some of Dendrite's efforts. She instructed the computer to go ahead.

What else? The museum had received a lot of press coverage over the years, so between the CDC and the local branches she should be able to get a number of flat photographs, a few Sunday supplement 3Vs, and some physical description. She would instruct her local to search for references to the Papandreou and to correlate them with the official plans. That would help pinpoint size discrepancies. If she could locate the false walls, she could decide how much space was given over to service halls, which would help her evaluate the extent of the security systems.

The terminal beeped at her and she took the "chicken" from the bin where it had been prepared and moved it to the oven. She didn't check the temperature. She knew it was right; she'd programmed the kitchen herself.

A check of incoming and outgoing mail and telephone calls for the Papandreou family would give an indication of the electronic firms the museum had contacted, including those which had been consulted more than once. She might widen the search to include Papandreou subsidiaries—which would increase the chance of seeing a pattern, but lessen the chance that the pattern would apply only to the museum—but that could wait until she had her initial results. It would be nice to find a disgruntled ex-employee, but that was unlikely.

Too much information to remember: she brought out her template and began writing a rough outline of the information she had and what she still needed. The result was sparse, but at least she had a working guide. She transferred the file to the computer, corrected an entry where the machine had been unable to read her handwriting, and lifted the cover sheet to erase the template. The entire process had taken only a few minutes, but Lys was uncomfortably aware of how much work it represented for her in the morning. This style of larceny was more trouble than it was worth, and she fervently wished Jason would find another hobby.

The terminal beeped again. Lys looked up, annoyed, realized it was time to put the vegetables on, and got the platter from the cooler. It was a nice assortment, lots of greens with a few bright yellow and red peppers for color. It had been a peace-making gift from M'orru; it hadn't worked. Lys had tried more than once to convince Jason to buy out M'orru's contract, considering her a disruptive influence within the crew. For, though she'd made some surprising contributions to the *Argo* (like the time she'd Tasted contaminants, olfactorily neutral, in fuel which had already been passed by Kenot), she never seemed willing to *work* at anything. If a project didn't come easily, she abandoned it. It made Lys angry: if *she* could wear that wonderful, coltish body, she often thought, *she* wouldn't waste it as M'orru did. It didn't help that she knew she was alone in her feelings; everyone else liked M'orru and got along well with her.

Lys had to stretch to reach the wok, grumbling at the thoughtlessness of people who stored things out of her reach. She set it on the magnetic ring, squeezed in oil, and turned on the burner, waited, and stirred in the vegetables. The wok was invaluable; even Denny could cook with one.

Lys remembered one morning on Helios, with the sun shining through the observation blister. M'orru had been sleeping in Jason's pilot's chair, her gold hair spun out against the fine red leather, her legs tucked under her. Asleep she was beautiful, and Lys had stayed, watching her quietly. Then Denny had dropped something in the galley; when Lys turned back, M'orru was awake and watching with her disingenuous, sideways glance, lips slightly parted as though she were waiting anxiously for anything you'd have to say. What had once been charming had worn thin; by then it was merely irritating.

Irritated, Lys had rolled past her across the floor, past the worn spot on the rug, and had set to work, grumpily, at her terminal. She hadn't looked up when M'orru had padded past her, or when she'd stood waiting for Lys to finish her work. Stubbornly Lys had continued to look for something that would engage her attention sufficiently that she could continue to ignore the disingenuous, graceless, arrogant . . . seductive person behind her.

That had been a month before, and Lys still couldn't explain her feelings. God knew, Jason had asked her often enough. She knew it made her job harder, and when she was honest with herself she had to admit that it made M'orru's job more difficult too—which was why Lys was standing over a stove with a panful of fresh produce. Well, she'd accept the offering because she couldn't waste good food, but she still wouldn't talk to the woman if she could help it!

If Denny got back in time and *if* she remembered she had galley duty, *then* Jason would be angry at Lys for eating alone. Jason liked to think of the ship as a family, and she had somewhere acquired the idea that families ate at least one meal a day together. The idea amazed Lys; her family never had, and she had trouble imagining them all gathered together, to sit at one table without an argument. She wondered who'd crack first, her orthofather or her great-aunt. She let herself descend to fantasy: maybe they'd fight and kill each other; that would be nice.

She'd found one thing about the Papandreou that surprised her, but pleased her sense of style. Now, who had thought to blanket a room with answer-back infrared? Marvelous! Everything and everyone in the galleries would be surrounded by a constant stream of invisible light, and anything larger than a dust mote would be immediately tagged and filed. It was elegant and expensive. Only the Papandreou could afford the luxury.

The computer sounded again: dinner was ready. She triggered the waldoes and was just transferring the vegetables to her plate as the chicken was delivered to the table. She'd forgotten wine. She tapped one of the hexagonal tiles on the table top to activate the plasma screen, touched the wine list on the directory, scrolled through slowly, and finally picked a split of Kokineli, left over from an earlier meal. There'd be just enough for her dinner.

With that she let herself relax. There'd be plenty to do in the morning, between scheduling Jason's trips to her mining properties and her own trading activities. For now, unless Jason called, she could enjoy her meal in peace and then get some sleep.

___ 3 _____

JASON _____

AND FINALLY BEAR slept. Jason slipped out of the cabin, quietly closing the door. Later she would sleep; now she ached with undischarged tensions.

She rubbed her hand the length of the wooden panel along the galley, as she did each time she passed. Laser-cut across cells, just thick enough to show the grain, you could get thousands of similar panels from one of the huge old trees outside her father's California estate. The laminate sealing the wood was cell-thick, too, but tough enough to protect the wood for generations. Through it she thought she could feel each small blemish—a bad winter, a good fall—and the warmth of the wood as if it were still alive. Once every few years she went back to check on the subsiding waters and to see what wood could be sacrificed. Some trees, flood-damaged, still contained useful heartwood. These she chose to provide office facings for Horiuchi buildings, and for her own ships.

She passed by the galley and started down the ladder. Someone watching her would have seen her pause, her right foot suspended on a rung. But no one saw the secret smile which raised her high cheekbones so that her eyes, normally deep-set, were thrown even further into shadow. It was more than anything mischievous—"I'm going to do something I shouldn't't"—and the same expression had been caught once, when she was seven and secretive, in an old 3V photograph she had never seen. It rested now, with a miscellany of other forgotten items, in the attic of her home in Osaka. Tossing her pack down before her, she braced herself on the rails and slid down, letting go as she neared the floor. She bounced as she hit bottom, tucked herself in for a forward roll, into a forward flip—and nearly slammed into the lock, having misjudged the distance. She stopped her momentum, hard, with the heel of her hands. Not bad for a centenarian.

She picked up the pack and made her way through the port, eerily silent now in that predawn lull before the late ships come in and the early leave. In Metacenter this time would be as busy as any other, with the field bright with high-intensity lights and ships boosting with metronomic frequency; but farther out commerce seemed to follow each world's diurnal rhythm, and early mornings were usually quiet. Baggage loaders crisscrossed the tarmac, hardly disturbing the still air, and cargo doors rumbled in the distance, muffled and indistinct.

A chill rain swept the field intermittently, though the sky above was clearing. Charybdis was gibbous. She looked west, hoping to see Sol, but Sol was too dim and too distant. Her shadow flickered as a cloud passed overhead. She pulled the parka's hood close and buried her hands in fur pockets. So strange to be so warm during the day and so cold at night; but they were high in the hills surrounding Moulinos, itself rising sharply above the water.

It had seemed odd to her to find the planetary capital built on an island. But Moulinos depended on space travel for much of its vitality, and the mammoth flat tableland on which the spaceport lay had therefore made the island of Mykonos a tremendous attraction. Had there been rockets, of course, having the spaceport so near the capital would have been out of the question; but a ship with inertial drive could land in the town square and do little more than rip loose overhead wiring.

Jason neared the edge of the field and was caught in the bright flash of the guard's light. She took her hands from her pockets and spread her hood, nodding at the young boy in the shed. "Just out walking, Laökos," she said. "I'll be back before long."

She passed the perimeter and was out into the rough cobble leading to the Beehive. No buzzing yet, she thought; the lawyers were snug in their beds. Cobblestone gave way to brick, not pavement. The roads were designed to decrease vehicular traffic through the central core, and no one with business in Moulinos drove there. If you needed something, you hired someone to get it for you. The Beehive was a clean, pleasant, sterile place to walk.

After a time the tall buildings oppressed her, and she cut off on a diagonal toward the marshland on the city's edge. New Crete had learned lessons from Earth. Where many home-world cities had paved over marshland, Moulinos had left such land as nearly as possible alone, ensuring only that its waters bred little if any disease. Mosquitoes it had, but they were *healthy* mosquitoes.

The nacre of the sky was lightening into dawn as Jason stepped over the abrupt end of the pavement. She shifted the heavy pack on her back, grateful for its weight; it felt solid and substantial, and sometimes she liked the feeling of gravity, of something drawing her home, to the earth.

The wood had been quiet when Jason had entered; she noticed now only because as she walked she heard the harsh scream of a kite and the less dramatic call of a barbary partridge, sounding like an old engine badly in need of a tune-up. Bramble and bracken tangled beneath her feet, and she almost lost a boot in the mire.

Unexpectedly, a screen of underbrush gave way to a rocky promontory overlooking the sea. The water was a vivid shimmering gold in the morning sun. It was peaceful simply to rest, with no calls upon her attention and nothing, now, to worry about. She'd even taken out her silvertip. With its absence she felt a curious freedom. Today would be her own; Lys could do without her help this once. She perched on the edge of the cliff, rocking back and forth on her heels. In the distance, barely visible, a high tor was topped by a monastery, surrounded on three sides by tumultuous surf while on the fourth a narrow isthmus connected the isolated finger of land with the main body of the island. Below her, ivy crept into the crevices of gray volcanic rock, while the occasional emphatic asterisks of bright yellow daisies could be seen through the green carpet.

She was tired enough to sleep now, so walking had served its purpose, but Jason had no desire to push her way back through the dense undergrowth. Instead she searched until she found a path, old bog paved with the weight of many people walking over time, and followed the path to the shore, the shore to the road, and the road back to the port. Later she couldn't recall reaching the *Argo,* nor the moment when (as she was hanging her jacket in the clean closet, brushing loose the worst of the dust; the closet would take care of the rest, so that next morning it would be ready to wear again) she felt in one pocket cool metal and fine twisted chain.

The watch came loose first; it was lovely, handmade, handcrafted, a fine analog timepiece, absolutely useless off New Crete. She strapped it on. The ring she set aside. The knife she opened and (with the ball of her thumb she tested its edge) closed again. She counted out the coins and put them in a jar, half full, on her desk. Both business cards were useless, the speakers broken or the batteries low; she threw them away. Somewhere she'd acquired a key, not one of hers. She set it aside. The hologrammatic pendants with their mutually distorting images she left braided together. She'd give them to Lys in the morning.

A. J. Pandey took his turn at guard duty along with all his employees; it had taken Lys four trips to New Crete to learn that he owned the spaceport warehouse, as well as a substantial amount of the port land. She should have spoken to him when the *Argo* had first landed, but she'd put it off because he'd been at once attractive and intimidating to her. He was tall (the orange turban made him seem taller still), and his striking black beard and mustache, curried and combed into fierce arcs framing his face, contributed to the image, which was somehow even more advanced by his incongruous business suit—somehow she expected to see him in robes, or in some form of homespun, hand-dyed cotton.

He nodded politely when she asked. "Storage space? We have some, yes, miss; and for a very short time only. But your ship is not one of the great trading vessels, is it?"

He smiled to remove any possible offense from his words. She grinned back, because the *Argo* was visible from where they both stood, dwarfed by every vessel around her. She was designed solely to get Jason from place to place in her far-flung business empire as rapidly as possible; she leased storage space to Lys—and lab space to Kenot—as a matter of courtesy. If Lys had been primarily a trader, she would have looked for a larger ship, but because *Argo* had so little space she had to be extremely selective in what she bought and she liked it that way, because it forced her to think about every item she chose, whom it would attract and how it would be used. It was a discipline, very much like learning how to ask the right questions of information systems.

Lys thanked the guard, promised to have the materials she purchased delivered as soon as possible, and turned to go. Pandey called out. "My son must go *sto agora* to pick up a few items. Perhaps he might offer you a ride?"

She considered: she'd planned on taking a taxi down, but it would take time and cost money. Still, she'd seen Pandey's truck, which looked to be contemporary with the founding of Moulinos.

Time and money concerns won out, and she soon found herself jolting uncomfortably in the ancient truck, down the mesa road toward the marketplace. Pandey's sullen son resembled his father only in the intricacies of his massive black beard. He said hardly anything to her until they'd reached the docks and the beginning of the extensive outdoor market. As he removed the makeshift wooden ramp his only comment was terse. "I'm not public transportation. I'm not going to give you a ride back."

She rolled back to allow him room to maneuver. "I wouldn't expect it. But thanks anyway." His only answer was the glare which seemed to be his entire range of expression. He drove away and Lys turned toward the waterfront.

It was a beautiful place, chaotic and stimulating. The gleaming white buildings, windows and doors trimmed in bright primary colors, jumbled and jostled each other like eager puppies, right to the edge of the water. Power cables draped from building to building and were stapled to the fronts of each as if they were part of a deliberate rococo design. Balconies thrust over the roofs of some buildings and nudged against the sides of others, sometimes higher, sometimes lower, sometimes nearly the same height, so that people drinking at several different cafes could and did eavesdrop on the conversations of anyone nearby.

There were boats in the harbor, though there were no actual docks. Pilings supported a restaurant here, a hotel there, and visitors climbed ladders directly from the water to the nearest building. The beach nearby was crowded with boats drawn haphazardly onto the sand: turquoise and white, magenta and white, cyan and white, yellow and white, all colors that shone with a vibrant intensity. Even the sky was a vivid, preternatural blue, and the sun, warmer, was whiter than Earth's.

She took her time, moving from place to place as easily as possible, considering the incredible swarm of people. Not everyone made way for a woman in a wheelchair. This was a working market, from which many of the people of Moulinos bought their goods; but it was also a tremendous tourist attraction, and elderly men and women wearing plain denims, cottons, and corduroys moved restlessly among the more exotic programmed hologrammatic fabrics whose surfaces were designed to mimic sunrises and sunsets on distant, wasted worlds.

She stopped in front of one stall late in the morning, arrested by the color of a bolt of fabric suspended from a wooden dowel. Unlike similar fabrics nearby, it wasn't an assault to her eye, but it had a cool intensity of its own which Lys found attractive. More, she was willing to bet it was salable.

A thin young boy with thick ropes of old scars across his shoulders and chest and a mop of thick black hair indifferently cut and falling over his eyes sat watching the platform of a holovision, his palms holding him inches off the seat of a tall four-legged stool, his ankles dangling idly. Lys called out, "Anything interesting?"

The boy swiveled on his stool. His black eyes were lively, and the unlined olive of his face was the only visible part of him left unscarred. He pointed a toe at the screen. "That man there is occasionally one of my customers. He's too large; he intimidates me." Lys looked at the holo-v stage and realized that the tiny three-inch figure was A. J. Pandey from the port warehouse. Apparently there had been some sort of demonstration commemorating the four-hundredth anniversary of a Sikh civil victory, and Pandey was being interviewed as a spokesman of sorts. Lys listened for a moment, but lost interest quickly.

"He is large, isn't he? But then he's a security guard; he's supposed to be frightening." She spun the bolt of cloth on its dowel and held an edge of the fabric into the light. It was even more striking with the sun on it. "I'm interested in buying a quantity of this. What is it?"

Lys had picked one bolt of cloth from what seemed to be

hundreds, jammed into every conceivable area. Between them, suspended from makeshift hangers, were white cotton shirts intricately embroidered, but the embroidery, in general, was exactly like that in half the shops she'd visited this morning. She might wear such a shirt herself, but it wouldn't have been worth her while to purchase any for resale.

The boy vaulted from his perch and made his way through the narrow aisles of his crowded canvas-covered shop. "You don't want to know what it is, it's just challis, you can get it anywhere. You want to know who dyed it." He tapped his thin chest with a forefinger. "*I* did. It's cha-lyb-*e*-ous challis. I picked it because I like the name, but all it means is steel blue. But it's very nice, and *very* expensive."

He said the last hopefully. She rerolled the bolt and cheerfully said, "Then you won't sell much, will you?"

"Maybe not of the cloth alone, but perhaps there are some fringe benefits?" He licked his lips in an elaborate cartoon of lasciviousness, and Lys laughed then. She didn't laugh easily, but her grim square face was attractive when she did.

"Is that where you got these, *paidhaki mou?*" She rubbed an irregular knotted line blurring his trapezious.

"*Kyria paidhaki* to you, *dhespoinis.* Or 'Sabu.'" He shrugged. "I *earned* those!" His outflung hand took in the confines of his cluttered canvas stall. "Do you think I learned the craft needed for this all by myself?" And then he looked down at the dirt floor, a dusty clay just drying out from the mire of yesterday's rain. His pose was submissive, but he spoiled it by looking at her from under lowered brows, and light danced in his eyes. "*Maybe* I liked it." Then he looked up, his submissive pose forgotten. "What do you think of my stock?"

She laughed again and the grim lines softened further. "I think I'm glad I only want one thing, and that I have very little time. Otherwise you might talk so fast that I'd find myself owning a merchant's stall in Moulinos. But I've seen what I want, and I still have to search this market for spices. So: let's discuss prices."

He was hardly more than a boy, and he gave the impression of being flighty and frivolous, but he drove a hard bargain. In the end Lys had agreed to buy all the chalybeous fabric he had in stock and had made arrangements to have it shipped to

Pandey's warehouse; and, though she had gotten her money's worth, she definitely hadn't gotten any bargain.

Pandey seemed more intimidating now that she'd seen him on the CDC news. It must have been some battle, she thought, to eclipse the Niarin war, analyses of which were still being shown daily on Moulinos's official network. (Of course, the fact that the Five Families had contributed heavily to the war, and that Papandreou et Cie had supplied mercenaries, might have had something to do with the endless recriminatory debates.)

She rolled forward. "Good afternoon, Mr. Pandey," she said, carefully cheerful. "Have my goods been delivered?"

He bowed from the waist, his hands stiffly at his sides. "Yes, miss. If you'll follow me?" He stepped aside to let her roll into the warehouse, carefully locking the door behind her. "We have little space left, as you see. It has been quite busy, in anticipation of the coming tricentennial. Many people, very proud of what we have done here, have begun their plans early, and we have as a result a great many things to store until next year." His teeth were very white; he turned to smile at her. "Nevertheless I have found space for you which, I hope, will be convenient."

The aisles of the warehouse were narrow, with high stacked material on each side casting shadows in the dim light. Her own boxes were by a large metal door of ribbed steel segments. They were carefully marked. Pandey obviously expected them to be moved soon. He handed her a handwritten inventory and stood, arms crossed, as she checked each item. She nodded and handed it back. "There should be a few more items to come," she said. "Nothing very large; I found some spices late this afternoon. Which for some reason are difficult to get here."

His white teeth gleamed. "We are proud of our spices, Miss Lyskopoulis. Mr. Papandreou has very strict rules telling us to whom we may sell, and we much prefer to accede to them. If you have bought such spices for resale, it is my hope that you will not diminish their value by disposing of them too cheaply, and that you will remember always that each spice is carefully grown and nurtured. But, of course, if you *have* bought such spices, the merchant has trusted that you will respect their quality."

She laughed. "Buy cheap, sell dear?"

"Very dear, yes." His smile was dazzling. "Now, when may we expect you to remove your goods?"

Lys rolled past the stacked pallets. "You must have moved something here; *Argo*'s right beyond the door, isn't it?" Pandey nodded. "Convenient. I should imagine we'll be gone by the end of the week." A week on New Crete was nine days long. New Crete was somewhat farther out from her sun than Earth was from Sol; her "year" was about 450 days, each day nearly two hours longer than Earth Standard. Lys sometimes wished she were a watchmaker; since the dawn of the interstellar age, their future had been assured. She'd lost count of the times she'd had her watch reset for local times before she'd started carrying several, one for Greenwich, one for whatever local time was in effect, and one for CDC Standard. (Which, honestly, was a nuisance, but some systems insisted on it. Government officials went merrily on their way, day and night, functioning on CDC Standard time, with an hour, a day, a week, or a month off periodically to adjust; while the people they governed—sensibly—based their day and times on the rotation of their planet around their sun. New Crete, fortunately, was ruled in this respect by reasonable people; they disliked and distrusted the CDC.) She also had a couple spares, in case any one watch broke.

"Captain Horiuchi had some business to attend to, but now we're only waiting until we have a full crew before we leave." She added anxiously, "It won't cause you any problem, will it?"

Pandey had carefully folded his inventory and put it in the large leather wallet clipped to his belt. "I should think not, unless you will be a great while longer. However, please let me know if you do extend your stay." He started walking back toward the entrance.

She rolled beside him, troubled. Finally she said, "A. J., you know the policies here. Why is it that the Papandreou family has so much power? I would think it was bad for this city, for New Crete."

He stared down at her. "Bad? If it were anyone but Dhimitri Papandreou, perhaps you would be right. Power is a dangerous thing, yes. But Mr. Papandreou is a very *strong* man, very exceptional. I am very, very happy to have him govern."

They'd reached the front. "I suppose I'm used to free

trade," she said. "It bothers me that one man—or one family —is responsible for the livelihood of a planet."

Pandey stroked his beard. "But he is a very *disciplined* man, miss." The distinction obviously was important to him. *"Not* like his son," he continued with distaste. *My* son tells me that boy kills animals, for pleasure." He opened the door, closing off further discussion. Strong shadows cast by the afternoon sun were crawling across the field. Dust motes danced in the rectangle of light from the door; Lys and Pandey passed through like fronds through water.

"Look below and you will see a city," he said. "You have heard that we make our living selling spice. I have said so myself. But spice is only a little part of the commerce of a city, and an even smaller part of the commerce of a world." He closed the door behind them and stepped slowly down the stairs as she rolled to and down the concrete ramp.

"Mr. Papandreou, he is concerned that we are, as much as is practicable, self-sufficient. Self-sufficiency, though, he knows, as do we all, here on nearly the newest of the new planets, is not a product easily wrought, nor is it easily maintained once it is, with difficulty, attained." They moved together out of the shadow of the warehouse. The day was ending and night fell quickly in Moulinos; this high, at the edge of the mesa that was the spaceport, the afternoon wind was chilly to anyone standing away from the direct sun. "So, out of patriotism—and, it must be admitted, perhaps proclaimed, out of enlightened self-interest as well—Mr. Papandreou, he supports many industries that are as yet marginal, and which are too often dependent on the vagaries of interstellar commerce.

"We are a small world yet. Not in terms of size, certainly; but, you see, our tricentennial marks the founding of Moulinos, which effectively was the founding of New Crete as well. We were the first city, after those decades of shaping and molding which created this world out of nothing, out of a sterile planet. It was a gift of God, and our peoples thanked Him, each in our own way, and turned rough stone into the jewel you see." He shaded his eyes in the strong sun. "We have few cities as yet, but we have many, many plantations where we grow food, and though they are necessary to our survival, they are not necessarily self-supporting. You see the difficulty, perhaps? The rice crop exceeds expectations? The farmers cannot then receive enough income to repay their in-

vestment. Mr. Papandreou graciously lends them the money
so that next year, when crops are not so plentiful and the price
of rice as a result rises, these growers will still be in business
and will grow more rice to feed our peoples. If he does not
lend them the money, at low interest, they fail; and the next
year there is no rice and a famine thereby ensues.

"So, too, with the equatorial lands, not tropic but desert,
where we have begun to grow what was called on Earth 'teff';
it is a difficult grain that requires sun at certain times and rain
at certain times, that is difficult to harvest and difficult, too, to
store. Yet it is a very *popular* grain, and those who harvest it
claim that it will in time be very profitable, for there are mil-
lions of people throughout God's gracious universe who are
fond of its taste and who will willingly pay so that they may
have it to eat on a regular basis." He paused. "I myself have
tried teff, in the form called 'injera.' It was very, very tasty. I
have only had it the once, though."

Lys looked interested. "Do you know of a restaurant that
serves it, A. K.? I've never heard of it. I'd like to try some."
If it was good, maybe there was a market for it.

He stroked his beard, considering. "That I do not know,
although I suppose there would be, in the Fagiton Exthesis,
such a specialized restaurant." He smiled down at her. "I shall
check, Miss Lyskopoulis."

He walked a little farther. "But to continue. Also in the
warmer climates, there are coffee plantations. Coffee is a risk
here; the soil, due to the presence of many different minerals,
creates coffees that taste stronger or weaker, more bitter or
more acid, than those we are used to, you are used to, the
people whom we wish to buy our coffees are used to; and so
they do not sell well. Someday we will find the patch of land
which will grow coffees that will rival those from legendary
Colombia, before it was destroyed. For now, we haven't. Very
well. Mr. Papandreou, mindful that in the future his interest
may generate a substantial return, continues to underwrite
the growing of coffee. And meanwhile we drink the results
of experiments—because, really, few people actually *taste*
coffee. They know, of course, when it is too hot, but otherwise . . . ?"

" 'I like it hot and sweet, just like my lovers'?"

"Exactly."

I thought I was afeared, she thought, until I saw his beard;

then wondered where the thought had come from. Really, she was getting as bad as Jason. Exposure, no doubt.

"This continues for many, many industries, and for many people who would, without the aid of Mr. Papandreou and those he—ah—*persuades* to help, be quite unable to live on what is still, despite the appearance of our beautiful Moulinos, a new and raw planet. You understand. We must have help to sell our goods; we must have help to market them on any world but our own. We—and I speak now, I must now say, for many people across the cities and towns we have forged, as well as those on the plantations and farms, the mines and quarries—need someone to whom we can turn until such time as we are able to rely not on the vagaries of the marketplace but on the quality of our goods. Till such time, in short, when you from Ilios, and your Jason from Earth, and Bear from Cameron, and, indeed, my own family from Krsna, will be willing to come to New Crete solely because you have heard of our merchandise and wish to buy some." His smile now was dazzling, framed by splendid black hair. He made Lys nervous; she was too attracted to him. "This is what Mr. Papandreou has done and is doing for us.

"I am not saying, I must add, that Mr. Papandreou is a paragon or in any way a holy man. He is human and has his share of venality, concupiscence, avariciousness, and other sins to which we all, even under the eyes of God, fall prey. But he wishes New Crete and his city, Moulinos, to succeed, to be an example of all struggling colonies in our expanding universe. May we all find glory in God!"

Troubled, she struggled to find words to express herself without explaining that, simply, she was worried that her captain would finally run up against an obstacle she couldn't sidestep or overleap. Loyalty prevented her from overtly criticizing Jason to anyone not on the crew. Slowly, thinking about each word before she said it, she asked, "Is it *necessary,* in bringing about this self-sufficiency you want, that Moulinos be so . . . highly regulated? It seems to me that there are laws against nearly everything." She paused, frustrated. Damn. If only she could think more clearly. She wondered when he got off shift, and whether he'd like to come back to the ship with her. She could cook up some fejoada, assuming he liked pork. What did Sikhs eat, anyway? "It seems like if you trip crossing the street, you'll be breaking some rule, somewhere."

He nodded his head very slowly, considering. "I suppose it must seem so to those who only visit. But then I suspect many cities, on many worlds, must be the same. Should you read their books of statutes you would be appalled. 'But they cannot make *that* illegal. Can they?'" He chuckled. "There is a story that my father once told me; he was old when I learned it, and I suspect he learned it as a very young man. A gentleman is placed in a cell, and uses the visiphone therein to call his solicitor. 'They have arrested me,' the young sir says, at which his solicitor replies, 'What is the charge?' The young man tells her, and *she* says, 'They cannot arrest you for *that!'* The young sir replies, 'I agree they cannot, but they have.'" He nodded again ruminatively. "Very much so. You see, the codification of laws is often the result not so much of the wishes of the people, or of the administration which represents the people, but of the legislators who feel it incumbent upon them to act as if they were doing something at all times. Which means that they frequently pass meaningless albeit well-meaning laws which, they hope, will represent the populace at large. You must not take such things very seriously; we do not."

Lys pulled her coat more tightly around her. While they talked, the shadows had lengthened and now reached to where they stood. She rolled into the sunlight but Pandey, with a glance toward the warehouse door, remained where he was. Sighing, she rolled back. He had a peculiar and rigid concept of duty which would not allow him to stray too far from his post, and she'd exceeded his limit. It was too damn cold to stay talking, yet she was unwilling to stop the conversation. Then, because she resented having to stay in the chill shadows, she said with a touch of malice, "Then you don't take seriously the thieves I saw in the market this morning, who are missing a few fingers here and there, or the men and women who have scars because they've been publicly whipped?"

"Oh, no, miss. I take it very seriously indeed." He stood nearly at attention, his eyes fixed not on her but on the horizon behind her, on the building-block boxes making up Moulinos. "You are just visiting here, Miss Lyskopoulis; you will go away soon, and I cannot say and you cannot say, now, if you will ever be back. We live here. This is our home. And it is difficult to maintain one's home in the face of vandals who could easily tear it down. If you were to come home one day and find your house broken into and your belongings strewn across the room, some besmeared with excrement, some only ripped and torn, but nevertheless all rendered useless to you, it would be for you to say that the thief should be given a fine, suspended, and let off with a warning; that would be your right. Or you could insist that the thief be given a prison sentence, which would take him away from your ken but leave him to fester in a place where grievances could and would grow, and flower. Then, after a year or two with other men and women with grievances of their own, which they would share with him so that his would reach fruition in the humus of their opinion, he would be released. In the meantime you and all your friends and relations would have paid for his feeding and his care, with no guarantee—and much to gainsay—that his grievance would be lessened by his prison stay. Very expensive, yes.

"Here? We say, 'Well, you are perhaps a product of your environment, and perhaps it is we who have made you what you are. Nevertheless, we will whip you, sir, because you will then think twice about doing something we believe—and you have been told—is wrong.' He is whipped then and released. What is the cost? The pay of one flagellator; the professional fees of doctors and nurses, standing by to ensure we do no permanent harm; in the unlikely event a death should occur, death duty to the man's widow or the woman's widower, whichever it may be. Does that make us barbarians, miss? You may say so if you wish. But we are only protecting our home—our city and our culture—in the way that causes the least anguish to all." He paused. "Those that are missing fingers, or who are more seriously injured by the loss of a limb, are those who have had need of repeated instruction. In every classroom there is at least one child who will not listen to lessons." He touched a finger to his turban. "I must return to my duties. Good day, miss."

She nodded and muttered, "Good day." She watched as he walked back inside the warehouse, until he was hidden within its sheet metal sides. Then she turned and rolled across the tarmac to *Argo*'s landing slip.

4

JASON AND BEAR

JASON SHOOK HER. "Bear?" She got no response. "Bear, damn it, wake up." She shook her again. "Damn it, Bear, if you're not going to wake up, at least give me half the covers." She grabbed a handful and pulled, hard.

One hand came out from under Bear's body and pulled harder. A muffled, grumpy, sleepy voice said, "If you go out of your way to get me drunk, Captain, the least you can do is let me stay warm the next morning."

Jason slapped a bare patch of skin below Bear's coccyx. (The rest was covered in blankets or fur.) It made a satisfying sound, so she did it again. "I've already been up and walking this morning. The marshland north of the city is beautiful, Bear! And there's a view out over the ocean. We can take a lunch up there, the two of us. All you have to do is get up."

The pillow raised up slightly and one eye glared at her balefully. "You are so goddamn self-righteous about your god-damn allergy to goddamn alcohol. You can go to Hell. My head hurts. I already climbed a mountain with you, last night. Remember Mars? Remember Olympus Mons? The road here must be *at least* that high." The pillow dropped down again and a muffled voice said, "Go away."

"I'm not allergic, only sensitive. It enhances my natural caution."

"On the other hand," Bear said, "if I *don't* get up, you won't let me forget it for weeks. 'Here, Denny, you take the

63

helm; Bear's in no shape for such *strenuous* exercise'; 'Let Bear rest; she's still recuperating from last night'; 'We'll have to find some nice warm rock where Bear can sun herself; this life she's living is too hard for a woman her age'; et, as they say, cetera." She threw the covers into a pile on the floor. "All right. I'm up. Now what?"

Jason hugged Bear, pleased. "Now I see how far you can walk before you collapse," she said.

There was a lake, and in the distance the ocean shimmered, reflecting a pellucid sky. "It's not Mount Ida," Bear said, "but it'll have to do." She was still panting from the climb, like a dog on a hot day. The manipulative surgery that had created her pelt had involved radical alterations to her hypothalamus; an increase in sweat glands in her hands, forearms, and frontal torso provided benign hyperidrosis and that helped some, but to produce the fat and oil needed to keep her fur supple had meant taking some sweat glands and replacing them with sebaceous glands. She was well insulated but radiated badly.

Down below, at the edge of visibility, a small herd of ponies (stunted horses really) could be seen nibbling the coarse grass of an elevated lea. A small pond had formed at the lower edge, run-off from higher streams, and from its basin a miniature cataract fell to a still lower rocky plateau. "I could live in a valley like this, Jason," Bear said.

"I did, once." Jason picked up a rock and dropped it over the edge, and listened to it bounce, ledge by ledge, down the cliff face. "My father sent me to a boarding school on Earth, in the Andes near Tierra del Fuego." She picked idly at the yellow lithophytes growing through crevices in the stone.

She opened her eyes. "That's where I had my silvertip implanted, but they weren't called 'silvertips' yet, but 'Bach– Buckley intercranial neural monitors,' or something of the kind. My first lover had them. His mother was Bach, his father Buckley, they developed the original patent, and they implanted him almost as soon as he was born. He was scrawny, all ribbons and string, but I thought he was wonderful.

"When they said they wanted to put a silvertip in me, I thought that meant they'd put a wire in my head so they could somehow *control* me, like a robot. That has a lot to do with my attitude about using the Net in military service now, too;

the idea of control still scares me. Imagine being a private in battle, backing out of a certain-death situation, when some officer who's safe in a ship above you decides it's better for him if you walk on in and die."

"You were twelve? That was—when, about '271?"

"Yes," Jason said quietly. "A long time ago. So I hid," she added, "as much as I could. I explored the nearby caves, and found a half-dozen exits from the mountain, mostly following flowing water. I picked two or three of them and fixed them up with blankets and dried food and whatever else I could steal." Jason rolled onto her spine; her eyes were half closed; her voice for the last few minutes had been growing gradually softer. "I picked the deepest cave I'd found, a beautiful, big grotto with stalactites hanging down like chandeliers and a wonderful whispering river running, bam, right through the center." She raised up on her elbows. "I wanted to seduce my friend, you see.

"It worked. I liked it. So did he. We were both pretty clumsy at first, but once we learned how everything fitted together we had a fine time. That skinny little kid was a fast learner, and I guess I was, too. It was a long time before we ran out of things that we'd heard of and wanted to try. Later, when we were side by side in the dark, I remember laying astride him, listening to the sound of his heart mixing with the sound of running water. And I said, 'I wish I could feel it from *your* side.'

"And *he* said, 'Well, they should have today's tape in the library by tomorrow afternoon, and then you can.' They were world builders, you see, his parents and the others at Tierra del Fuego. They wanted to record the experiences of everyone, because they thought the Net would lead to some unambiguous Utopian society in which everyone was equal because of pooled experiences, shared indiscriminately.

"I'd wanted my affair to be private. That's why I took him down into the caverns; I thought they'd insulate against transmission, as though the Net operated on radio waves. I'd wanted the experience to be *mine;* and the next day anyone at the school could visit the library and find out what a good screw I was.

"I didn't think. I just grabbed the lantern and ran back through the caverns to my room, where I locked the door and cried myself to sleep."

She was silent for a moment. Bear said, "What happened to the kid?"

Jason took a deep breath and let it out slowly. "He died. And now I can't even recall his name. Kimo? Robin? No, I don't remember."

Bear tossed a rock and watched it bounce down the cliff face. "Why should you? That was more than a hundred years ago. Unless it's an obsession."

"An obsession? No. But I saw someone last night who reminded me of him, and I've been thinking about it ever since." She brushed leaves from her clothing. "I talk too much. Let's go back to the ship."

The cabin was like a sauna when Jason emerged, toweling herself vigorously. Clothing accented her gender; naked, she was nearly androgynous, with small, muscular breasts, a narrow waist, and slim hips. Her upper arm and thigh muscles were well developed as the result both of diligent exercise and genetic predisposition, and if she carried any superfluous weight it wasn't immediately evident. Bear, in contrast, seemed overweight and ungainly—an illusion created by the combination of her pelt and a protective subcutaneous layer of fatty tissue.

Bear was at the desk, separating strands of chain. She held up one of the pendants. "These are new. Where'd you get them?"

"Last night. I found them after I left you at Fibi's. They're for Lys. And I've got a ring for you." She took it out of the drawer.

Bear looked at it critically. "It's a little small," she said. "Maybe I can wear it on a chain around my neck." She put it in her pocket. "Thanks. I like it. You get ready; I'm hungry. I'll see you at breakfast."

A quarter of an hour passed before Jason made her way downstairs. M'orru waved a piece of toast in greeting (because it was in her hand at the time). Rat continued to eat with passionless intensity. (He often seemed to consider meals a grim but unavoidable necessity.) Bear (not, surprisingly, Denny) was talking quietly to Capella, who sat in a chair too small for him, his knees bumping the undersurface of the galley table. Even Kenot was there (not because he enjoyed the communal meals but because it was easier than arguing).

"Listen to this, Jason!" Bear said. (It must have been important; Bear had interrupted eating to talk.) She sang a note and held it; Capella came in with the first overtone of the harmonic. When he had held his note as long as she held hers before he joined in, she switched to the third overtone. They worked their way up and down the scale, in perfect harmony. The music (yes: only apparently simple) was seamless and serene.

Bear's breath control Jason knew from experience; Capella was her match. They had to breathe sometime, of course; and with only two voices, she would hear the gap in sound, or a slight gasp for air.

She didn't.

They finally rolled to a stop, simply; simultaneously. Jason shivered slightly. "What *was* that?"

Bear's eyes were nearly squeezed shut as maxillary muscles flexed to accommodate a huge smile. "A voice exercise. But *what* an exercise! When *he* hits an A you could measure it out at four hundred forty hertz ex*act*ly." She ruffled his hair. "He's going to study with me, Jason. I always wanted a student with perfect pitch. He can sing, too." She frowned. "Though I should have gotten you earlier, Senhor Capella. You have a smooth voice; if I had only met you when you were younger!"

"You two got together in the ten minutes I spent getting ready? And where'd you learn to sing like that, Capella?"

"I trained at the Levka Vourna, on the western shore of Mykonos. I was in the choir; that's where I first heard Bear Vouris, from her recordings."

"Ah. I have some disks myself; you may want to borrow them later." Jason tapped the table to bring up the computer screen. She ordered a hedgehog omelette because Lys had programmed the chef to make them, and Jason was fascinated that it could be successful with such a delicate thing. "What time is it?"

Automatically, Capella answered, "Three hours, ten minutes to meridian."

"It's early yet. Where's Lys?"

"She's gone to pick up trade goods," Bear said. She was back to work on her second helping of bacon and eggs, and a great mound of buttered toast. "I tried to talk to her before she left, but she had her goddamn timetable in hand. You're the one who described her as a harried March hare; then you had to tell me the reference. Do you know how she started our conversation when I called yesterday? Not 'Hello' or 'I've missed you, how have you been?' I'd barely said, 'This is Bear' when she said, 'Oh, good. Jason's meeting Alecko Papandreou in the Beehive, and you should go there and provide backup.' "

"Lys always assumes you know she's glad you're back, and that a greeting would therefore waste your time and hers. She may be right." Jason pushed her plate away untasted and rose from the table. The motion tripped a circuit; the galley waldoes waited for a moment to see if she'd change her mind then retrieved her plate and silverware. They left her coffee cup, because it still rested within the sphere which the computer defined as "in use" for each place setting.

Capella looked up from his plate, a ruin of broken yolk and grated fried potatoes stirred together. He wasn't neat when he ate. "I have some things to do in the city before I leave. *If* I join you."

"I thought you'd already made up your mind." Jason rinsed her cup and put it down to drain. "I don't have much use for people who vacillate. You're with me or you're not. Let me know by tonight." She turned to Denny. "I thought I'd drive up to the Papandreou Museum this morning. Would you like to come with me?"

Denny frowned. "I'm not much on museums, Captain. Everything there is, you know, dead." And then she looked at Jason, tongue tip just edging past the curve of her lip, a smile starting, suppressed, and starting again, showing on her face. "Maybe this time, though. *This* museum's supposed to be really something!"

Kenot had left the table to fetch a glass of juice. As Jason headed for her cabin to dress, he said, "I've still got some zero-G meds incubating. I'd like to get back to them soon; I don't like leaving them in free orbit."

"Why? It shouldn't be that difficult to pick it up, no matter how long we're here. Unless they're unstable . . . ?"

Kenot shook his head. "No. But someone stole a culture from me once." He was silhouetted by the incandescent light above the stove, and his forehead was surrounded by a radiant nimbus. "If it happens again, I'm prepared. I'll have to report a *tragic* accident to the CDC." A smile drew his thin lips tighter. "I'd enjoy that. Still, I have a tremendous amount invested in those meds, and I'd hate to lose the time."

Jason considered. Today she'd check some of her own sources, while tonight she would go through the information Lys had found. A day to make preparations, and a night to carry them out. "I'll be conducting a test flight for Capella later, and—I hope—a new Sight as well. We'll be out of here within three days, four at the most," she said. "If you want to check your incubator, Kenot, the test flight would be a good time." She looked at her watch. "It's a long drive to the Papandreou. Let me dress. Denny, you go down to the port office and arrange for a car. I'll be down in a few minutes."

Jason promised herself never to let Denny rent a car again without supervision. But she let an attendant park the fiery red convertible, and she and Denny followed a suave Alecko Papandreou, perfectly dressed in a formal jacket and linen waistcoat. Jason was wearing her dress uniform, milk white with a brilliant scarlet sunburst on her left breast pocket; but Denny, slightly subdued, was wearing jeans and a blue cotton pullover. The sleeves were pushed up past her elbows, and she'd unbuttoned the top so that the turtleneck collar flopped loosely down her back like a miniature cape, leaving her neck exposed. She'd left her coat in the car because the weather was hot, even this high up in the hills. She tripped as she climbed the rough stone stairs. "You'd think with all your money you'd repair those things," she said.

Alecko's lips thinned, a disapproving expression which he turned, with effort, into a slight smile. "Those steps are over two thousand years old. My family rescued them, at great expense, from a place called the Aghia Triada, on Earth. If you have no respect for their beauty, then you must respect their antiquity."

"I guess so," Denny said dubiously. But she walked more carefully then, looking where she stepped.

"My grandparents started the museum with a seed grant a hundred years ago. I don't think even they knew how it would grow in the time since." Alecko guided them up the newer, more regular marble staircase into an immense chamber, the vaulted ceiling of which seemed curiously delicate and insubstantial until Jason looked more closely at the pillars which supported it and realized how small they looked at their apexes. Because they were so massive at their bases, she suddenly realized how far away the ceiling must be. It was overwhelming, although a part of Jason's mind noticed the sudden pressure gradient as they stepped across the threshold and said: airlock.

Alecko evidently loved the museum and loved showing it off to visitors. "If you don't mind, we'll pass by the first few rooms. There is a great deal of pleasant painting there, but nothing significant. I would rather begin my tour with some items of which I'm quite proud."

He led the way to a grander gallery. Once the opulence of the hall itself had seeped in, there was room for the sculpture to make an impression. Jason walked close to a bronze statue of a young boy who appeared poised to run. She didn't notice Alecko standing behind her until he spoke. "It's called 'The Jockey of Artemision.' It was in the National Museum until the Long Winter forced closure. We acquired it soon after." He reached out and touched it gently, lovingly. "This young boy is over twenty-five centuries old. Except for a little mottling of the flesh, he's still quite attractive."

They both turned at a cry from Denny. She was sitting on the floor, stunned. "Damn! These things *bite!*" She looked ruefully at a statue of a nude woman whose head and arms were missing, leaving the legs and a flawless white marble torso.

"Be careful, young woman." Alecko helped her to her feet. (Jason, quietly, walked near the statue of the Jockey again. With Alecko some distance away she could feel the subsonic. Cautiously she reached a hand forward until the sensation became painful, then backed away until it ceased. Satisfied, she turned aside.) "We have electronic devices near all the art," Alecko explained. "First, of course, there's the problem of theft; but also, if we let everyone who wished feel the sculptures, they would eventually be worn away to nothing. I'm surprised you were able to get so near. Didn't you feel the warning?"

"Yeah. But that marble looks so smooth I had to touch it." She looked wistful. Alecko laughed. "Here, take my hand. As long as we're in contact, you can approach any exhibit you want; the touch-me-nots won't affect me."

Denny closed her eyes then and stroked the marble torso with voluptuary pleasure. "If I had this in my house, I wouldn't keep it hidden. I'd put up a sign that said 'Touch

Me!' It might wear away, but it would still do a lot of good for people."

"Then I shouldn't ever ask you to be my curator."

Alecko was enjoying his guide's role. He escorted them through the museum like a small child showing off toys, beaming paternally as Denny, rapt, fondled the mammoth carved Vegan worry wood, and becoming patronizing as Jason involuntarily reacted to the desolation radiating from a Tikelian sound sculpture. If Jason felt occasional impatience—if she wished, more than once, to be taken directly to the jewel gallery and the case which held *her* ruby (for she already considered it to be her property)—she could see that Denny felt nothing of the kind. In fact, she was enjoying Alecko's attention, listening intently to his explanations and looking at each painting or ceramic or sculpture as he pointed them out.

Denny had been staring at a picture, a landscape. At a casual glance it contained nothing unusual, although the lighting was odd and the two figures walking were tall—taller, even, then Capella. She giggled. "I know them. They're Rolands. I saw a couple of Rolands and some Gethnians making it on stage once. Have you ever met a Roland?" She turned to Jason to ask, but her question could as easily have been directed at Alecko. "They're mostly thin, real tall, and almost all angles. If you're like me, you get an elbow in the eye a lot, riding public transit with one of them.

"They're hermaphroditic." She stumbled slightly over the word. "And any one can have sex with himself—herself?—itself? The Kai Sisters, the ones who are always getting busted? They have a Roland stripper once in a while."

Jason, worried, watched Alecko. His tolerant smile had frozen, and he'd taken his hand away from Denny's. He said with cold grace, "I would very much rather not talk about either Rolands or Gethnians."

Denny grabbed his hand again, and held it in her own and started stroking it, with just the tips of the fingers of her other hand. "I didn't mean to get you upset, really. This is a funny story. You'll see. But you have to know about Gethnians; they're kind of either-or. They don't fuck much, but when they do it's something, because they change from something about as sexy as a statue to something real hot; it's not even that they look all that different, but everything comes on intense, like a fire you don't want to douse because it's too good at burning."

Jason looked at Denny with surprise; the idiom seemed both out of place and oddly natural, but Denny gave no indication she'd said anything unusual. "Sometimes Gethnians are the one (which I think of as male) and sometimes they're the other (which I think of as female); but whatever they are, when I see it it makes my gut hurt with wanting it so bad.

"Now four of them got together—two of each—this time I'm talking about, and it's like wet cats spitting at each other: mad at being wet; mad at being *seen* wet; and mad at whoever was seeing them. That's how it was. All four shouting, those Gethnian eyes like ice, Rolands' eyes red: 'What are you *freaks* doing here?' And they started fighting, out on the street. And it was so intense that when the cops came, why, they sat and watched, too, like me.

"Because the Rolands were hot to begin with. They'd just put on a show and, believe me, they were never acting but were really into it on stage. I *know*. And the Gethnians? Well, that fight lasted long enough for them to warm up, too, and then warm up some more; and then one of them—she was definitely a she by then—hooked one finger into a Roland's shirt and tore it straight down, like her finger was a razor. A minute later she was biting; but he—it?—wasn't objecting. Oh, no.

"Ten minutes later and those four didn't know any of us were there, oh, no. One of the cops said, 'Jesus,' and I think, you know, he really *was* praying."

Denny grinned, pure enjoyment at her own story, and seemed startled to see Alecko's cold, hostile stare. Jason quickly stepped between them, afraid that Alecko's anger would erupt into violence. Instead he stopped, closed his eyes for a moment, and when he reopened them he seemed calmer. "I'm sorry. But I'm not used to such . . . direct discussion of sexuality. I envy you your freedom of expression." He didn't sound envious. His complexion had paled slightly and he radiated subdued tension, but his voice was charming as he took her arm again. "This way, Kyria Dendrite. We'll continue the tour—if your captain will indulge me?"

Before all he had displayed was a silver lure; now barbs broke through everything Alecko said. Jason rather liked the change. She showed her teeth in a smile. "So far I'm enjoying myself, *kyrie*."

Alecko bowed. He had his arm around Denny again, but she seemed disturbed by the attention and made occasional, minor efforts to step away. "When the Museion ton Papandreou was first begun, no one had the foresight to consider a direction. The curators were given an open purse and were instructed simply to buy 'the best.' That was meaningless, of course, and so we ended up with an exotic collection of furbelows and galletyles—material that was expensive and unique, but often had no other value." Alecko released Denny's shoulder to reach for the bare skin at her elbow. "Down this ramp, please. Captain?"

Jason would have liked to follow one or two interesting hallways. But she joined Alecko and Denny instead, down a gradually sloping ramp. Jason estimated they had descended two stories before Alecko again changed direction. He opened an inconspicuous panel on one wall and tripped a series of switches, one after another, and the darkened wing became comfortably bright. "Natural light," he said proudly. "At least it's natural for Earth, where most of these paintings originated.

"This wing, and most of the museum, in fact, has been designed to minimize spectra which might bleach or darken any pigments. Some color changes are inevitable, of course, with the passage of time. Some of the older artists painted on wood, which cracks and dries with age. But most of these paintings will last as long as the museum stands." He opened a door, and Denny took the opportunity to slip away from his sheltering arm. She made no fuss about it, but she stayed out of his reach. "Eventually they settled on two goals, which the curators considered compatible. Because we were Hellenic, and proud of our background, it was decided to dedicate part of the museum to Greek antiquities. You've seen some of them today—hardly all! It would take months to properly catalog any one section.

"They also hoped to encourage new artists, of whatever background. Your brother was one of them, *kyria*." He nodded to Jason. Somehow he'd managed to slip close to Denny again, and had his arm around her waist. There was none of the pleasure she normally showed in physical contact, though Denny let Alecko guide her from place to place without moving away.

When he put a pair of hands on Denny's shoulders, she squirmed, but looked where he directed her. "This is one of the failures," he said in genial contempt. "Captain Horiuchi's brother created it." With hands bracketing her ears he moved her head from side to side; up, then down. "You see how the picture changes? That's a three-dimensional matrix, painted with the aid of lasers and a microscope. That's not art, that's artifice." The contempt was stronger. "Technically, of course, it's quite good, but there's more to art than technique. Don't you agree, Captain?"

Jason said mildly, "I'm not an artist. I don't make the distinction."

Alecko smiled, but between his brows lines met and expressed puzzlement; he had expected Jason to defend her brother's art. When she didn't he seemed to dismiss the subject. He released his hold on Denny's arm and moved slowly down the hall. Jason and Denny kept pace. "You saw some of the other failures when you entered the museum," he said. "Pretty paintings—the tourists like them—but they're hardly great art." With a flourish he threw open a set of double doors. "This is one of the successes. I was here almost every day when I was younger, because it fascinated me. There's nothing about it in any museum brochure, and there never will be, not if I have anything to say about it. Although you're getting the lesson free."

He spread his four arms wide, taking in all of the immense vaulted chamber. They were underground now, but there were several large windows, and each was apparently open to the surface. Near each window was a painting—scenes of a dog running, a couple strolling, another couple vigorously arguing beneath a shade tree. Papandreou looked at his watch. "We're here at the wrong time. Come by later in the day and look out the window by each painting; you'll see the scene come to life."

There was a stone bench, painted white, its supports decorated with Corinthian capitals. Alecko sat down, his legs spread wide, two palms resting on his knees. "Sit down and rest for a while; we've walked quite a distance."

Jason shook her head and remained standing; Denny found another bench across the room but still close enough to hear. It was clear how little she'd liked Alecko's attention; she had rolled down her sleeves so her arms were no longer bare, and had fastened the three buttons that converted the sweater to an enveloping turtleneck. He could hold her hands if he chose, or the sides of her head as he'd done before, but otherwise Denny was completely and uncharacteristically enclosed.

If he noticed he didn't comment. "At first the museum hired actors," he said, "but it was too much of an expense. Now we use doppelgängers created by a family of clockmakers on Keppler. The artist's original proposal had said that she hoped to define, in a small way, the difference between 'art' and 'artifice'—as your brother attempted, *kyria,* and failed.

"I've always liked this room. I'd sit by a painting for hours and wait for the moment when it would come alive outside the window." With that he seemed to forget, momentarily, not that Jason and Denny were present, but that they were antagonists. His face seemed younger, the unlined olive of a Greek boy about to steal an apple from a cart.

As the image surfaced she saw him look up, darting her a playful look. Then he stood. "We'll make one last stop, *kyries,* and then I must go." He was suddenly abrupt, as though he had become bored. That suited Jason, who had seen what she could hope to see in one trip and was eager to be on to something else. She beckoned to Denny, who followed, letting Jason form a bulwark between Alecko and herself.

There were no lectures now, and no side trips to favorite galleries; Alecko led them up flights of utility stairs and directly to Dhimitri Papandreou's jewel gallery. He didn't explain what they were seeing, but took a set of keys from his pocket, selected one, and turned it in a lock by the main entrance to the room. "I have no interest in any of this," he explained. "I'll let the museum's doyen answer your questions." He leaned against a marble pillar, four arms crossed, and apparently ignored them; but his eyes, half closed, watched them wherever they walked.

When he'd turned the key a quiet, assured voice had begun to speak in a language neither Jason nor Denny understood. When it said, "Would you like to hear a lecture in English?" Jason realized that it was repeating the same sentence, over and over, in various languages. She said "English" at the same time as Denny, and the voice cut off in mid-sentence, to begin again as she neared a display case. It wasn't a voice at all but a directed sonic burst which discretely stimulated the auricle.

Denny stared at each case, bemused, and her expression clearly said, "That thing is responsible for *all that?*" After watching her for a while, Jason smiled. "Gemstones have probably been responsible for more bloody murders than gold or silver. Jewels are supposed to bring luck, or give misfortune; they're symbols both of fertility and procreation. A pale diamond was supposed to be a sign of a lover's infidelity, but a luminous diamond enhanced the love of both parties. Amethysts cured drunkenness, emeralds foretold the future, onyx was anaphrodisiac." She grinned. "Sometimes I've thought of giving you a casket of onyx as a present."

Alecko's voice drifted lazily through the vast gallery. "And what's a ruby good for?"

Jason ticked off qualities on her fingers. "It provides mental and physical health. It protects the owner from all harm. It shines in darkness and cannot be hidden because its light penetrates any container. Whoever owns a brilliant ruby will live in peace, prosper in business, triumph over her enemies. The ruby will guard house, hearth, and homeland, and protect all from tempests. And a great deal more as well. In addition to all that, they're beautiful—more beautiful than diamonds. And more rare."

In the background, the lecture droned on. She heard the name of Catherine the Great. In the case, on velvet, the ruby lay resting. After a moment she remembered to breathe. She got as close to the case as she could before the touch-me-not field began to hurt, and then stayed, ignoring the pain.

"I want it, Alecko. You knew I would." She walked away. "I've toured your museum with you. My ears ache from the pressure changes, from room to room and hall to hall. I'm standing close to a force field, and it's painful. There are locks on all the doors; there's a computer-scanning ray surveying the room now. I can feel it; I'm more sensitive, I suspect, after years in the Net.

"It's a complex security system, and a good one. You designed it? I'll beat it. Denny, we're leaving. Alecko: good night."

___ 5 _____

DENNY AND JASON _____

DESPITE THE HEAT, Denny shivered. "I guess I shouldn't have told that story back there, huh? I just thought it was funny, but Mr. Papandreou, he looked like he'd bit into an egg that'd gone bad." She piloted the car expertly, effortlessly.

Jason was preoccupied. It bothered her that Alecko had known her so well, or had guessed so accurately. After a moment she realized that Denny was waiting for a response. "You couldn't know. He did overreact, didn't he? He must know about the parahuman races; there're enough of them passing through Moulinos each year."

Denny thought about it for a moment, then laughed. "That might be the problem, Captain. Last time we came here, I walked through the Old Town. I saw a lot of signs for live sex shows, human and alien, alien and alien. I bet he doesn't like that at all." She brought the car speeding around a corner and slowed as the road seemed to drop away, revealing a deep bowl framed by mountains, filled by gnarled olive trees and open fields and the distant, indistinct haze of wild rockroses.

Denny slowed the car and stopped. "That's really something. Where I come from the land's flat. I've never lived anywhere where the horizon was up instead of down." After a moment she engaged the frictionless drive and they continued on down. The sound of the motor was an almost inaudible electric whirring which never seemed right to Jason, for whom driving a car was inextricably linked to the sound and smell of an internal combustion engine.

On a relatively straight section, Denny risked looking at Jason. "I'm sorry if I fucked things up back there. I just couldn't stand him touching me after a while."

"Don't second-guess me, Denny. I get enough of that from Lys. If you ask why I wanted you along, I may tell you. But don't try to think of what I might want from you and wonder if I got it." She slouched down in her seat. "I didn't much like the way he was grabbing you either, Denny. Not sexual; it was something else."

Denny raised both eyebrows. "It was sexual at first, Captain. You can take my word for that. If you hadn't of been there I might have tripped him, right there on the floor. Later, yeah. After talking about the Rolands—then he felt like he was leaving little slug trails wherever he touched me."

The convertible was a relatively new model, as New Crete cars went, and a map was built into the instrument panel next to the odometer. Denny glanced down. "We're almost to your friend's house. You sure you don't want me to take you all the way there?"

Jason shook her head. "No. The walk will do me good, and I'm sure you can put the time to good use. Maybe Capella would like a drive in this thing."

Denny's grin was wide in her broad, flat face. "Well, you *did* tell me to pick out a car, Captain, and I thought you'd want to go in style." She patted the sleek calamander-wood dashboard. A few minutes later she pulled to the roadside and Jason stepped out. There was no curb; the pavement gave way to densely packed, dusty clay almost as hard as the road itself. "Capella said he'd meet me if I got back soon enough. Thanks for letting me keep the car, Captain." Denny waved and drove off.

The hour-long walk to Niko's home would take Jason through the Arkaikon, the "old town." She found it amusing that on a planet so newly settled as New Crete, on a world which had yet to celebrate its tricentennial, there was still the distinction between the "new" and the "old."

She shouldered her pack and began walking along the narrow shoulderless road. Chronological considerations aside, the Arkaikon did recall old Crete. The low buildings were nearly all white, either painted brick or stucco, and few were over three stories. In many buildings, holes cut into featureless walls were glazed or not as suited the owners; in others, Byzantine design framed windows with lavender balconies tricked out with intense magenta, cerulean, or saffron highlights; there were even buildings the cornices of which were precise and geometrical, whose colors were muted where they weren't simply black.

Niko's home was high on a hillside overlooking the bay and a series of terraces where olive trees had once grown. Now there were only a few trees left, and woven between their boles were intertwined flats of acanthus. Nearby was a warren of passages and alleyways, from which his property was separated by a fence, more decorative than purposeful. The cornices were of huge square bricks, whitewashed.

Niko was unusually solemn. Jason followed his corpulent, white-suited frame down the dark pathway leading from the entry to his front room, touching the stuccoed wall less for balance than for a sense of grounding, in much the same way as she ran her palm along the wooden paneling of her ship each time she walked by. There the grain was subtle, reassuring; here, the deliberately irregular surface was comfortable and warm.

Niko lead her down a short flight of wooden stairs to a long low room lined with books and pictures and littered with yet more books, magazines, and assorted paper piles. He walked to one chair and shoved aside a stack of debris, clearing a space just large enough for one person to sit, moved to another chair and did the same, then picked up a large tumbler from beside the second chair and left to fuss in the kitchen.

On the ship, only Denny approached this disorder, and Denny kept her debris contained inside her cabin. Niko emerged with a tray containing two glasses, a pitcher of ice, a pair of tongs, and a tall clear bottle and rested it atop a lopsided stack of books, where it remained at a jaunty angle. "Don't you ever lose anything?" Jason asked.

"All the time," he said. "But, you see, when I look for things I've lost I find things I'd forgotten I had. I am fascinated by the sheer diversity of the things I own." He held up the bottle. "Ouzo. Today we drink to forgetfulness and youth. Here's to both." He filled one glass with ice and alcohol, and handed the milky mixture to Jason. His own tumbler he downed neat.

Jason sipped more carefully, feeling the sweet licorice sting fill her mouth and nostrils. She'd forgotten what it was like, that sudden, intense blossoming of flavor. She set the glass down carefully. "Just this one glass, Niko. More and I'll be sick all the day." It was an exaggeration; Bear overdramatized everything, including Jason's allergy and her own occasional hangover. Still, a little alcohol went an awfully long way.

"I remember, Jason. We sailed together how many years?" His eyes half closed, lost in folds of fat as he smiled. "But Kazantzakis once said ouzo proved there was a God; here's to God!" He poured another and drank more slowly. He turned to Jason again and, with a very slight smile, said, "You come here at a bad time. Last night I find—once again—that love doesn't last forever. And today I feel old and fat and useless. Poor Niko; they should take me now and put me in a grave." He set down the glass, crossed to the other chair he'd cleared, and started to sit. Instead he brushed a long-haired orange cat away before he sank down heavily into the cushions. He tugged at his linen suit but gave up without doing more than increasing the bag at his knees.

The cat looked first startled, then disdainful; then, nonchalantly, it began to clean its fur. It was the most disorderly feline Jason had ever seen, with fur that popped up in spikes all over its body, a neck ruff like a monitor lizard, and an unbelievably fluffy tail, the color of orange sherbet spun into cotton candy. "You watch," Niko said. "Half a minute of that and he'll decide to join me."

The cat suddenly paused, paw in midair. Its tongue was still extended, giving it a particularly half-witted expression. It twisted backward from a sitting position and flowed up Niko's leg into his lap. "You see? Predictable as clockwork. Like my loves."

She grinned. "How many cats have you now?"

He shrugged. "Five? Six? Some may have wandered in since I last counted." He rubbed the top of the orange cat's skull with a thumb and scratched under its chin with the fingers of his other hand. "Sebastian here is new; for the first few weeks he looked as though he expected to be pierced by arrows at any moment. Hence the name." An audible rumble emerged from Sebastian, the loudest purr Jason had ever heard from a cat. "Now the worst thing that happens to him is he rolls over, expecting my arm. If I don't notice and put my arm out, he falls off the chair. He's very trusting. Aren't you, dear?" He used both hands to smooth the cat's fur, stroking from head to tail. "Would you mind pouring me another glass? My hands are full.

"But you didn't come to speak of cats. You want to know about this boy, this Lynch who was arrested last night."

"Lynch? Is that his name? I never learned it."

Niko nodded, flesh pouching below his chin. "A strange young man, that one—very lonely, very bright. Not very civilized. Like you, Kyria Horiuchi. Excuse me, Sebastian." As the cat reproachfully slipped to the floor, Niko levered his bulk from the chair, two pudgy hands set on the arms for balance. "Lynch Lysikomos. He's what I'd call *apóvlitos*—an outcast. His name he received in an orphanage; he showed up one day, alone, unable or unwilling to talk. The name means 'disheveled,' by the way; apparently he was no beauty even then. At a guess, he was six then."

Niko picked through a stack of papers. He seemed to be searching for something, but in a moment he was distracted and when he looked up again he had a book in his hand which he fondled lovingly. "Kipling. I read it again recently. Wonderful writer. A lovely imagination. There's one story about a man inhabited by the ghost of the poet John Keats that brings me to tears whenever I read it."

When Niko was distracted it was best to humor him. He'd return to the subject in his own time. "I would have thought you'd want your books in perfect shape," she said. "Most of yours look ready to be thrown out."

He tapped the volume. "Like this?" The orange cover was torn and tattered, the spine showed cracked through the dust wrapper, and the edges of the book were dented and splayed. He laughed. "When I was younger, I was more careful. When I read books I held them open like so"—he opened the book gently, just enough to shed light on the pages—"and read them so that when I was finished they seemed as though they were still new. But then, as I got older, I thought, What if the writer were to visit me? What if a man or woman I admired were to come to my house? Should I show them a book that looked new, or should I bring out a book that looked as though it had been read many times, as though it had been carried from place to place, opened with more attention to the contents than to the cover, marked to show favorite passages?

What would *I* want if I were a writer? The books I love are the books I read over and over again, and so they look." He stepped to the nearest shelf and waggled his palm between two books to make room, then pressed the Kipling volume into the space left. "Come here, I want to show you something."

He moved ponderously to an antique oaken partner's desk with larger drawers on all four sides; two tall stand lamps, brass, rested on either side, each simply a long tube on a large flat base, flaring to a tulip-shaped shade at the top. A crystal bowl at one corner of the desk was filled with yellow and white asphodel. With one hand resting on the desk for balance, he leaned down and pulled open a wide, shallow drawer. A flat square inset into the top of the desk swung up: a plasma screen. He reached under the desk and brought up a slim keyboard. "I don't like having one of these in my home," he explained, "but I sometimes require it, and this one is very nice. It goes away when I don't want it."

He leaned forward, wheezing, and expertly typed in a series of commands. "Ah." He turned to Jason. "Here is the boy's entire file—and little enough there is of it, too. You may read it if you like." Jason shook her head, and Niko pulled at the bottom of the keyboard, sliding it back under the surface of the desk, and reached into the drawer. The screen faded to a neutral gray and slipped into place flush against the desktop. "And I wonder how he has remained hidden in the time since. He's deposited no payroll checks; whatever he does, he's paid in cash. He has no bank account. The address he gave to the arresting officers was fictitious. His arrest record lists his profession as 'messenger'; that's a nice title, but it could mean anything." He slid the drawer closed and straightened, groaning. "I'm glad you asked me to check. The boy fascinates me."

He walked laboriously back to his chair and leaned down for his glass. When he lifted the bottle he frowned. "My doctor tells me once again that I am exceeding the limit that is good for me. I tell my doctor I have made my living by exceeding such limits, and that is why I'm as old as I am. He doesn't listen to me, either; we have a very good relationship." He took the empty bottle in one hand and the glass in the other. "I'll be right back."

While he was gone Jason prowled restlessly around the room, removing books from the shelves and returning them, looking through scattered papers, straightening piles that had fallen. She stopped before a large brick fireplace fronted by gray slate tiles and framed by mammoth andirons. A polished brass globe was mounted on each andiron. She was delighted to discover that each bore an intricate and faithful chart of New Crete. I'll have to tell Lys, Jason thought; she'd like a pair. And then she thought of constructing a fireplace for the *Argo,* and laughed aloud.

Niko came back, carrying two tumblers and trailed by a tortoiseshell cat which twined itself between his feet, looking up with anticipation. "I'm glad you're so cheerful," he said and held up one glass. "In case you finish your ouzo. No, Sasha, it isn't for you." He set her fresh drink on the table beside the old, and crossed to sit down heavily in his own chair. "I made the mistake once of leaving a full tumbler of water in the bathroom. Now all my cats insist on drinking from glasses. It's a sobering sight to wake up in the morning to see a cat's head wedged in an old jelly jar." He closed one eye and opened it slowly, in an old, familiar gesture of consideration. "Someday, maybe, I will return to Smyrna where I will look out each day on blue waters, drink ouzo, and dream. Much as I do now; but I will be home then."

With the callused tip of a finger, Jason was tracing the line of a continent on a bright brass globe. She said, "About the boy."

Niko exhaled. "Yes. About the boy. Lynch. He seems well-read, but not very well adjusted. He tries too hard to be liked, and when it doesn't work he tries to act as though it doesn't matter, he doesn't need anyone, all he needs is to be left alone.

"Another point: he hasn't had his eyes replaced. It's unlikely that his condition is so rare or so far advanced that to correct it wouldn't be comparatively easy. Such correction is not routine, but neither is it uncommon, and the cost would be small. Therefore, he has some aversion to having surgery.

"Or it may be that he doesn't wish to call any attention to himself, even to the extent of consulting a doctor." Jason crossed the room to listen, and was standing above him now, arms folded. The creases in his neck smoothed as he looked up at her. "Do you want him as Sight for your crew? I'm guessing."

"I don't know. Let's say I'm exploring the idea."

"In that case, he could be an asset. He might be willing to sacrifice a great deal in order to be able to see without surgery; to be Sight, with all that implies, might make him considerably less antisocial."

Jason looked down at Niko. Her eyes were shadowed and she was frowning, concentrating. "That's quite an evaluation. You didn't get all that from your computer."

"You're quite right." He heaved himself to his feet and walked to the foyer. One hand braced on the polished mahogany doorjamb, he leaned into the long hallway and called: "Kyrie Lysikomos? You may come out now." He beamed at her, his face roseate with exertion. "You see? You did take my mind off my troubles."

"The boy's here?" She turned as a door opened down the hall. His spiky hair was greasy from a night in jail, his complexion was pallid, and his eyes, magnified behind thick glass lenses, were a pale periwinkle blue, now bloodshot. He was still wearing the black pants and white cotton shirt in which he'd been arrested, but now one sleeve was torn and there was an irregular black stain like a smear of tar across his side.

Niko took another long swallow of ouzo. "I knew last night you would want the boy's release. I knew also that I could arrange it easily and you could not. I admit I also was curious to find what you saw in young Lynch last night." He said the latter guilelessly and raised his eyes to meet Jason's stare. "I don't know that I have discovered anything of the kind, but he and I have had some interesting discussions before you arrived. Because I had the opportunity and the means, I also replaced his spectacles. I was fortunate to find an optical grinder who considered the project a challenge."

Jason said, "He'll need implants. Have you made arrangements?"

"Of course. However, I haven't explained to Lynch what that means. Here. The doctor's name is Vernon Kalb. He's the best Net surgeon in Moulinos; one of the only ones, in fact. You won't find many implants here yet." He handed Jason a dog-eared business card. It had been creased so badly that it skipped when she tried to play it, the announcer's voice slurring drunkenly over the address and comm line numbers. Still, it was readable so it was of some use. She put it in her own pocket, to look at later.

Lynch was standing nervously, shifting from foot to foot.

"Has the *kyrie* told you what to expect?" Jason asked.

Niko answered. "I've told him very little. I believed you would prefer to talk to him yourself."

Jason nodded. "Is there anything else I need to know now, before we leave?" Niko shook his head. "Good." She turned to the boy. "Your name is Lynch Lysikomos?"

Lynch looked up at Jason and the light glinted off his lenses so that his eyes were blank spheres. "Yes. But no one ever calls me Lysikomos." Lynch looked from Jason to Niko. "He says you want to take me off-planet." His voice was high and shrill, like a clarinet with a split reed, and his tone was aggressive.

Her own tone was sharp. "At most he said I *may* want to hire you. Niko is careful with his words. Yes, it's a possibility. Is that what you want?"

He had spirit; or he was too dense to react to her sharpness. "More than anything! If you take me away from here, Captain Horiuchi, I'll do whatever you want." He should have been pathetic, in his cheap, old, soiled and torn clothing, but his intensity gave him a certain precarious dignity.

Jason watched him, considering. "What training have you had, son? What kind of schooling?"

He answered reluctantly. "Almost none." And angrily: "They don't give training to orphans on New Crete. You have to belong to the Five Families before you get anything at all."

"Can you read? Write? Do you know basic mathematics?" He nodded reluctantly. "Don't look so contemptuous," Jason said. "You'd be surprised how many people can't. As long as you can understand screen symbology, who needs literacy?— that's an attitude you'll encounter frequently if you travel with me. Many of Horiuchi's employees are facile with computers, but they couldn't read a book to save their lives. Can you cook?"

He shrugged. "A little."

"Another plus, *paidhia mou*. You're full of skills you don't recognize."

He bristled at the diminutive. "Don't call me that! I've been on my own since I—I've been on my own for five years. I'm not a child anymore!"

Jason almost laughed. *"Child,"* she said, "nearly everyone is younger than I am. You're sixteen? I have a century and more on you! I saw Niko there grow from a boy smaller and younger than you into that great hulking dreamer. I still forget his age at times and address him as I used to. Don't take offense or you'll be storing up resentment with no place to spend it."

Niko sighed dramatically. "You forget my age, and have no respect for it, either. I am an old man, and tired, and if I must listen to you talk on and on, then I will sit while I am doing so and be comfortable." His voice was slightly slurred and Jason knew then that he was quite drunk. Youth had always been a valuable commodity to Niko, and he regarded Jason's near agelessness with increasing bitterness as he grew older and fatter and more infirm. He moved, not stumbling, but walking somewhat unevenly, back to his chair.

Jason turned back to Lynch. "Niko told me you were a messenger. What exactly does that mean?"

His expression was sullen, but he answered without hesitation. "You've probably seen us and didn't know it. When you're downtown, you'll be walking and maybe almost get run over by some guy on a bicycle? Well, that's one of us. People aren't supposed to drive through the business district, so they hire people like me to deliver packages back and forth between the buildings. Artwork for magazines, documents that need an original signature so they can't be faxed, product samples, things like that. When you need something in a hurry, you call a bike messenger and we get it there." Lynch was obviously proud of his work. "We know the city better than anyone, even the Papandreou family. I bet none of them could find half the alleys and dead-end streets I know about, not without spending hours at it. _I_ can deliver a package from any point to any other point in a half hour maximum. Other people, too: if you give me an address, I can tell you what it's near and how to get there the fastest way possible, even if I've never been there myself."

Jason was pleased with his answer. Good topological coordination was a definite asset. "I'll ask more later, but unless you've got a problem with the implant, you've got yourself a job. You can start now." She dug the battered business card out of her pocket. "We're going here next. Is it within walking distance, or should I call a taxi?"

"In Moulinos?" His voice was disdainful. "Have you ever seen one? You're lucky if it doesn't break down more than once on a trip. The trains will get you within a few blocks. The buses are a little more reliable than the taxis. Not much." He handed back the card. "This isn't far. Three or four kilometers."

"Then we'll walk. Niko, thank you. You're always a help, and this time you've done more than I expected. I had hoped to spend more time with you. Before I leave again I hope to come back."

Niko bowed without getting up and raised his glass in a salute. He would drink himself into melancholia today, and tomorrow remember better times.

She waved her own hand in farewell, and she and Lynch made their way out the dim hallway into the midafternoon sun.

__ 6 _____

LYS _____

As Lys REACHED the gantry she frowned, shaded her eyes with one hand, and looked up. Because the late afternoon sun was silhouetting the ship it was difficult to see, but it looked as if the cargo hatch was open. It was. It had probably been left unlocked by Denny, who liked riding the chain-driven elevator in preference to either the ladder or the counterbalanced rope loop near the smaller front hatch. Lys's reaction was largely frustration. Denny wasn't thoughtless, she simply disagreed as to the importance of things—and let her disagreement translate into inaction. She didn't think it was important that the crew should eat together, so she was often gone when it was her turn to cook; she didn't think it necessary to lock the ship when the entire port was guarded, so she left the hatch undogged. (To her credit, she never shirked the duties that were *necessary*, and she was an alert and diligent presence on the crew in space.)

From long habit, Lys made a quick tour of the ship, checking the more valuable items of equipment, but nothing seemed out of place. She returned to the hatch, sealed it, and returned to her terminal. She knew the timing of the orbiting satellites, and one should be passing overhead soon. It was a simple matter then to plug into the satellite transmission and lock onto its internal cameras. It was an expensive operation, but the entire transaction would be billed to a thoroughly fictitious d/b/a, one of many Lys had established over the years.

She found that with patience she could even focus from her terminal, which had to class as an extraordinary security breach. Someone would lose a job when it was discovered what she'd done, but by then Lys and the *Argo* would be long gone.

The initial image showed the entire southern coast of the major continent below, an arm of the subcontinent above, and centered in the picture were the sparkling waters of the inland sea where Mykonos was situated. By increments she narrowed the frame until she could see only the island; and then only the highlands to the northeast; and finally the Museion ton Papandreou filled her screen, appearing as a series of regular blocks set into an irregular plateau. She stepped up the resolution, casting the resulting picture on a grid to get a better idea of its size. Involuntarily she whistled. Because the surrounding peaks were so large, her first rough estimate had been drastically low. The place was huge! She looked at the scale and whistled again: the main building was over a mile square.

She stepped up to the next order of magnification. Now all she saw was the main bulk of the museum. She left the wings until later. Gradually, working with the information she'd found the night before, she built up a convincing blueprint of the entire structure. It might not be complete, but she'd lay odds it was reasonably accurate.

She dumped the material to a graphics plotter, and listened to the almost inaudible hiss while it printed. She'd now gotten as much information as she could without visiting the museum directly. Which, come to think of it, was not a bad idea. She glanced at her watch. It was late, but if she scouted the landscape tonight, she'd have that much more information for Jason tomorrow, and a day's less waiting meant that much less risk as well.

She couldn't make the trip alone, but she knew whom she could ask: Rat. Few people liked the wizened old man, but she was one of them. More, he had practical experience in areas where Lys's own knowledge was largely theoretical.

She put out a call through the Net, and he answered so quickly she realized he'd had his silvertip in place, waiting for her. Rat was often prescient, and his anticipation was occasionally disquieting. Tonight she was reassured by it.

She explained why she wanted to travel more than a

hundred kilometers in the middle of the night. Bear would have argued and Denny would have asked questions until Lys was rigid with suppressed tension, but Rat only said, «It's a good night for a long drive,» and agreed to meet her at the port gate. «I've already found a car,» he added. «It's not much, but it will get us there and back.»

Next came the hard part. Lys's fractured back she'd gotten when she was younger, in an accident which had been no one's fault; but while she'd been in the hospital her former shipmates had brought her a caudal walker and had made her promise to use it. She'd tried repeatedly, but though she enjoyed the sensation of walking again once she adjusted to it, the process of adjustment itself was so traumatic that she'd abandoned the frame after several tries. The trauma didn't lessen, either; every time she'd tried since, it had been just as bad. After a time she'd gotten used to her wheelchair, and now there was seldom any real need to walk anywhere. The few places she couldn't reach in a chair were places where, generally, she didn't want to go.

A more minor problem was that Lys felt a little like Mary Shelley's monster every time she wore the frame. Lys wouldn't admit it, but she was vain about her appearance, and it was impossible to be suave when you were wearing a construction project, partially completed, suspended from your neck. Unfortunately, Lys couldn't get to the land around the museum in her wheelchair—unless, of course, she wanted to be as conspicuous as possible.

The damn thing was in storage, and she called up her files to locate it. Lys hated the walker so much that she'd buried it deep in a cargo bay, under a half ton of miscellaneous emergency supplies which were to be used only if the *Argo* had to remain underway for an extraordinary length of time. It took her an hour and a half to shift cargo, lift out the box, and replace everything, and then she had to check each circuit to see that it was still working. Lys spent an additional hour adjusting the rig; she began to worry that someone would come in and ask what she was doing. No one on the *Argo* had ever seen her walking; no one but Jason and Rat knew she could.

She squirmed in her chair. No matter how she changed the settings, she kept feeling phantom pains along pressure points. Finally Lys turned to her terminal and adjusted the exoskeleton bit by bit, in line with the computer display. As she suspected, it showed a perfect fit; yet it still didn't feel right. The arms had been easy, like pulling on gloves. She'd straightened the seams along the radial artery to the brachial bifurcation, and then smoothed the fabric up to her armpit. On either side, a single connection plugged into her cervical collar. She wiggled her fingers, watching the video display with satisfaction. She tried to ignore the spasms in her calf, tibia, and thigh.

Eventually Lys realized it wouldn't get any more comfortable until she was used to wearing it, and she stopped fiddling with the adjustment.

She typed in a brief message for Jason, explaining that she'd be out all night. She tore off the stack of neatly printed blueprints and rolled them into a tube which she stuck into a canvas carryall. Then she logged out and, a little clumsily, stood. For a moment she wavered until the gyros kicked in, correcting her center of balance. The rush of blood startled her and she hesitated until some of the dizziness passed. She stopped down again to normal vision and started to stride forward, realized that her lumbering johnwayne stride was a little ridiculous, and corrected to a more regular gait. By the time she was halfway down the corridor she was walking almost normally as her own natural rhythms returned and joined with the computer's own learn-by-doing regimen.

Lys had ridden down in the cargo hatch so often that she'd forgotten the galley stairs, a modified ladder leading to A Deck and the crew's entrance. For a moment she stood looking at the ladder in dismay. But she felt cocky enough now that not even the thought of stairs bothered her; she simply moved step by step, carefully, bracing her arms on the railings.

She didn't realize how hard it had been until she reached the lower deck and found the contact alarms triggering because of the sweat under her arms. Thoughtfully, she queued into the computer and issued a monitor command. Now, if her heart rate became too high, an audible alarm would signal her it was time to rest. At the moment, despite the sweat and the drumming pulse in her forehead, she felt more exhilarated than she had in years, and she wondered (as she always did, each time she ventured out of her cocoon on shipboard) why she didn't do this more often.

The galley was empty. With any luck at all, she'd be out of port and into the hills above the city before Jason knew she'd gone. Her own sense of self-justification kept her moving: she was used to computer alarm circuits, and not even Jason could come as close as she could to anticipating where and when—and how—an erratically programmed security system would trigger itself.

She was afraid of falling from the three-story catwalk, but the sling was in place so Lys hooked one foot in the stirrup, held on to the leather strap, and rode down. It was, she decided, fun. But as she neared the pavement she heard Capella say in mild surprise, "Hey! What are you doing out here? And what *is* that thing?"

She wasn't yet confident enough to turn; instead she swiveled from her waist, carefully repositioning herself so she faced him. "You've never seen a Petrovsky frame before?" She said it acidly, which wasn't fair. They weren't common. But he was so goddamn tall.

With an effort she bent at the waist and sat on a rung, patting the ground beside her. "Sit. I'll tell you about it." She had set the ship's clock, which periodically reminded her that time was passing faster than she liked; yet she didn't want a curious, suspicious Capella (who, for all she knew, was an expert computer programmer; she hadn't had the time to delve into his past yet) reading back her files to see what she'd been investigating. She had, of course, left a simple block, but the key word was simple. Anyone with knowledge and a little diligence could break through.

"I'm supposed to exercise in this thing more often than I do," she said once Capella was settled beside her, "but it hurts. I *know* it's phantom pain, because the nerves are severed. But I still feel it."

"I'd think you'd *want* to use it," Capella said. "I know I would. It would frustrate me, not to be able to go where I wanted, when I wanted to. You didn't see me, but I saw you today, trying to shop *sto agora*. You have more patience than I do. I would have yelled at the people who wouldn't get out of my way."

"I used to. It doesn't work, believe me. But look at this thing." She raised her arm, flexed to show the exoskeletal connections. "What would happen if I were in a crowd and the power failed? In a wheelchair I can at least move, no matter how long it might take."

He nodded slowly. "There is that. But couldn't you have

surgery of some sort? I'd have thought fixing a spinal injury would be relatively easy for a Net surgeon."

She was becoming more used to the Petrovsky now, and chanced leaning forward with her elbows on her knees. "It is, and I had it done once, but it didn't take. I think there was some kind of neural misalignment, but the surgeons said it was me, that I wasn't giving the graft a chance. All I know is that for the next several weeks I was in constant pain, it never lessened, and I never got used to it; and after two months I told them forget it, cut the cord, get me out of this, I was better off unable to walk.

"My doctor was more than reluctant. She told me I was a damned fool, and that it would just be harder the next time around."

Capella said, not unkindly, "Do you ever think she could have been right?"

"Well, of course she was right! But it was my body. I knew what my limits were then—I know what they are now—and I'd have reached my limit long before I reached the equilibrium they promised. So I made the decision while I still had the strength and desire to adjust." She patted the grotesque neck brace. "And, after all, I think I've adjusted pretty well."

Capella was quiet for a moment. "You know," he said at last, "I think so, too."

He rose and she moved away so he could climb the ladder into the ship. As she'd talked to Capella, a plan had formed and crystallized, and tomorrow morning (with luck!) she might easily have a surprise for Jason. Lys shaded her eyes to look up at the *Argo,* and then turned and carefully made her way through the maze of ships to the gate.

__ 7 _____

JASON AND LYNCH _____

"WHAT DO YOU know about your implant?" Jason asked as they walked down the dusty Arkaikon road toward the Beehive.

Lynch raised a hand to the nape of his neck. "Hardly anything. They made me get it for work, but I don't like it much. It's hard to keep clean."

She looked at his neck, startled. In the light the metal O-ring was brightly polished. She hadn't noticed it last night, or in Niko's home. "You must burnish it. You're not supposed to, you know. If you leave it alone, it'll grow a layer of pseudoskin that'll seal the graft so it's permanent."

He had a loose rambling gait that wasted a lot of energy, and he was walking ahead of her, slightly faster, and stopping periodically to wait. He stopped now and looked back. "Maybe I don't want it permanent."

"If you don't you might as well stop now and go back home. The Sensory Net's a career, not a job. If you're implanted for Sight, it's not a temporary modification. More nerves grow, to handle the increased information." They'd started walking again, and now Jason stopped. "When you get on board, Lynch, when you get out in free space and see— really see—for the first time in your life, you won't want to come back. You *will* do anything to stay sailing. I know; I did. My father wanted me to come home, to work in the office, to learn the business. And I did, for a while. But since I first set

95

sail, that's where I wanted to be. When we had our fight over control of Horiuchi, it was because I wanted to run the company my way, and my way was to leave the office work to others, to get out and visit the branches on my own."

They stood together on the hard-packed clay, Jason staring out in the distance, remembering, while Lynch shifted uneasily beside her, moving from one foot to the other and kicking the dirt on occasion with the toe of a worn canvas shoe. He stood it as long as he could, then asked, "Do we need to see this doctor right away?"

"I'd like to. Soon, anyway. Then we can arrange for a training flight. I've got one scheduled. I'd planned to give the cells a chance to root, then get you in the Net as quickly as possible, to make sure the graft has taken before we have an actual flight. Why?"

He tugged at the tails of his shirt ruefully. "I'd like to go home, if I could. To change my clothes and take a shower."

She considered. "That's a good idea. While we're there you can pick the things you want to bring with you. I'll send some crew up later to pack up the rest. And how far in advance have you paid your rent? If necessary, I'll buy out your lease."

"I've paid through until Kyriaki next," he said. In his only display of humor so far, Lynch added, "If you want to give the money to *me*, I can use the cash."

Kyriaki was Sunday, literally the Lord's day. The New Crete calendar sandwiched two days between Saturday and Sunday; Savvatokyriakon was the weekend, given over to religious celebration—and, not coincidentally, absorbing the extra days of New Crete's nine-day week. It made little difference except during the High Holy Days of Easter, when religious penitents took to the streets in alarming numbers.

Jason calculated an amount equivalent to two weeks' wages (including the two extra Cretan days) and handed it to Lynch. "Consider this an advance on your wages; it's yours to keep whether or not your implant is successful. If your boniface will refund your rent monies, you may keep that as well; but that's between the two of you."

"She won't," Lynch said confidently. "I've heard her argue with people about rent." His apartment building was at the head of shallow stone stairs cut into a hillside. Inside the stairs were even steeper, almost a ladder between floors, and the hallways were dim and dirty and depressing. So it was a surprise when he opened the door shyly, and Jason stepped past him into a bright apartment whose muted orange walls were cheerful and scrupulously clean. There was a small bed—sitting room and a kitchen, from which light poured through two windows whose panes were irregular rectangles of cobalt blue, scarlet, and clear leaded glass, the clear glass cut into a diamond set into the rough crown formed by the blue and scarlet. Not a pan was out of place, and an old, worn couch —the only furniture other than a kitchen table and two chairs, painted the same enameled orange as the walls—was carefully covered with a white lace cloth.

"Make yourself at home, Captain. The shower's upstairs. I'll be right back."

"You've got your own shower?" Jason was impressed; that was highly unusual in a building like this.

Surprisingly, he laughed. "I've been asked that before. I don't like sharing. I looked for a long time until I found this room, and I paid extra for the water closet." He ascended narrow, steep stairs (leaving Jason wondering if they led to still steeper stairs, vertical rungs perhaps, on a landing above) which twisted back on themselves within the space of five feet, creating a cubby into which was built a small cupboard. It looked as though Lynch used it as a desk, although the area was cramped and it would have been uncomfortable even for Jason, who was smaller than average.

Jason followed him; but the door at the top was closed, and a moment later she heard running water. As she had done earlier at Niko's, she prowled, opening closet and cupboard doors at random. One was a wardrobe, filled with clothes that were mostly worn but well tended, pressed and neatly hung on wire hangers. Her opinion of him had changed. Jason had judged him to be careless and indifferent about clothing on the basis of seeing him before his arrest, and had let her impression be confirmed by his appearance at Niko's.

Behind her, he coughed. "Can you turn your back, please? I'd like to get dressed."

He was clutching a towel around his mid-section with an air that indicated he didn't intend to let it slip. She faced the window, but said, "There's a lot of room on the *Argo*, Lynch, but it's not *that* big. If you have qualms about being naked, in front of me or anyone else, I'd like to know."

She waited out his silence. Finally he said, "You can turn around now, Captain. I got rid of the towel." His tone was resigned. She faced him. It wasn't being nude, she discovered, but that he was ashamed of a network of very faint scars which covered his chest, back, buttocks, and thighs.

"Well?" he asked challengingly. "Do you like them? Or do they make you ill?"

"I've seen worse," she said, "in the mornings, in the mirror. Look." His slight intake of breath was a satisfactory response and she buttoned her shirt again. "I got mine fighting," she said, not unkindly. "Where'd you get yours?"

"Not fighting. I mean, I didn't fight, and that's why I got them." He was dressing slowly. "I was in an orphanage. My eyes were so bad that I couldn't see anything unless I held it right in front of my face, and even then it was blurry. And I didn't want them to operate because no one I talked to could tell me I *wouldn't* go blind, and even if I couldn't see very much I could see a little.

"I didn't have any money, either. I didn't know then that no one pays for medical care on Moulinos, and the Master made me think treatment would cost a lot. Then one day he called me in. He said he had a surprise for me, and he held up a pair of glasses. He even let me try them on." He put his arms through the sleeves of a white shirt embroidered with blue and red. His glasses came off in the process, and he put them on again. "I could see clearly for the first time in over a year. 'I went to considerable difficulty to get these, young man,' he told me. 'I had them made illegally by someone, you don't need to know who it was.'"

Lynch threw himself down on the couch. "Today I learned how he lied to me. Your friend Niko took my glasses, and the broken lens, and a couple hours later I had a new pair. *He* made it so I wouldn't know who to go to if the *doctor* took my glasses away. He let me get used to them. He took me to his window, which was high up on the hillside, looking out over the rest of the orphanage, and let me see things. Just see things. And then he said he'd let me keep them if I was nice to him." He said bitterly, "I was 'nice' to him until I ran away. But for a year the only one who wanted me wanted to hurt me.

"I suppose he's got someone else to be 'nice' for him now," Lynch added. "He wouldn't go long without it."

Jason sat on the far end of the couch, facing Lynch. "Is

that why you have no bank account, why you pay for everything in cash?"

"Who told you that? Oh. It must have been Niko again. He learned a lot, didn't he? That's part of it. But I couldn't get any credit, either, or find a bank that would open an account for me, because I didn't have enough identification. I didn't think *you'd* hire me, because of that, but Niko said I was wrong."

"He was right. I don't care much about official standing; I'm more concerned with how people feel to me. I think you'll work out well. We'll see." She sat quietly for a moment, then said, in a question that wasn't really a change of thought, "Lynch, what happened to you last night?"

His arms were crossed over his chest protectively, and he was staring at the floor. At first, he mumbled so that she didn't hear him, but when she didn't respond he turned and said loudly, "I got drunk."

"Does that happen often?"

It surprised her that he smiled. "Not as often as I'd like," he said.

The answer was pleasing; it was honest, and he hadn't hesitated before he said it. Nevertheless she said, "It can't happen at all when you're on board ship."

Very seriously Lynch said, "I don't think it will, Captain Horiuchi. I hope it won't."

He knew enough not to promise, then. That was good. She moved to the window. One of the clear panes gave her a view over the rooftops of buildings to the waterfront, diamond-hazed in the afternoon sun. "You have a beautiful apartment."

He sounded pleased. "I fixed it up myself. The tile was here when I came, but I painted the whole place and fixed the broken stairs, and put in the cupboards and closets. I made some of them, and found the rest thrown out on the street." He said proudly, "They look pretty good with a coat of paint." He ran a toe over the rhomboid tiles which, in patterns of yellow and light and dark brown, gave the illusion of advancing and retreating hexahedrons. "I'll be sorry to leave this place—but not much. I'm ready to leave."

"Aren't you going to pack?"

Lynch was bleak. "There's nothing I want. Maybe I'll come back for my clothes." He looked around the room one last time.

Jason put a hand on his shoulder then, squeezed it gently, and said, "Come on. Let's get your implants."

The doctor examined the spinal socket carefully, pushing Lynch's head from side to side casually, as though he were manipulating a doll. Vernon Kalb was an unprepossessing man whose dignity had been learned in a classroom. He was a few inches over five feet, and his nondescript pepper-colored hair would be little more than a tonsure in a few years. He had thick, shaggy eyebrows that crossed his face in a solid bar, lessening only slightly across the bridge of his thin, sharp nose, so that his deep-set brown eyes were constantly in shadow.

His hands, disconcertingly, were beautiful, with slim fingers, long and hairless, tapering to even, well-manicured nails. His palms were pink and free of calluses. He put his thumbs to the edge of the organic plastic housing and pressed, then nodded to himself. "Good job, this. Local?" Lynch shook his head, to the right and upward, a classic Hellenic "yes" that had survived the transition to space. "It's taken well. Seems to have grown along with you. Neat. Scar tissue sometimes puckers; this is clean. Do you remember who did it?"

Lynch shrugged. "Just a doctor. I didn't pay much attention."

"It doesn't matter. But I appreciate good workmanship. Makes my job easier. You just use it for messages?"

Lynch had thought the question was rhetorical until Jason tapped his arm. "Answer him, Lynch." Then he looked up. "Yes. I didn't know you could use it for anything else. The dispatcher calls me and tells me where to go. When I pick up or deliver something, I call him back so he can give me another job." He squirmed a little under Kalb's sometimes painful touch, and was quiet. But finally his curiosity prompted him to ask: "What else can I do with it?"

Kalb took a diagnostic probe from a rack hung with a variety of instruments like dentists' drills. "Hmm? Lean forward a little, son." He popped the probe into place and flipped a switch on the underside of one arm of the examining chair. "Depends on what they've built into you. For now, I suspect there's nothing much you can do." He fiddled with a dial and watched the response on a tiny monitor. "Like I thought: all you've got is a simple two-way, purely mechanical. Stimulates the auricles directly so you get sympathetic vibrations that sound like sound." He heard what he'd just said and seemed slightly embarrassed. "Well, they *are* sound, of course, but no one else can 'hear' them. They're doing their little timpani inside your head. No air movement on the eardrum; nothing for anyone else to notice." He tapped Lynch on the shoulder. "Sit up straight now.

"Of course, it'd be easy to do a full modification now, shoot you full of bacteria and let them eat their way to the right parts of your skull. It would take a few weeks for it all to gel, though, and I think your captain is in a hurry." He raised his shaggy eyebrows questioningly and Jason nodded. "So right now, all we'll do is release two sets, one batch that's specific to your ocular nerves, another that transmits physical sensation—very important, I'm told; I wouldn't know myself —and in a day or so you'll have a good myelenic sheath pathway."

Lynch squirmed more vigorously and Kalb said, irritated. "What's the matter with you, son?"

Jason answered, "He's worried about his eyes. Apparently they've been getting worse, and he doesn't want to go blind."

The doctor's irritation increased. "Yet you won't have surgery. You can't get better if you won't accept help." Then, more gently, he said, "This won't damage your eyes in any way. You've got a simple dysfunction, son, though it's rare; your eyes focus light so that it falls short of the retina. But your ocular nerves are fine. What I'm doing will affect you here"—he tapped the medulla—"not here"—and his finger brushed Lynch's right eye so that he blinked and slightly recoiled.

"Bend your head again, young man. I'm going to give you a local anesthetic first; we'll wait for a bit until it takes, and then I'll inject the bacteria." He moved Lynch so that his chin was resting on his scapular notch. Then, without looking, Kalb reached behind him to a small metal tray covered with a neutral gray cloth and littered with an array of syringes, scalpels, and clamps, each in their own neat little pile. His slim fingers fell on a syringe; he picked it up, looked at it, nodded, and said, "This will sting a little. Try not to move." To his evident surprise, and to Jason's, Lynch stayed perfectly still while the doctor probed, injected a small amount of a colorless solution, and then probed again. He made four injections in all while Lynch sat motionless.

The doctor, pleased, said, "Very good," and then pressed hard directly on the spinal socket. "Can you feel that?"

"I can feel you pushing," Lynch said. "It doesn't hurt or anything."

Kalb's voice was smug. "I know. If the anesthetic hadn't taken hold, you would have jumped through the roof when I did that."

He set down the small syringe and picked up another, filled with a pale yellowish solution. On the floor beneath his examining chair were several foot pedals connected to his examining couch, surgical spotlight, and to several pieces of equipment around the room. He nudged two into position with his right foot. One controlled a miniature tomograph and manipulated its image on his monitor. Kalb clicked on the control, looked toward the apparatus, and watched it sway from side to side as he depressed the foot pedal. Satisfied, he stretched the skin on Lynch's neck between his thumb and forefinger until it was taut. Holding the needle in his other hand, he tapped another foot control until the spotlight dimmed and the monitor image was the strongest light in the room.

Kalb was careful; he spent several moments picking his injection site, and more time still injecting the fluid slowly, almost imperceptibly. When the syringe was empty he pulled the needle free with a quick, abrupt motion and wiped his forehead with the sleeve of his right arm.

"Well, that's done," he said cheerfully. "You're a good patient, Mr. Lysikomos. How do you feel?" Kalb had set the needle down and was holding a cotton swab against the small puncture wound.

Lynch shook his head. "Like someone shot off a flashbulb in my eyes, and I'm still seeing the light."

Kalb nodded. "That's fairly common. It will wear off after a while. We'll monitor you for a few minutes, to make sure your pulse rate and blood pressure stay within acceptable limits. That's a formality; I can see you'll be fine. But don't do anything that'll strain your eyes for the next few hours. Don't drive, for instance, or try to read anything. It won't cause any harm, but it will give you a tremendous headache. It's also possible the nerves will continue producing pseudo-flashes until the myelin sheath is completely formed. It grows very fast, but it's not instantaneous."

He snapped off the monitor, raised the lights, and swung the small metal table away against the wall. "That's it. If you're still in the area next week, stop by for a checkup; if not, any competent doctor can make sure that the nerve graft has healed properly." He helped Lynch out of the chair. "Congratulations, and welcome to the Net."

The afternoon sun had baked the brick roads so that a shimmer of heat struck her forcibly, and even the sea breeze was hot. "I need your expertise," Jason told Lynch. "Late last night I met an old woman who takes cube portraits, in a place called Fibi's. Do you know where I might find her?"

"Is she short, with hair that sticks out to here"—Lynch spread his hands wide an improbable distance from the sides of his head—"a whole bunch of sweaters, and a watch that costs a fortune?"

"That's the one, yes."

"That's Mara. She goes to all the bars. This time of day, she'd probably be in a coffee shop somewhere in the Arkaikon." His receding chin stuck out stubbornly. "Why don't you tell me what you want instead of heading back and forth from the Arkaikon to the Beehive all day?"

"There's some justice in that," Jason admitted. Her eyes were half closed in the heat and she stood for a minute, considering. "I want Mara to make a three-D portrait of me, as clear as she can make it. Then I'm going to find four or five captains, owners if possible, who will help me on a private project. Later, after we've initialized your implant to the *Argo*'s subroutine, I'll tell you more about what I'm planning. But until I know that you can function in my Net, I'd rather not let you know what I have in mind. Fair?"

He was leaning against the side of the office building, staring down at the sidewalk. "What if I *can't* do what you want me to? I don't even know what 'Seeing' means, the way you're using it. I don't want to come this far and not go any farther."

Several people passing by glared at Jason with annoyance, and she eventually stepped out of the pedestrian traffic pattern and leaned against the wall near Lynch. "I've never had an

implant fail initialization," she said. "There's always a first
time. *If* it happens, it may be fixable. I'll take you back to Dr.
Kalb and we'll try again. If it fails a second time—even more
unlikely—there may be a genetic incompatibility. In that
case, I'll try to find you a job on another ship. If I can't, I'll
take you aboard as a passenger until we get to Metacenter,
where I know there are jobs available. In any event, if you
decide you do want to go, I'll find a way to get you off-planet.
Now, is *that* fair?"

Lynch tried to talk and couldn't; and swallowed; and tried
again. His voice was hoarse. "Yes. Thank you."

"Now let's find this Mara of yours."

Later they returned to the port. Jason asked for and received a permanent badge for Lynch and showed him how to
use it. "There's a fairly brisk black market trade in them,"
Jason explained, "so don't lose it."

But she'd lost his attention. Lynch was trying to see everything at once, to make up for the times he'd been to the
spaceport and seen nothing at all. "They don't let messengers
into the port," he said. "The closest I've ever gotten is that
guard shack we passed."

"There's a lot of valuable merchandise changing hands
here," Jason explained. "We lose enough of it as it is; we'd
lose more if we opened these ports."

"Sure, but most people don't want to steal anything. They
just want to look. You can climb above, on the hill, and look
down; but the port's so small from there you can't see anything."

"It must be a high hill," Jason commented. "The field's
over ten kilometers square."

Lynch's look of anticipation had given way to disappointment. They were passing through row after row of bare-bones
trading vessels, mammoth and skeletal. "These don't look like
spaceships," he complained. "They look like oil rigs. Or
bridges under construction." Then they passed out of the
shadow of another massive vehicle. Lynch's comment was
simple and straightforward. "Wow."

"Wow indeed." Jason followed his glance, pleased. "That's
the *Argo*. My ship. She's beautiful, isn't she?"

He nodded his head vigorously. "But why does it look like
that, when the rest of them are so . . ."

"Ugly? Functional?" He bobbed his head again, like a jack-in-the-box. Jason looked at the tall, slim missile balanced on three vertical jacks, like a fletched arrow. The hull was burnished to a mirror finish and the conn bubble was sealed seamlessly in a broad band circling the forward third. "The ships here are made to carry cargo in space. They don't need to be aerodynamically sound; all they really need is one flat space to land on. I wanted a ship that was practical *and* aesthetic, and I had the money to have one designed and built. The inside is beautiful, too; I'll show you when we come back this way."

Lynch kept looking back until the *Argo* was out of sight. "That's what spaceships *should* look like," he finally said.

"I know. That's what they looked like in my father's fiches. I read them all when I was a kid—his collection went back over two hundred years—so I had a lot of models to choose from."

Jason consulted her list of ships in port. For what she had planned, Jason would need at least four backup supercomputers, and she consulted the list now for the names of people who might owe her favors. There were few people who would willingly donate computer service for an afternoon; most captains had a superstitious horror of being off-line.

The *Iraklion* was in, but she was home-ported for Moulinos. Jason thought about it, but even if her captain was willing, the crew had to live here—or at least return periodically for repairs and re-registration. If Papandreou found out they'd helped Jason help herself to his museum, losing their registry would be the least of their worries. She crossed it off with a sigh.

Scapegoat. Had Bear not been doing military service, and hence somewhat out of touch, she would have known what had happened to the Hasiqi kids she'd captured. Panos Benali, a young trader, had read about them and brought them aboard as his crew. From rumors, he considered them his children, and the children themselves were fanatically devoted to him. Bear's ignorance may have been engineered, as she had continued to work for the Niarin after the engagement in question. To Jason's possible benefit, the adolescent army had been trained, and abandoned, by mercenaries working for Papandreou et Cie.

It was worth a try. Jason brought out her map, punched in the field coordinates, and requested a path to the *Scapegoat*'s berth. "Damn it." She held out the map to Lynch. "The shortest distance is a straight line. I can even see his ship from here, but I can't get to it without traveling halfway around the field. Did you have problems like this when you were delivering your messages?"

He bent down to study the two green pulses, nearly side by side, and the snaking trail of phosphorescence that connected them. Interlocking gates blocked their most direct route. "All the time, Captain Horiuchi. The city's building something, so you have to go a kilometer out of your way just to cross the street."

They reached the ship eventually, but her captain was anything but receptive. Big and burly, he sat in his command chair glowering at Jason through a thick nimbus of black beard. He slapped his leg, an emphatic parenthesis. "You want a favor from me, and I have not seen you but in passing for years? No."

A young woman had waited at the cabin door while Jason was introduced. She was wearing a set of combat fatigues and a fiery, defiant expression; both appeared habitual. Her complexion was so clear her skin was lustrous, like close-grained wood lovingly polished by hand. "Pardon me, Captain Benali." She turned to Jason. "You are from the *Argo?* And you have someone on your crew, a woman named Vouris?"

Jason nodded to both questions.

"Then, Captain Benali, the crew asks that you grant this woman's request." She faced Jason again. "The Sergeant Vouris was a brave woman, and fought for our rights, even when it was to her disadvantage. We were not treated well, but it was through no fault of hers. If Captain Benali will agree, perhaps this one favor will be partial repayment."

Benali frowned, his lips thin beneath his black mustache. "Is it important to you?" It was apparent he wanted her—and was giving her the opportunity—to say no.

She didn't. "To us all, it would mean a great deal. But we will do as you say."

He frowned again. "She makes me decide, Captain. Well, she should; that is my role. But if I decide against you, I will have hurt my crew, and if I decide for you I will place my ship in jeopardy, no matter how slight. You do not dispute this? No. Then tell me: what is it you will need? I will listen, Captain Horiuchi, and if I can I will give you an answer tonight; or, if not tonight, tomorrow."

Jason said, "I need your high-speed computer, for a few hours only."

"Out of the question. I am sorry. I have projects generating in the cray, and I would have to download them to a machine that is slower and less versatile. That would take time, and more time to boot, and even *more* time before I was convinced everything was operational. No. Again, I am sorry." But then, curiously: "What do you want it for? You've your own."

"I need several."

"Several? Good my God, why? One has more power than even a ship my size can use."

"I'll show you. I'm not as good as Lys, my Second; but I can give you a rough idea." She opened her pack and pulled free the small three-D statue. "Have someone digitize this for me, please? And I'd like to use your terminal for a moment."

Benali took the statue and looked at it critically, then tossed it to his crew member. "My myrmidon, please take this to Kalish and have it entered into the computer." The woman bowed and left. "Why naked?" he asked.

"I didn't want to have to wear the same clothing, in case it were noticed. I'm going to break into the Papandreou Museum."

"The devil you say! I'm delighted! I think it's wonderful. I wish you the best of luck. But that, again, would put me and my ship at risk. You cannot use my computer. I'm sorry."

"You keep saying that, Ben. Wait and see. Move away, please, and let me at your terminal." Benali shook his head, but he stood, grunting a bit with effort. The keyboard was active. She swiveled in the chair. "Lynch, come here and plug in."

He hesitated. "Why?"

"Because I told you to." An audible signal told her the digitation was complete. She called up the model. "Good. Lights off." The bridge darkened, except for necessary terminal illumination. "I want you to get used to the probe, Lynch; the feeling is much different from the simple radio you're used to. It's like a muscle—the more you use it, the easier it becomes. And, like a muscle, it may be uncomfortable the first few times you exercise it. I'd rather you start now, rather than risk fatigue when you're actually in the Net with me.

"I got this idea from Bear Vouris," she said to Benali. "You know Bear? She insisted we pose for a street artist. I hadn't had such a portrait done in years, and when the woman handed me the plaque, I was startled. Excuse me a moment." She called the computer room. "This is Horiuchi on the bridge. Am I on line to the cray yet?"

"You seem to know my ship well," Benali said. He seemed slightly put out by the idea.

"I should. I own a fleet of them. I brought the first few up active myself. How are you doing, Lynch?"

He was rubbing his neck. "It itches."

"It will. Where was I? Yes: I was startled. It was much more detailed than the 3Vs I'd seen when I was younger, and every detail was sharp. There were no blurs or loss of definition.

"Now. Remember that Lys is the expert. She'll be performing the actual animation. This will only be a rough estimation." The bridge was horseshoe-shaped, with a cleared circle set below the working level to allow crew members free access to each terminal. On that darkened stage, a little unsteadily at first, a small figure was dancing. Its movements were graceless, jerky, as though controlled by an unsure puppeteer, but the figure was obviously Jason Horiuchi. When the short dance was done, the figure bowed and disappeared.

"That was harder than I thought it would be," Jason commented. "But that was with only one cray, and I'm inexperienced. Can you imagine what an expert would do?"

"I can." Benali rubbed his chin. "I would like to see it. Still. Tomorrow, Captain. I will give you an answer then."

She didn't push. She waited while Lynch disconnected from the terminal, and took Benali's proffered hand. "Whatever your decision, Captain, I thank you for your time."

Lynch was quiet until they were on the gantry platform and the airlock was cycling closed behind them. Then he said excitedly, "That woman? I've seen her uniform! She was Hasiqi, wasn't she? But she's younger than I am! Was she in the war? Are children really fighting, like it says on the news?"

"Yes, she was fighting. And she was captured by the Niarin and abandoned. She and her friends are lucky they've found someone to help them. There are hundreds of such children still in the field, and most of them will die.

"And I'm fortunate Bear helped them at first; that may work in my favor."

She was talking more to herself than to Lynch, but Lynch seized on the unfamiliar name. "Who's this Bear?"

"Bear? She's an animated fur coat with a tremendous sense of humor, a background in opera, and a lot of skills she takes entirely for granted. She's also one of my oldest friends, and (currently) a member of my crew. You'll like her." She consulted her map. "You *won't* like this next ship, though."

The lock was cycled by a black girl in a calico pinafore over a ruffled, frilled dress. Her hair was done in braids and she had braces on her teeth. "Mith-ter Thi-mon is bu-thy," she said in a grotesque, parodic lisp. "Who shall I thay is calling?" She curtsied and the curtsy, too, was parody.

"You know me, Flossie. Captain Horiuchi. I can do without your act; just tell him I'm here."

"All right. *Cap*-tain *Jay*-son Hori-*u*-chi, the scourge of space. I'll let him know. Stay in the lounge until I get him." At the door she turned, hesitated, and stuck out her tongue.

They had settled down with coffee when a little boy came in. He looked to be about six. "Oh, you're pretty," he told Jason. "I like you. You know what? I've got a little wee-wee—Mr. Simon says I must never call it a cock—and I'll show it to you for a dollar." He turned to Lynch. "You look like a creep. I *don't* like you." He kicked the table so that Lynch's coffee spilled and said, "Oh-oh. Mr. Simon will punish me. He'll take down my trousers and whip my ass. Excuse me, my bummy. But then he makes it all better again." He leered.

"Tommy, you're being bad. Go to your room right now." The corpulent, greasy voice belonged to a man who was thin and elegant, clad in a full dress uniform with scarlet sunburst and the scrambled egg epaulets of military service. "Captain Horiuchi. I'm pleased to meet you once again."

He extended his hand. Jason ignored it. "You owe me a favor, Captain Simon. I've come to collect. We can then go our separate ways, thank God. And what right have you to wear that uniform? It must be earned!"

"Oddly enough, Captain, I have earned it. Years ago. I have the papers to prove it."

"You use kids for crew?" That was Lynch, unable any longer to refrain from asking.

"I do, yes. Do you want a job? You're a little old, but I can compensate for that." He looked suddenly as though he were judging fresh market produce. "If you like, I'll tell you more. Please feel free to come back anytime—with or without your charming companion. Captain Horiuchi: you're requesting a favor?"

"It's not a request. You will keep your cray ready, and sometime in the next several days I will use it for several hours. I will compensate you for any time you lose on specific projects, if you submit an itemized bill. And thereafter your debt to me will be canceled."

"You offer me little choice."

"None at all."

"Very well. I agree. My cray is at your disposal, until further notice. Flossie?" The black child was peeking in the door. "Their business here is done. Show these two to the door, please. Captain, good day." He bowed and left.

As they moved down the corridor another child walked up. She seemed to be about ten. "Tommy said you were a creep," she said to Lynch, "but he's just being a numbnuts like always. *I've* got something better than he does. Want to see?" She began to lift the hem of her skirt.

"No." Lynch walked away fast; Jason walked faster. The *Pan* was a LHRH ship, and all such ships were staffed by volunteers; though she knew this, it didn't decrease her discomfort. Soon she was walking so rapidly that Lynch was nearly running in an effort to keep up with her.

He had tried to puzzle out her reaction, and his own, and reached a conclusion: "He sleeps with those kids, and you don't like it. I don't either."

She stopped. "I was twelve when I first got laid. It was my choice, and I liked it. No, it's not that. They aren't children, Lynch. The youngest is over thirty. The miracles of modern chemistry: Simon's introduced them to a drug which inhibits the onset of puberty—and which, in some cases, can actually reverse it. Lutenizing hormone-reducing hormone: LHRH.

Hence 'LutHorH.' The *Pan* is part of a network of ships that include the *Pied Piper* and the *S. Temple, Esq*. They publish newsletters which they send to each other, explaining the cute things their 'kids' have done.

"But they're *not* children. They're adults who have chosen to live in a world where they don't have to make any decisions, they don't have to grow older, and the only thing they need to do is bargain. Like the master of your orphanage, except they're the ones doing the bargaining. I'm not even certain they actually are offering sex; it might be more palatable if they were."

Lynch considered. "Tommy seemed pretty specific about what he was offering *you*."

"Yes, but I suspect that if I'd taken him up on his offer, he'd have withdrawn it, or found a way to turn it into something else. Everything those 'children' say has double and triple meanings, most of them foul. Real children grow and change, and learn from experience. These children don't."

And then she was walking rapidly not to escape the *Pan* but because she was approaching an old friend, a squat ship that looked less like an oil rig and more like a steel-coated warehouse. "That's the *Mya Lin*," she said. "My old ship."

"They named a ship 'myelin'? Why?"

"Not myelin; Mya Lin. Two words. She was a woman who designed an antiwar monument on Earth. I think it's even more effective now that it's sunken. The water magnifies the black marble.

"I sailed on her when I was about your age, before I challenged Osamu Horiuchi, my father, for control of our company. We'd fought so often that everyone assumed I was out of the line of succession, so I had a lot more freedom to do what I wanted. There was a period, when I had just become the chief executive, when I couldn't leave the office because my okay was needed on every decision, no matter how small. That's the way my father ran Horiuchi, and that's why I took over. Now I delegate, and things run much more smoothly. When I die, the company will still continue.

"The *Lin*'s a traveling art show," Jason continued, "with a little street theater thrown in. I used to run props, design lighting for some of their shows, and for a while I had a hell of a good time trying to program the impossible special effects the actors, directors, and writers routinely requested."

Xaviera Watteau owned the *Lin*. She had light brown hair which rippled in an oscilloscopic wave reaching almost to the base of her spine. "I saw you coming across the port," she said. "Someone tried to break in recently, so we've left the external cameras scanning." Her tiny triangular face and large brown eyes gave her a deceptively naïf look which had taken in many people with whom she traded, some more than once. "Have you come back to show us more tricks, Jason? My mother often talked about you."

"You're the master illusionist, aren't you? What could I teach you? But I may have something new, yes." Carefully she unwrapped the statue again, and brought out a Bernoulli box she'd brought from the *Scapegoat*. The brief animated sequence was now preprogrammed, so she simply played it back—and very nearly regretted it, for Watteau wanted Jason to stay and outline the technique.

"Xaviera," she said finally, "it's simple. If I succeed I'll come back later and discuss it with you at length. If I fail, the question will be moot: the technique won't have worked well enough. Now: do I get the cray?"

Watteau seemed shocked. "Of course, Captain! That goes without saying. Your plans have brought this ship luck in the past, and luck we can always use."

The sun was lower now, and stark shadows were latticed across the walkways. Lynch's tone was glum. "You know a lot of people, don't you, Captain?"

He hadn't complained until then, which Jason appreciated. She would have quit long ago were she in his position. "I've been doing this for a century, Lynch. You can meet a lot of people in that time. Take Sae Hoon Hwang; we'll meet him next. I want you to keep something in mind when we do: in twenty years of sailing, he's always claimed that he was on the edge of both disaster and bankruptcy, but he's never even lost a cargo or defaulted on a contract."

They were brought to the off-bridge lounge of the *Mehitabel*, where Jason wasted no time. "I want to borrow your cray for an hour or two tomorrow evening, Si, under the direction of Lys Lyskopoulis, my Vector and Second. There will be no risk involved." (Well, not much, she amended silently.) "And

I'll personally compensate you for the time and any inconvenience."

Hwang's face normally had a pinched look, like a grape trying hard to become a raisin. It was more so now. "I would like to help, Jason, but I can't. I have a time-factored load to be delivered, and I may have to default on the contract. In which case I will also have to sell the *Mehitabel*, because I'm over margin and they may call my note." He was sitting with slumped shoulders, so tense he was vibrating. "We had an accident in an E-R Bridge. It took longer to cross than I thought, and my Sight decided to open her Eyes in the middle, to See where we were. She had a seizure and somehow cut an artery when her arm hit the terminal. I could feel it, of course, but I didn't know how serious it was until she blacked out and I was flying blind. I had to cut too close to the singularity and ruined my engines getting out; and then we had to lay to and repair, so we couldn't take Seyed to hospital."

He held his head in his hands, looking depressed. "We were out of commission anyway, and none of us shared Seyed's hemotype. So we had to shut down the cray, drain it, and use the coolant as a blood substitute. So now the manufacturer says we've broken the warranty, and the MMA wants to sue me for practicing medicine without a license."

"How's Seyed?"

"Oh, she's fine. But now she wants to transfer to another ship."

Jason stood. This was impressive, even for Hwang. It might even be serious this time. "Well, thanks for listening anyway, Si." But Hwang had already returned to his gloomy contemplation of his open voyage log.

On the tarmac again, Lynch giggled, the first real sign that he'd paid attention to anything that afternoon. "I'm sorry. That sounded serious. You say he's never had anything really bad happen to him?"

"Never." Jason consulted her map again and turned aside into another corridor of ships. "Core captains have traded Hwang stories for years. I hope he doesn't ever learn about them; it would hurt his feelings, for one thing. If Seyed had been seriously hurt, it would be another matter; but this is just another case of Si's Jonah complex with some genuine bad luck thrown in."

They visited three other ships without result. She'd expected to be turned down by the *Tom Paine*, because it was a Patrol ship, but Commander Dodson was an old friend so she had stopped in to say hello. The other two ships' captains, though, owed Jason—or Horiuchi, through Jason—a multitude of favors, and her irritation increased as first one and then the other turned her down without an explanation or an apology. She thanked them for their time—and made a note to have Lys pull them from Horiuchi bid lists.

The sun was below the horizon now, and deep shadows made each ship seem threatening. Even the more modest frames of the trade ships Jason was visiting—comparatively tiny, at no more than three stories tall and no wider than an average house—managed to seem intimidating in the uncertain light. Lynch was also getting cold. Jason noticed him shivering in his cotton shirt which hadn't been made for the thin, chill air of the mesa. But he followed Jason doggedly.

They were met at the *Mahayana* by an apparently nude woman who greeted Jason effusively, hugged her fiercely, and then released her abruptly. And then (it seemed to Lynch) her skin moved. It was clothing, some sort of form-fitting hologram. As she talked, unconcerned, vivid simulacra fled across her torso, hands cupping her breasts, squeezing her nipples; fingers disappearing into her groin and reappearing again.

Satter Das, the ship's owner, was marginally less enthusiastic in greeting Jason, in deference to the boy's presence.

"His name is Lynch," Jason told Das, and added that she planned to hire him. Jason continued to talk quietly but as she did she kept an eye on Lynch. If he could survive meeting the crew of the *Mahayana*, he could handle anything on board the *Argo*.

Jason enjoyed the atmosphere of the *Mahayana*. The crew worked hard, and they were among the most industrious people she knew. But when they had been sailing for several months they pulled the ship into the nearest port, and their method of relaxation was, to say the least, strenuous. She was rather partial to the oiled, ebony-skinned man herself, and looked forward with a certain amount of anticipation to the moment when Lynch noticed what was happening in the far corner of the room.

A woman walked through, carrying a tray pungent with sharp, attractive odors. Lynch watched the woman until she disappeared into a passageway. "Was that food?" he asked abruptly. "Please, may I have some? I haven't eaten all day."

Das, shocked, said "Jason!" in an accusatory tone.

"I'm sorry," Jason said. "You didn't say anything, Lynch, and I didn't notice."

Das gave orders and in a few moments a young man, slim, shy, offered Lynch a glass of lhassi and a tray of sweetmeats. "I would sooner run out of fuel than food," Das explained. "Take what you like; there will always be more."

Lynch looked at the assortment suspiciously, but the young man bowed and set them on a table at his side, and after a moment he took one and nibbled. "That's besan laddu," Das said. "Cardamom, cashews, almonds, and sweet butter, among other things. You'll like it." He did. Thereafter he busied himself with the tray, sampling one item after another, many of which he left alone after the first bite, washing away the taste with a sip of the slightly sour yogurt drink. He ate each item rapidly, ravenously, before he went on to the next.

Sattar Das had agreed to open his equipment for her use, and had even offered backup personnel, something the others had not done. "Perhaps you'll teach us something new," he said, his strong white teeth gleaming in a face the color of walnut. "Then we'll use what we learn to take profits from your Lys, as we've done in the past."

More seriously, he said, "You aren't the only one who has had trouble with Alecko Papandreou, you know. On several ports, my taxes were extraordinarily high, and at first I couldn't discover why. I learned that Papandreou controlled the ports in question, and I was carrying cargo in competition with his own ships. It hurt me financially, Jason, and it was so unnecessary. At its best, the *Mahayana* is no competition to a fleet of Papandreou cargo ships."

He stood and held her in a tight bear hug for several moments. "Come back later, please, if you can. My daughter is too shy to say anything, but she's been following you like a stricken calf since you entered, and I'd enjoy spending the night with you as well. I haven't forgotten the things you taught me, and I'd welcome the chance to show how much better I've gotten with practice!"

There was a young woman hovering around the edges of the room. Jason glanced at her now. "You're Sattar's daughter?"

She was small all over, from her tiny feet to her breasts to the top of her delicate, elfin face. A blush wouldn't show on her dark skin, but Jason could almost feel the heat of embarrassment radiating from her. She nodded with her head bowed, so that her eyes never met Jason's. "I am Kala Das. My father is right. I am very young—but I am eager to learn, and he has told me about you." She hesitated. "In detail. My father was especially complimentary about your thighs. He said they were strong, and that once you held him close when he wanted to get away."

"Sattar Das exaggerates; he has never wanted to get away when he was with me. Your breasts are small, like mine; I would like the opportunity to compare sometime. Perhaps Lynch and I could spend the night soon."

Kala looked at Lynch, hesitated, and said, "You look as though you would be clumsy at first with a new lover, because of eagerness, but pleasantly clumsy; and later it would be very nice." She waited as if expecting an answer, but Lynch was staring at the deck with fixed intensity. After a moment she shrugged, smiled again with shyness at Jason, and left the room.

Das, not obviously, moved away so that Jason could speak to Lynch. Lynch, agonized, said, "She was talking about spending the night with me, and I don't even know her!"

"She was making conversation; in her culture, sexual comments are meant as compliments. Did you think she was pretty? Then you should have said so. You could have said you liked her hair, or her eyes, or that you thought she could teach you a lot. It's a matter of politeness."

Sattar Das returned. "I have spoken to my crew. Any time you are ready, call and they will turn the highspeed over to Lys." He glanced at Lynch. "You hurt my daughter's feelings, young man."

"I didn't mean to."

"I will apologize for you. I will tell her you were thirsty for her taste, and the thought tied your tongue. She'll like that. Jason, again: please come back soon."

Outside Lynch said, "I'm sorry if I did something wrong back there. But all of this is so different; it's not like I'm used to at all."

"At least you tried, Lynch. That's a good sign. We'll visit one last ship and then I'll take you home to the *Argo*."

She plotted a course through the port maze to the *Carolyn*

Wild. Ordinarily Jason wouldn't have attempted to enlist her help, any more than she'd done with the *Tom Paine*, because the *Wild* was a security ship and so tied into the CDC, but the *Wild* had been Lys's ship before she joined the *Argo*. She explained as she walked.

Lynch looked at her oddly. "You were on the *Mya Lin*. The captain of the *Scapegoat* knew that woman, Bear. Now another member of your crew worked on *this* ship. Are there any ships here you *don't* know?"

"A few. But there are over three hundred ships here, Lynch, and we've visited fewer than a dozen. I'm only calling on those ships where I think I'll be successful."

He thought about it for a moment. "So why do you think you'll be successful with this one?"

"My Second broke her back aboard the *Wild*. Natalia Tereshkova—that's her captain—had engaged the ship's drive while the *Wild* was in port—and while Lys was relading. A pallet of cargo swung out of position, and torque placed Lys and the pallet in the same space at the same time." She stopped at the gantry and rang the buzzer. "They may give me access to their cray without the prodding, but if they don't I'll remind them—gently, of course—of the accident."

"Isn't that blackmail?" Lynch asked.

The platform door opened and they stepped in. "Of course," Jason answered. "But I've never had qualms about blackmail."

She hadn't needed the threat. Tereshkova followed the dancing figurine with delight. "Wonderful," she said. "I can predict other applications already. Of course, professionally I see nothing. Indeed, you are not even here, because at this moment I am at my terminal going over the logistics of our security arrangements for the Tricentennial." She chuckled. "Mr. Alecko Papandreou has been quite critical of our efforts, and I'm sure he'll be pleased to learn of my skull-cracking session tonight." She had a pleasant alto voice, greatly at odds with her square muscularity and her flat, Tartar features. Her iron gray hair was close-cropped an even half inch around her skull, except for a braided pigtail down her back. She swung in her chair. "I didn't know, Captain Horiuchi, that you had such criminal tendencies. Perhaps I should not have released Ms. Lyskopoulis so easily to your charge." She stood. "Allow us an hour to prepare one of the machines for release. Good luck."

* * *

A sleepy Denny cycled the lock. "Where's Lys?" Jason asked in some surprise. "I thought she had duty tonight."

Denny waved a hand vaguely and yawned. "Capella said she left an hour ago, and she was walking. I didn't know she could." She yawned again.

"Why are you still up if you're so tired? Lys stands watch, but that's just habit."

"I went to return the car, and when I got back Capella was asleep in my bunk. I don't really mind." Her tone said she did. "But I kind of want it to be my choice, you know? So then I decided to take a shower, but I couldn't get to my clothes so I got a shirt from Bear." She tugged at the plain cotton shirt draped around her like a painter's smock. Then she indicated Lynch with a tilt of her chin. "Who's the kid?"

Jason was standing to Lynch's side, and she could see resentment flicker across his face. "Given standard years, he's older than you are. Lynch Lysikomos, meet Denny. No last name: she calls herself Dendrite. Later you can ask her why. He's our new Sight, Denny. Tomorrow you can show him the ship. Tonight, just find him an empty cabin and some linen. Find yourself some, too. There's ten cabins aboard; you don't need to wait for Capella unless you want to." She shouldered past the two of them.

"Did Lys leave a message?" The question was tossed over Jason's shoulder, like a rag. Denny caught it. "She didn't put it on the bulletin board. She might have keyed it to your file."

Jason nodded. She was already at the terminal, leaning on one hand while she tapped in commands, a little slowly, with the other. Gone, no forwarding: the message said Lys would be out all night, but not where she was. Annoyed, Jason tried to reconstruct the last commands Lys had executed, but Lys was too thorough. She'd even reset the screen before she'd left.

Jason slapped the terminal into its resting position and walked toward the ladder to the upper deck. Lynch was staring through the crystal port at the mesa and the lights of the city below. Denny was watching, too, her weight resting on one leg, her left arm behind her back and clasping the crook of her right elbow. Lynch glanced at her and turned back to the window.

Halfway up the ladder Jason paused, considering. Lynch

would need new clothes and at least some tack to get him
started. She called across the chamber. "Lynch! I gave you an
advance. Have Denny take you out tomorrow to buy what
you'll need for work. You can show her where to buy it
cheaply. I'll see you in the morning. Good night."

As she climbed the ladder she heard him ask Denny, "Is
she always that abrupt?" She grinned. He'd get used to it. And
Denny would learn more about his background in an afternoon
than she could in a week.

The bed was warm, but slightly cooler than her body temperature. And comfortable. (It should have been; she'd designed it herself.) She pillowed her head on her arms and
stared up at the ceiling, letting her mind drift. "My toes are
relaxed," she murmured sleepily. "My ankles are relaxed. My
calves are relaxed." Drowsily she nestled more deeply into the
forgiving mattress. Tomorrow she'd talk to Lynch. She was
glad Niko had bailed him out, but a night in a cell wouldn't
have hurt him, and it might even have given him something to
brag about later. Hell, most of her crew had been in jail at
least once. It came of being crew. "My thighs are relaxed."
They tended to get a bit wild in port, but then they often spent
much of a voyage with their own personalities subsumed into
hers, acting only as a focus for her own sensibilities. "My
genitals are relaxed." As always, a wash of pleasure suffused
her then, as though she were being reminded that, relaxed as
she might be, arousal was always a possibility. As always, she
flowed with the feeling, let its warmth contribute to her relaxation.

She tried to imagine what it would be like to surrender
herself so completely, to allow someone else to control her.
She'd tried once, years ago. It hadn't worked out well, but it
was fun while it lasted. "My abdomen is relaxed."

She felt herself growing tense. Unconsciously she drew in
several deep breaths and let them out slowly, following an old
count. Breathe deep. In two three four. Out two three four five
six. Rest. Breathe.

Lynch, now. He was going to be interesting. She hadn't
seen anyone with glasses . . . and she realized suddenly that the
last person she'd seen with glasses had been her father, as he
was dying, still stubbornly ordering her as though he would go
on forever. She remembered light from the lantern in his bed-

room (an oil lamp, in a paper lantern, late in the twenty-second century; her father had worn his idiosyncracy until he had worn thin) flaring off the flat glass of his gold-rimmed spectacles. All she could see of his right eye was a circle of white that flashed and glittered as he spoke. He had been trying to tell her something, order her, *force* her, to do something for him. He'd died instead.

She breathed. "My breasts are relaxed. My neck is relaxed." She could feel the muscles loosening, the tight band at the base of her neck gradually easing. The slight pucker of the living plastic tugged slightly on the socket. It might be time to have it checked again. The stuff had a long life, but when it started to break down it practically whistled for bacteria to invade.

She heard sounds in the galley below, but the warmth of the bed and her increasing torpor made her reluctant to react. It had been a long day; it would be longer tomorrow. "My eyes are relaxed. My jaw is relaxed." She felt, rather distantly, her mouth hang open slightly.

It was pleasant to lie, drifting, watching the neutral gray ceiling and listening to... ah, to Denny and Bear. Odd. Denny should be asleep. Maybe she should get up and check. But her absolute lethargy made it out of the question. Tomorrow would be time enough.

Perhaps that was why it took her so long to understand when Denny and Bear burst in. She didn't even hear what they said at first, only an unpleasant buzz which brought her back from the soft edge of sleep. But finally she sat up, blinking her eyes against the light from the corridor. "What? Tell me that again."

Bear's voice was bleak. "It's Alecko, by holo transmission. Lys and Rat have been arrested."

_ 8

JASON, RAT, LYS

IT TOOK JASON a moment to focus. "What? What time is it?"

"Nearly four," Bear said. "Local time. They were arrested hours ago, before midnight, but Alecko didn't call until a few minutes ago. He's apparently removed their silvertips, or they've been confiscated at the jail."

"Five hours." Jason was pensive. "And he's—_just_ called?" She swung her legs free of the tangle of blanket. "It's too bad Lys never got the mandibular phone; I could call her."

The closet was locked but she wanted her uniform so she interrupted the cleaning cycle. "What do you think, Bear? What have they done?"

Bear leaned against the wall, arms across her broad chest. "You can't guess?"

Jason balanced on one foot, one leg thrust into her uniform pants. "I'm tired. I'm not in the mood for guessing."

"And I'm not the captain, Jason. I'm an underling; Alecko wouldn't talk to me. He's a major-general—or thinks he is. He's not what I'd pick as the model for a modern major-general—_my_ troops wouldn't follow him—but he's got the salad, he's wearing it tonight, and I suppose he's earned it." She laughed suddenly, a short bark, bitten off. _"I_ would guess, then, that Lys tried to break into the museum and that Rat agreed to help her. She's foolhardy when she believes she's protecting you; he's suicidal. She'd think she was helping you; he'd be along for the ride. And Rat is sufficiently fatalistic that he wouldn't much care how things worked out. I don't *know* anything, it's speculation. But soundly based, I think."

Jason tucked her tie neatly between her third and fourth shirt studs. "I agree: if it were a routine arrest, Alecko wouldn't be involved." She tapped the closet door to vary the polarity, combed her hair in the resulting mirror, and bound it loosely with an onyx clip, a gift from her father. "I want to control this interview as much as possible," she said. "Which may mean only that I'll terminate it when *I* choose." She straightened the collar of her jacket. "So be ready to cut the transmission when I give you the signal. Let's go."

Alecko was wearing olive drab, well and expensively cut, but obviously a uniform. Wire-spring tension propelled him around the room restlessly. "I've interrupted a training exercise to speak with you," he said. "I dislike wasting my time this way."

"You could have called five hours ago," Jason answered mildly.

Alecko stopped in the middle of a restless circuit of the room. "I had to question your crew. I did not believe they'd act for you. If I had thought you'd order your crew to steal for you," he said, perplexed, "I would have never proposed our agreement."

"Bear." Jason's voice was sharp. "Record this, please. Kyrie Papandreou, as of this moment the only thing I *know* is that two members of my crew have been arrested and that you've held them incommunicado for several hours. But I would not order—and I have not ordered—anyone who works for me to perform any unlawful act. Now: why have you arrested Kyria Lyskopoulis and Kyrie Sanjuli?"

His arms were moving like those of a spider drunk on caffeine: spasmodically, jerkily, as though each arm was separately alive and not under his control. "They were acting for you, Captain! *They were acting for you!* I have proof!"

Bear and Jason exchanged glances. Jason said cautiously, "Of what sort?"

"Auditory, visual; voice prints; blood sonograms, cardiotomography; basilar metabolic scans. Do you need more? I have cubes of their process through the museum. Let me show you." He lowered an upper arm slowly. "I made two sets; the first is sealed for the court. Here are portions of the second."

The light surrounding Alecko dimmed; responsive, the *Argo*'s computer matched the new lumen level. "This is one of the hills above the museum," Alecko said. "The vehicle you see was rented by your Kyrie Sanjuli late this afternoon." A tiny car rolled into view on a moonlit mesa, suspended in the air beside Alecko's hologram image, rendered ghostly in the dim light. Two figures emerged, barely identifiable as Lys and the Rat.

Alecko looked toward Jason. "I'll skip forward." The video blurred and slowed to show Lys alone within the museum. "Kyria Lyskopoulis liked this statue as well as you did, Captain Horiuchi. She told Kyrie Sanjuli about it at length." The miniature of Lys stood rapt before the "Jockey of Artemision," fingers extended but not quite touching the small figure. "Before this point, your two thieves had stayed together. My museum staff had followed their progress with interest. But when they split up, and your Kyrie Sanjuli set about disabling some of our potentially lethal devices while Kyria Lyskopoulis ventured into the jewel gallery alone, my security officer made the decision to call me."

Jason watched Lys pry open a locked case. "We needn't see this next," Alecko said, and skipped forward to a point where two small figures scrambled on loose shale. One— Lys—reached the summit, and stood—

—and the lights came on. In miniature, Alecko entered while his larger doppelgänger gazed fondly down at the scene played out before him. What followed seemed to continue for hours. Alecko watched himself with fascination, now smiling, now nodding with satisfaction, once laughing aloud. The process— arrest, interrogation, prolonged and repeated physical examinations—was geared obviously to produce *some* discomfort, *some* pain, and, more importantly, fear and humiliation.

Alecko himself had administered Lys's second urine test, and he'd enjoyed the process. At that point Jason called a halt to the transcription. "This proves nothing but your sadism. Very well. I want them released. To that end, what do you want from me?"

Alecko raised four hands, palms upward. "Nothing. You've misunderstood me, Captain. You cannot have them released at all, until after they are sentenced, and that is now out of my hands. As I said, I've sent a more complete version of the tape you've just seen to court, with a notary's statement that it represents a true and correct record. Yes, and any cove-

124   LOREN J. MACGREGOR

nant we may have had is canceled by what I consider your bad-faith dealing."

A wrinkle in his uniform appeared to capture his attention and he pulled the fabric of his blouse tight with two hands while a third probed the seam with a delicate, callus-free finger. "I'll arrange for you to visit them, of course," he said. He smiled. "It's the least I could do." The complexion of a shrug was much different with four arms. "But when the courts open in the morning I will remand, and by late morning the State *versus* Lyskopoulis and Sanjuli will be officially filed. It's a formality only; they will both be sentenced. For a first offense, the penalty is fairly mild. They will each receive fifteen lashes in the public arena. It will be difficult for them. I hope they are in good physical condition. Good day."

Bear cut the transmission. "Well?" she asked. "What now?"

"If we can, we free Lys and Rat. It may not be possible; I'll have to talk with Wolde Dawit." Dawit was her lawyer, one of several used by Horiuchi, Pte., but the only one she used personally. Together with Kin N'Lopez, her accountant, they formed the triumvir that guided Horiuchi's policies. "And we start working on my own plan. Damn it, I wanted more time. I've talked to several people already. The list, and my notes, are stored on my terminal in an invisible file. Ask for 'Stoplight.'"

Bear nodded. "'Stoplight.' What then?"

"I'll need Denny's help, and yours. Possibly the new boy, Capella—I don't know yet. And there's someone else I want you to meet. His name is Lynch; I hired him last night. He'll be our Sight—and I'll definitely need him. So he'll need a training flight; Capella, too. You've run the introductory sequences before, so I want you to work with Lynch at first. Arrange with the tower for clearance sometime tonight or tomorrow. And one more thing."

Bear raised an eyebrow. "Yes?"

Jason put her hands behind Bear's neck and pulled until Bear's head was on her level, kissed her quickly but thoroughly, and abruptly released her again. "We'll have more time later. I've missed you, and I'm glad you're back. Now I've got to go." She sighed. "I have to sound reasonably intelligent when I talk to Wolde, even though my blood sugar feels as if it were somewhere in the negative numbers."

* * *

An hour later she was at a Trans-Core office, where she demanded a hookup to Dawit. (The *Argo* could manage local hologrammatic transmission without difficulty, but exoplanetary messages were beyond its capability.) Trans-Core employees were inclined toward a stuffy and pedantic adherence to written procedures which, if not forestalled, could and frequently did mean that an hour-long procedure would drag on for days. Today she hadn't the patience; and when the very pale, almost tubercular receptionist began to argue with her she simply stared him down until he subsided, and then handed him Dawit's card, complete with his comm number. Finally, reluctantly, the young man agreed to put the call through, and Jason followed his directions to an empty conference room.

She had barely seated herself, her black boots stretched out to the light gray square set into the darker slate of the rest of the carpet, when the slight subsonic of the hologrammatic projector started. Her boots disappeared at the edge of a test pattern. The gray was gone; in its place was a pale carpet, in color like Japanese broom, blooming. "Good morning, Wolde. It's good to see you."

A comfortable chair, leather, of the same warm yellow, solidified, and with it Wolde Dawit. Ebony highlights gleamed high on his forehead, by his middle ear, and against the line of his jaw, framed by a gray steel-wool fringe and marked by a shimmer of sweat. Barely perceptible along the left side of his face were three etched lines, nearly parallel, the scars of an old wound.

"Good morning, Jason. It's later here; I was just preparing to leave." His teeth gleamed. "The overtime will, of course, show up on your bill. Now tell me, what was so urgent?"

"Lys and Rat—you remember them?—have been arrested, Wolde. I want them released."

One corner of Wolde's lip lifted, perhaps an eighth of an inch. "'These are rather alarming prolocutions,'" he said somberly, "'and if there are in your story any little jostles to the law, I would beg you to bear in mind that I am a lawyer, and pass lightly.'"

"You're quoting. Dickens?"

"Stevenson. *Kidnapped.*" Dawit had met Jason Horiuchi in a bookstore, where they had wrangled over an elderly and

unreadable copy of Wilkie Collins. They had found a mutual
interest in Victorian literature and the Neo-Victorian Society,
but Dawit had the better memory for quotation. He frankly
grinned. "The selection seemed apropos. Can you outline the
problem?"

Jason had learned long ago not to keep bad news from
lawyers; it only interfered with their ability to help. If you
were going to break the law, it was simpler to tell your lawyer,
and generally it was cheaper. She was nevertheless not comfortable as she explained about Alecko and the ruby, and her
plan to steal it, forestalled by Lys's own attempt.

Dawit sat back, considering. After a time he said, "Let me
give you some advice, Jason. If you can avoid dealing with
that—with Alecko Papandreou, do so."

She leaned forward eagerly. "Why?"

"He's a lizard. His blood is the temperature of whatever
rock he's hiding under and he sheds his skin twice a year.
Don't talk to him without witnesses. Don't agree to anything
without having it in writing. Don't accept anything he says
without having it independently verified."

"This sounds like personal experience," Jason commented.

"Oh, it is. I didn't pay attention to venue once, and relied
on his personal guaranty. I had dealt with Dhimitri Papandreou
in similar situations without difficulty, and apparently Alecko
knew this, or suspected it. As a result the deal was struck
under corporate rules with which I was unfamiliar, and Alecko
foreswore his guaranty in such a way that the cost of litigation
would have been much higher than any possible return. My
client lost a great deal of money, and I lost a client.

"Dhimitri is reputedly grooming him to take over the Papandreou business," he continued, "which is understandable
but foolish. On rare occasions he can be a charming host and a
good businessman, but he's been in the same position within
the Papandreou organization for twelve years, for good reason. He isn't stable enough to handle more responsibility. But
one day he will try to take over, and the good lord help anyone
who attempts to stand in his way."

Dawit stood. "I'll spend as much time as I can working for
your crew's release, but I won't hold out much hope. Good
luck, and please give Ms. Lyskopoulis my regards."

As he stepped away the screen went dark and the square
became pastel gray once again. The subsonic whine ceased,

much to Jason's relief. She tapped the timer, which spit out an impossibly high fee statement. At least now she knew how Trans-Core could afford the Tooker lithograph in the entrance hall.

Bear and Denny joined Jason in front of the jail. Denny acted as if the meeting were an accident, but Bear was more straightforward. "I wanted to see Lys," she said. "I wanted to make sure they were treating her well."

The jail wasn't much, an old converted house, with any decorative frills long since removed. Lys's cell was plain, square, with a wooden slat bed, a washstand, a toilet, and nothing else. No pictures interrupted the whitewashed walls; the only light came from the small barred window or from the low-wattage bulb in the corridor. There wasn't even a chair. Lys was lying supine on the bed, her face turned to the wall.

Jason saw the jailer was a middle-aged woman whose hair, dirty gray, hung in limp, greasy strands. She was corpulent, not in any pleasing way like Denny or Bear—or even Niko— but with vast pockets of flesh that sagged from her arms and neck in pendulous folds. The seams of her blue dress uniform bulged; the cuffs and collar were dingy with ground-in grime.

Lys had turned at the sound of Jason's voice. She threw her pillow against the wall of the cell, then dragged herself up on her elbows until she was leaning against it, sitting. "Hello, Jason. Bear, Denny. You saw the video Alecko made? I was sure he'd show it to you. He was awfully proud of it. I'm sorry, Jason. I took what I thought were adequate precautions. I was wrong." And, more quietly: "I did the best I could."

"I know you did, Lys. I appreciate it." She'd hoped that being near Lys might somehow compensate for the lack of a silvertip—sometimes, when she was close to her crew, she could subvocalize and make herself understood without the probe—but it wasn't working. She could feel a little of Lys's fear and tension, but none of the frisson of true contact. "We'll talk about it later. How have they treated you otherwise?"

"Not badly. Though it's embarrassing to ask their help for everything." She glanced at the toilet and back. "There's nothing to do here, Jason. I don't even have anything to read."

"Never mind," Jason said again. "I've got Wolde Dawit working exclusively for your release." A minor exaggeration wouldn't hurt, and might raise Lys's spirits. "He's turned the rest of his practice over to his partner. He sent his best wishes."

It was difficult to see, but Jason thought Lys smiled. "Thank him for me. But I think the only way Rat or I will get out of here is through the Arena." She indicated the jailer. "Ask her."

But the woman only said, "Time's up," and, "Do you want to see the other prisoner now?" Jason nodded and the woman led the way down a short flight of steps.

But Denny hung back, tugging on Jason's sleeve. "I brought this," she whispered and handed Jason two sterile silvertips, temporaries only, with short-term battery packs the size of small coins. Unlike the more sophisticated probes used on the *Argo*, this was a simple set, with limited range, used only for sending and receiving messages. "They're a matched set," Denny said.

"Denny, you're wonderful," Jason said. She took one of the probes. "Can you get this to Lys without anyone seeing you?"

"Me? Sure. That's why I brought it."

"Good. Then do it, and follow us as quickly as you can." She hurried to join the jailer and Bear in another row of cells set at right angles to the first. Rat was in the last, farthest from the light, and his cell had no window. He was lying on his bunk, knees up, head cradled in his hands. He was smoking a cigarette, and the only light in the cell came from the red ember at the end. Jason turned angrily. "You could at least get him some light."

In the darkness Rat laughed. "It's all right, Captain. I do my best thinking at night anyway. Now I can think all I want, any time." His face was a pale blot, darker than the pillow, lighter than his clothes. "Lys and me, we had a time of it last night. You should have been there." He chuckled and coughed, lightly at first, then rackingly. That kind of cough, prolonged, could tear the intercostals. Jason suggested as much.

The jailer said, "He'll be checked thoroughly before he goes into the Arena. They all are."

Rat made an effort and stopped coughing. "It's all right, Jason. It's been with me for years. It's no better and no worse now. 'The Arena'—that'll be interesting. I saw it from 'tother side some time back when I was visiting. Now I'll see it from the stage." He flicked the cigarette accurately through the bars. It missed the jailer, who growled. "Sailing with you has been worth it. A man my age doesn't have the chance for much to happen." He lit another cigarette and the brief flare of the match was startling in the dark. "I have no regrets. Watching you is like watching a river, *neh i ohi?* You flow along, moving over or around anything in your way. Lys, now, she's a riverbed. She can guide you sometimes. But you remember, Captain; you're wearing her away, too.

"Bear's there, isn't she? I can't see very well. Now you're a granite cliff. Odds are you'll outlast all of us. You're big enough to endure anything, any way you want to think of it."

He coughed again. Jason waited until he'd stopped and asked, "Does Alecko fit into your pattern?"

"Papandreou?" He was contemptuous. "He's just a storm, Captain. Leave him be and he'll blow himself out."

She walked out into the sun, shivering. "I don't like that woman, the jailer," she stated as they walked away from the courthouse square. "She's mean, evil, avaricious, and small-minded."

Denny said, "She is not."

Bear said, "This isn't a good time, Denny."

"I don't care." Denny faced Jason angrily. "You don't like her because she's Lys's jailer, and that's the only reason. She's an old woman who probably doesn't make much money, and she's tired and her feet hurt, and she doesn't eat well because she's broke all the time, and her uniforms are filthy because she can't afford to buy new ones, which she would if she could, and she really doesn't like people to visit the jail because she's ashamed of it, and she's sorry that she has to put people in a place that dirty and dingy, but it's all she's got, and tries to keep it up, but she can't, because they never give her any money for paint or new brooms or any of the stuff she needs, and she doesn't have the staff to do the job right anyway, and most of the time she's on shift alone, and it's just not fair!"

Jason looked at her, astonished. "Denny!"

"I'm *sorry,* Jason, but that's how I feel! She was a nice lady—I could tell—and I don't want you to hate her just because Lys and Rat are in trouble."

Jason hugged her. "Okay. I promise. But now I'm going to

try to get Lys and Rat out—and I won't make any trouble for your old woman while I'm doing it. The probe you brought will help. I'll have Lys get rid of it when we're done. At least she's got a window. She can break it and toss it out on the street. It won't look like much more than a wire then, and with the transmitter cracked, if it's found, Alecko can suspect but not know it's from me.

"Now I'm going to see Alecko's father. If anyone can overrule Alecko, it's Dhimitri Papandreou. But it's best that I see him alone. Maybe I can convince him to listen to reason."

She may have overestimated him. Papandreou looked out over the bowl of ocean, his eyes reflecting the cerulean sea. He was older than she remembered, and lines of stress were drawn tight at the edge of each eye. The memory of Alecko's projection was still vivid and it was somewhat disconcerting to see him when she could still recall how it felt to be, briefly, Dhimitri Papandreou. On an impulse she asked after Irena and was startled by his reaction.

"Do you know her? Do you know where she's gone? But I see you don't. My son must have suggested you ask." He was bitter. "She was someone I cared for a great deal, but now she's gone. Never mind, it's unimportant. How may I help you?"

Papandreou listened carefully while she spoke. Occasionally he nodded, and once or twice he frowned, as if in concentration. "I like you a great deal, Captain Horiuchi," he said finally. "I admire you. You're strong. You're forceful. You run your companies as they should be run; you know how to delegate authority, and to whom." He turned away from the water and leaned against the railing, two-by-fours and two-by-sixes the only barrier against a thousand-foot drop. "Perhaps you rely too much on that device in your neck, which I confess I don't understand."

If he could stand it she could; she joined him. Chin cradled on her clasped hands, she leaned her elbows on the railing and gazed out and down, drinking in the incredible lavender, crimson, fuchsia, and lilac colors of the mountain stone, so deeply faceted that if she climbed over the railing and down the cliffside, she could easily lose herself in the stria. "I've told you before, Dhimitri, and I'll repeat it until you're tired of hearing it—if you're not already. The Net represents the future. You've seen how it's spread in the last fifty years. There isn't a trading vessel today whose captain would sail without a Net-linked crew." The whitewashed walls of Papandreou's villa seemed to grow out of the cliffs, which towered for a thousand feet above; below, rock dropped away to the ocean. Looking down, she could see minuscule whitecaps seething around stone spires. On the horizon deep blue met the lighter, kinder blue of the sky. "People use it in different ways. I know some captains who drug their crews, keep them in sensory deprivation chambers, and discard crew members like batteries when they're all used up. To me that's criminal, and I'm working with several other owners to get the practice outlawed." She leaned against the rail. "But I can do on my ship, with five people or fewer, what you need an entire crew, sometimes of hundreds, to do. I can lade cargo, pilot, tune the engines, manage the respiratory systems, adjust the fuel mixtures, even clean and polish the ship, while it's in flight, using only the services of Sight, Sound, Taste, Touch, and Smell. Sometimes I have more crew; sometimes I have less, and double up duties. More importantly, you have no idea how exhilarating being head of such a team can be, both physically and emotionally."

Dhimitri shuddered convulsively. "Perhaps so, Captain; but you have no idea how appalling the idea seems to me. In my mind, that socket in your neck is some form of horrible mutilating surgery, and I would never have it performed; nor, I'm sure, would anyone in my family. Look around New Crete; you'll find few such devices here, except among the lower strata of the working class, stevedores and such."

Jason shook her head, shivering. "I'm not here to argue the virtues or faults of the Net now, Dhimitri. I'm here to free members of my crew. If I had taken Alecko's challenge and failed, I wouldn't ask you to intercede. But *i kyria* Lyskopoulis and *o kyrios* Sanjuli were trying to help me. If they picked a poor way of doing so, I still don't want them hurt because of it." After a moment she said, "I'm pleading with you Dhimitri."

The silence trailed. Finally he said simply, "I know." He looked out over the water. "Back in the city I could look out my window at this time of day and see a beggar down below. The man has been whipped so often that it's broken down his immune system. Recently he had a foot removed as the result of gangrene.

"May I get you a drink? No? I hope you won't mind, then, if I have one myself."

He moved away from the railing and walked inside to the sleek black marble bar. He poured liquor over the ice in a chased silver shaker, agitated it briefly, strained it into a chilled glass, and carried the glass back to the railing.

"I've talked to the man once or twice, because he interested me. It takes a great many assaults to break down the human system, which means that he has been whipped regularly for years. He considers it all a mistake, of course, and he blames my administrator, Akie Todheou, and his predecessors." He leaned out over the railing, looking down placidly into the ocean below.

"The people here are not ignorant but *untutored*, if I might make the distinction—they are innocent in the best sense, they cannot understand breaking the law, not in any *serious* way—and they look at this man and say, 'If I'm ever punished I may wind up like *him*.'

"And so he is an object lesson." He turned and faced her, his hands clasped behind his back, his legs spread slightly, like a military officer at an official briefing. "I am not a monster, Captain. I don't like inflicting unnecessary pain. No one is punished here who hasn't broken the law. If they choose to break the law and are caught, they know the punishment. It is always the same; so many lashes for this offense, so many for that, and then a period of parole, more as a cautionary measure than for any other reason.

"No, Captain. I appreciate what you're asking, and if it were in my power I would grant it. But the law here is specific and inflexible, and not even I may break it. Because if we were to make exceptions, the balance here, which is precarious enough anyway, might give way entirely."

Jason sat quietly. "Nonsense," she said after a moment.

"Do you think so?" An odd, crooked grin made an appearance and was gone, leaving only pain. "Then how about this." He set his glass down carefully, but his hands were shaking slightly and a small amount of liquor spilled onto the wooden railing. He was, Jason realized, not just aging but *old;* she had never noticed it before.

"I heard that your crewmen had been arrested on the news

this morning. The information should have been on my desk when I arrived at the office, but it wasn't. Earlier today I went to the museum." His voice was hoarse. He cleared his throat and tried again. "But my key wouldn't work, and I had to summon a guard. I didn't recognize him, although all the personnel files are supposed to pass to my desk. I like to be able to address everyone by name," he explained. "I feel it increases rapport with my staff."

He coughed. "I'm sorry. This is . . . difficult. The guard knew me, though—and he wouldn't allow me inside. There had been break-ins recently, he said, breaches of security. I hadn't heard of them. He explained—patiently, as though he was talking to a senile old man—that Alecko had reminded me of them on several occasions, but that I had failed to respond. Alecko knows my fears," he said bitterly. "He knows that I dread the thought of losing my memory. The guard, it seems, had been very well coached. So. Now the museum is staffed by people I do not know, and I cannot visit my own treasures without asking my son's permission." He cradled his drink in his hands, staring at the floor. "What has happened to Martin, to Jean-Marie, to Jovanie, to Natalja, to Mischa? I don't know. Perhaps my son is right. If they could all be replaced without my knowledge, then I am too old to maintain control."

He looked up. "Do you see why I cannot help you, Jason Horiuchi? I cannot even help myself."

Jason sat in the chair silently for a moment. He looked down at her, possibly asking for her understanding. "So I can do nothing but let my crewmen be flogged in public," she said. "You'll do nothing to stop it."

He bowed his head. "Correct, Captain Horiuchi. I'll do nothing to stop it."

"Then there's nothing else I need talk to you about." But she waited. "You realize this will precipitate the conflict we've been trying to avoid for years."

"I realize that. I'm looking forward to it, I suppose." They walked into the house.

"I have no one to whom I may will my power. You may yet have an heir, I don't know. But as it presently stands my empire will be carved from within by individuals who cannot control the whole, but who would not believe me if I told them so; and your own family is simply waiting, like vultures, until they can descend on your carcass. The trust you've administered has kept them at bay so far, but I don't believe the integrity of the trust will survive you."

He stopped pacing in front of a massive painting, the white of his linens contrasting with the surprisingly harsh earth tones. Brown gauntleted hands grasped columnar branches growing from cylindrical trunks: three nudes in a forest. Elsewhere the same colors might be warm. Here they were powerful and threatening. "So why not throw it to the wolves now?" This time he didn't hesitate, but poured a large tumbler of bourbon. "Why not scatter the pieces and stand on a hill where we can watch the blood flow?"

"Dhimitri, do you race horses?"

He shook his head, perplexed. "No, I never have. Why?"

"Someday I may tell you. And have you ever heard of a tavern called *Kenicki's*?"

He considered for a moment. "Yes," he said. "I own it. And Alecko is titular manager, although I doubt he spends much time there."

"I see," Jason said. "Thank you. That clears away some underbrush." She moved to the door. Dhimitri took her hand briefly. "Savvatokyriakon is fast approaching. I hope you will find an answer for your troubles before then."

Jason called Niko, using the mandibular circuit and enjoying the grate of bone against bone which fit in well with her current mood. He sounded half asleep, and she wondered if he were still drunk. But he listened, and as he listened, occasionally asking questions, he began to sound more alert. Yet he had no advice to offer her. "I was lucky with the boy. But Lynch had no previous record, and I had been able to do a favor once for the duty sergeant. So he had no arrest record to tamper with, no intake interview, and the written reports were destroyed. Therefore, he never existed. I can do nothing for Lys and Rat, especially if Alecko Papandreou is involved. I'm sorry. To help in this might not only place me in jeopardy, but your brother and his children. We will still need to live here after you've gone. Again, I'm sorry. If I could help, I would."

She walked through rows of cedars which provided shade for the granite bricks of a public plaza, and the late morning light created irises of color as it was focused by the prisms of mist from a half-dozen graceful fountains. But Jason saw none of it, and when she finally said good-bye to Niko she was no longer among the welcoming cedars but had passed into an area of shabby red brick and dirty wooden siding, through which old newspapers and other debris blew in a constant, eddying swirl which seemed to move old garbage only to replace it with new. It suited her mood.

At a bench she sat and ripped open the sterile silvertip package. Unlike her own probe, it wasn't custom-made and she had difficulty inserting it. But she managed.

«Is that you, Captain?» Lys. Thank God.

«Who else? Can you talk now? I want to know about the Papandreou, Lys. From the time you and Rat left the hillside above the museum. Take me through, step by step.»

«It may take all night, Jason.» Jason missed the full Net connection, because she wanted to know what Lys was feeling. But a few seconds later Lys's voice resumed. «I've been over this material before, in jail and on the flight back, wondering what went wrong. We found several levels of defense, but we evidently missed some. Cameras surround the ruby galleries, and wave detectors blanket each room with multi-planal sonic, thermal, and visual spectra. Everything larger than a dust mote and more substantial than a current of air is recorded and evaluated by a central computer.

«That computer, by the way, is an idiot, but not obviously so. When it's overloaded it shuts down its receptors until it can process the flow. It takes a lot to overload, and it's remarkably fast for something that isn't a cray, but during the crisis period it's essentially helpless. That's not common knowledge; I found out by accident, using a similar system once. But I didn't think we'd need to take advantage of that particular flaw. Apparently I was wrong.»

«I'll have at least five crays to play with,» Jason said. « We should be able to keep Alecko's computer as active as a flea on a griddle. What about the museum proper? Did you feel the pressure changes as you were going from level to level?»

«To be honest, I didn't notice. I felt vaguely sacrilegious walking through it. That huge marble floor reminded me too much of a mausoleum. And I kept thinking I'd reach the ruby without any trouble, but that my shoe would squeak just as I opened the jewelry case.» She laughed. «I may have been too tense. The alarm kept going off on my Petrovsky frame because I was sweating so much. I remember telling myself, 'Jason meditates to calm her. You can, too.' But it didn't work. I kept wishing something would *happen*.

«Rat and I had talked about shutting off the ventilators, but we'd decided it wouldn't serve any purpose and it might have alerted the guards. But after a while all I could hear was my own breathing and the air-conditioning, and it started to drive me nuts. It was okay, though; by the time I got to the trophy case, my heart was hammering so loud I was sure the guards could hear it, and then when I found out the case wasn't even locked I was convinced I was going to have a coronary then and there. You think I should have suspected something, with that open case?» Her voice was self-mocking. «I had to keep from giggling then; the whole thing seemed suddenly ludicrous. For one thing, my cervical collar kept pulling against my neck, and I had to keep adjusting it.»

«You should have worn a nullsuit,» Jason commented. «Your Petrovsky frame showed up on every monitor in the museum.»

«I thought I had it shielded,» Lys said. «I was wrong. Next time I'll know better. In any event, I grabbed the ruby and the velvet it was lying on, shoved it in my pocket, and ran. 'Just let me keep going until I get back to Rat,' I said. 'Let me just get out of this building, off this hillside, out of this area, and back to my ship where I'll happily go to sleep and no more a-roving go.' And I remember thinking, *'This* is how Jason relaxes, this is how she enjoys herself?' I think I called you a lunatic along about then, I'm not sure.»

«And that's when Alecko arrested you.»

«No. Didn't he show you that part? He waited until we'd left the museum and had gotten all the way up to the mesa. We couldn't see him until we were actually at the car; he was leaning against the hood, with a half-dozen security guards to back him up. Rat and I had been quiet all the way up the hill, because we didn't want to give ourselves away at the last minute.» She laughed bitterly. «And he just stood there. 'Good evening,' he said. 'I think you've got something of mine.'»

The contact was beginning to grow faint; Jason was some distance away from the jail, and the batteries weren't very strong to begin with. «Thanks, Lys,» she said. «I'm not sure how helpful that will be, but it gives me something to work with.» She said good-bye before the contact failed entirely.

With Lys on board there would always be an answer when she called, but now she was half anticipating silence when she inserted her silvertip and hunched her shoulders to make the connection. Yet Bear answered.

«I've been waiting, Jason. Any news?»

She was sour. «No. I'll continue working, of course. But no matter what happens, I want the ship ready to sail on a moment's notice.»

Lys on the Net was businesslike; Bear was very different. Her exuberance rattled through Jason. «I've already run the boy through the initialization sequence. He did fine. He and Capella don't get along, though. Too bad; I was hoping for a trio. We could sing in bars, make up for the slow times.

«If there's anything I can help you with,» she said more seriously, «please let me know.»

«I will, Bear. Thanks. But I'll be home in only a few minutes. Jason out.» Feeling slightly better, she removed her probe, recoiled the wire, and stored it in her battery pack. Bear's voice had been somewhat distant, so she checked the battery at the same time, and found it needed charging. Of course. Everything else was going haywire; why shouldn't her lifetime battery fail as well?

Bear had understated the tension between her two newest crew members. Lynch may have been watching for her to arrive; he came up as soon as Jason had cleared the hatch.

"I don't think I fit in here, Captain," he said. "Everyone knows more than I do, even Denny. You were right. She's younger than I am. But they've been talking over my head all day." He pointed at Bear. "And when *she* hooked me up to your computer, it *hurt!* I thought my head would come apart!"

Capella said, "He squealed like a stuck pig, Captain Horiuchi, and started yelling that we'd blinded him, that he'd never see again, and that it was all your fault. He's a coward, and I don't intend to ship with him."

Jason said, "Read the forfeiture clause in your contract, Capella. I'm perfectly willing to let you break that contract. All you have to do is write me a check for the entire amount and let Bear debit it from your account before you leave the ship."

He looked stunned. "That clause is never invoked," he said.

"It is on my ships," she answered. She turned her attention back to Lynch. "I'm sorry you were hurt. Sometimes it happens that way. But Bear said you did fine, and I trust her judgment. Your implant is still new, and it may hurt, just as it would if you were exercising a new muscle. Eventually the feeling will pass. As for talking over your head, don't worry about it. You're on a new job, and the jargon is unfamiliar. In a few weeks you'll be using the same language and you won't notice it." Jason glanced at Bear. "How did it go otherwise?"

"Fine. High marks in all spectra, quick recovery from photometric stimulation, rapid assimilation of data." She grinned down at Lynch. "Actually, young man, you adjusted more rapidly than I ever did when I had my first implants. I was sick for weeks, and every time I tried to get out of bed I lost my equilibrium and fell."

Lynch looked at her shyly. "Really?"

"Yep. I'd given up singing professionally by then, but I was still trying to teach, and I was afraid I'd have to give up that, too, because everything I heard was distorted and too loud, so that even people talking made me nauseous. But eventually I got used to it, and now I can even hear a greater range of tones. And I've still got perfect pitch," she said proudly.

"You were a singer?" She nodded. "What kind?"

"Mostly opera. But that was a long time ago."

"Why'd you quit? If you don't mind me asking."

She ruffled her pelt. "I had all this put on, and I didn't think the process through. Here, touch my arm."

She held it out, and Lynch stroked the fur shyly. "I like it," he said. "It feels nice."

"I like it, too, but there's a problem. See, a pelt like this needs something to keep it supple, and so the doctors had to mess with my hypothalamus so I could produce fats and oil for my fur. That meant they had to cut down on my sweat glands and replace them with sebacious glands, and *that* means I'm pretty well insulated, but I radiate badly. So I overheat." Her raucous laugh boomed through the galley. "Ever seen a dog on a hot day, Lynch? She pants like this." Bear demonstrated. "So do I. It cools me down. But when I sing on stage, boy! do I overheat. And for some reason, no one wants a shaggy opera singer who sticks her tongue out and goes *a-heh a-heh a-heh* after every aria." She laughed again.

"But don't you miss it?" Lynch asked seriously.

Bear said equally seriously, "Every minute I'm awake. I love to sing. But I love what I'm doing now, too. And honestly, I don't know what I'd do if the opportunity arose to go back now. I think I'd turn it down. The past is over with, dead and done. I have to live in the present, and I can only hope for the future. Whoops. I'm getting too serious. You strap in now, like I showed you; we're ready for your first trial run. Do you remember what to do?"

"I think so. I'm not sure."

"Don't worry. You'll know once you're in the Net. Ready, Jason?"

"As ready as I'll ever be." She hooked into her command chair. Everyone else was seated. She waited while Bear adjusted Lynch's silvertip and, over his protests, removed his glasses and placed them in a drawer by his side. Bear held up her hand. "No rings, see? No watch, either. I can feel them in the Net, and they break my concentration. Trust me. You won't want your glasses."

Once Bear was at her own post, Jason signaled the tower. "*Argo* ready for departure. Do I have a clearance for an excursion run?"

A bored voice echoed through the ship's intercom. "Ten · minutes, *Argo*. How long will you be?"

"Ten hours, roughly. We still have goods in storage, so I'll need the same berth on return."

"No problem. We'll hold it. Transmitting corridor information. Tower out."

Slowly she relaxed, letting her awareness of her own body dim and her awareness of the ship grow. Somewhere in the background Bear's personality rested, serene and comforting. She could hear the air moving throughout the ship now, and the sound of the struts cracking slightly in the heat of the tarmac.

The wind was warm on the shell of the ship, and she felt the breezes on the ship's "skin." Good: Dendrite was down, giving Jason a sense of Touch in the Net. Denny was loud and boisterous between runs, but when she was in the Net it was hard to notice her at all. Except for the heightened sense of Touch, it might be Jason's own sensation, expanded, to feel the ship around her and the space around the ship.

Kenot, too: she probed for his cynical presence. She could smell the acrid odor of the engines, now heating. The rotted vegetative smell of the field surprised her, as always. The sharp scent of the ship's air told her the recycling system was working efficiently and properly. But of Kenot there was hardly a trace.

In the Net, most members of the crew almost ceased to exist as they were subsumed within the nervous structure that was Horiuchi-plus, the sum of their parts and Jason's personality. Maybe that was why crews were so rowdy in port. Lynch might think he was unique, but almost everyone who had ever shipped with her had been arrested at one time or another. On most planets it took a lot to "disturb the peace," yet starship crews managed it routinely. The CDC kept a record of the worst offenders, and such ships were often required to post substantial good-faith bonds before they were allowed to land.

«Can't we start, Captain?» Lynch asked. «I want to see what New Crete looks like from space.»

She was startled. Lynch's personality remained intact, as though he were standing behind her, his head next to hers, watching what she watched, looking closely at everything she saw. Jason frowned: Lynch's hunger was an irritant, like an insect bite that itches more once scratched. Even Bear was quiet in the Net, her persona neatly tucked away and boxed. Of her crew, only Lys retained any awareness during a full cast of the Net though she, too, had learned over the years to surrender more completely. Maybe Lynch would learn, too. (Even so, she thought, the picture is so damn *clear!*) But she nodded. She planned no more now than a simple jump from Moulinos and a quick pass through a clear corridor to a point from which she could see the E–R Bridge.

She said aloud to Lynch: "Set your straps. Yes: we take off soon. You'll be able to See all you want once we're off." Then, realizing she must sound more harsh than she wished, she turned to him and smiled. "Enjoy what you can, Lynch; it'll get dull after a while."

He wasn't looking at her but was staring eagerly ahead,

Seeing through the ship itself out into the air surrounding. "No, it won't, Captain. Never. For me it'll never get dull. And, Captain?" He said it quietly, almost inaudibly. "Thank you."

She "opened" her "Eyes": Lynch was in the Net, and she felt his own expanded awareness, eagerly—avidly!—watching. She looked down the spectrum to see the pattern of air flowing past the ship and rising in sheets from the field. She looked up: a clear sky. Experimentally she swept through the ship, triggering each internal and external camera eye in sequence. All of them worked smoothly.

She had been the *Mya Lin*'s Sight for a while. Perhaps she had been as eager as Lynch then. She no longer recalled. But she guided him through the capabilities of the *Argo*, letting him See everything from the macroscopic view of New Crete's solar system to the microscopic focus which allowed her to examine the ship's welds for strain. "I've never seen things so clearly," he said, awed, while silently she agreed.

Their lift was without event, though Lynch had difficulty remaining focused on the cleared corridor provided by the port engineers. She had to remind him forcibly several times to let her control the visuals, as his enhanced senses wanted to follow every glittering trail of radiation.

Otherwise it was a long dull ride to the Dark Twin. The Einstein–Rosen Bridge, unstable this close, exhibited a rhythmic pulse that was both attractive and dangerous.

"It's beautiful." After a while Lynch remembered to breathe. "Does it always look like that?"

"I don't know; I don't know what you're Seeing. When there's something beyond your experience, your mind provides a convenient metaphor to explain it." To her augmented senses the bridge was always a kaleidoscope of intense color whose constantly shifting patterns were nearly hypnotic. She disliked watching a bridge for any length of time, because the effect was disturbing. The attraction to Jason was that the pulse would provide power for a long jump. The danger existed because the effects of an E–R transfer weren't always predictable.

Jason let Lynch watch because she remembered her own first reactions. If he had received the full neural network of implants, he would have perceived the bridge as seductive sound as well; the spectacular harmonies of escaping energy had inspired more than one symphony, but no composer had yet captured the raw vitality of that primitive sound.

Eventually Jason interrupted Lynch's reverie. This trip had been a trial of Lynch's performance, for she had no real doubts of Capella's ability. Capella's talents would also be useful in the Net, but a sense of duration was auxiliary to the ship's sensory functions, and Jason had hired him largely as a favor to Denny, secondarily as a possible backup second on prolonged voyages. But now Lynch had shown that he could See, and See well. As necessary as the excursion had been, it was time to return. "When we leave we'll travel through that. I'll need both you and Capella then, you to See a clear path and Capella to time it. It's not easy."

Lynch's voice was dreamy. "It looks impossible. I was digging in a garden once, and uncovered a nest of earthworms. It looked a lot like that, though not nearly so pretty."

He seemed content now to be simply an observer, and fell back into the Net almost passively, letting Jason See without protest. Jason had a tendency to forget the ship's attitude, because that had been within Lys's purview. But when the skin of the ship became hot, because one side had been facing the sun for too long a period, she felt it; and when the discomfort became too great, she rolled the *Argo* easily. With that reminder, figuring the vector became an autonetic function, akin to estimating the speed of an oncoming car while crossing the street.

They'd been sailing for three hours when she realized suddenly that she was too tired to continue. "Bear," she called. "Take over for me, please. I'm going to sleep for an hour or two. Kenot wants to visit his incubator. If we have time, and the positioning's right, let him do so. Run Lynch and Capella —especially Lynch—through maneuvers. And wake me when we're near port."

She drifted in and out of sleep, not uncomfortably so, but in a rhythm that seemed to complement the pulse from the engines. Perhaps she'd lived with the ship too long; they seemed in tune with each other. Lazily, she realized she was hungry but that she was unwilling to get something for herself. What the hell, she thought, I'm the captain, and slipped in her silvertip.

Bear was with Lynch. Jason listened for a few seconds, absorbing Bear's calm, patient instruction and Lynch's impa-

tience that he wasn't immediately getting something it sometimes took years to learn.

M'orru was with Kenot. Oh, yes; very much so, as the
spaceport's owner/guard might say. It always surprised Jason
when she felt Kenot's surging intensity, because it stood so
successfully behind his facade of cynical disinterest. Perhaps
more surprising was M'orru's response. She seemed both
bumptious and gentle in public, and the violence of their combined lovemaking was overwhelming.

Kenot was fully concentrated on what he was doing; there
lay a clue to his long list of accomplishments, because when
he decided to do something he did it well and completely.
M'orru was no less involved, but she was not as able to shut
out the rest of the world; she felt Jason's presence, and, somewhat timidly, invited her to participate. Lys would have been
appalled.

But Jason moved on. Denny and Capella were in the galley, talking in low voices. Interesting, to listen in. Capella
wasn't yet used to the eavesdropping possibilities of the Net,
it seemed; he didn't have the sixth sense that had let M'orru
recognize Jason's presence. Unusual but not unheard of, especially if his entire experience had been in school. "I just get
the impression you're going to tell Captain Horiuchi that I'm
signing on because of her." He was quiet for a moment.
"Now, your captain is certainly well known. But Bear! Good
God, she's the woman who knocked Bayreuth on its ass the
year she staged *Faust*—and played Mephistopheles." She
could picture him on his bunk, hands behind his head, knees
up and touching the bunk above, speaking with a quiet intensity that was almost frightening. "Jesus, Denny, but you
should have been there! She was perfect. She was *wonderful*
—and I'd gone there prepared to hate the production. So had
everyone else. A woman playing the devil! God, how sacrilegious!" He stopped, hearing what he'd just said. "Yes, that's
it. That's perfect! I hadn't thought it through like that, but I'm
sure she did. She didn't leave anything to chance. Her entrance on opening night was unannounced and unpreviewed.
'D'ou vient ta surprise?' And this huge, menacing *woman*
comes out in Satan's colors. Oh, the audience *hissed*. I can
still hear it; it sounded like King Cobra come to see an opera
and not liking what he saw. If you've never seen opera, you
don't know how fanatically we can cling to the forms we

know and love. Let them experiment with Shakespeare! Let them cut out all Mozart's 'extra' notes—'He wrote for the harpsichord, you see, and needed to disguise the lack of sustained tones like you'd get on a piano.' Shit." It was marvelous what contempt he could summon in a single word. "But leave our opera alone."

He laughed, no longer quietly but so that his voice boomed through the ship. It was Denny who was unusually quiet, possibly in complicity: "Now we both know something about Bear that the captain doesn't." Jason, above, smiled, and continued to drift into sleep.

"I can't imagine very many performers who could have continued." Jason could imagine Capella swinging his arms wildly now, trying to recreate for Denny the excitement of the evening. "Everyone was hostile! But Bear *used* that hostility, she worked with it so that you knew the Devil herself—and we all used the pronoun then, knowing it was right—was on stage, feeling our hate and loving it. 'You'll want me someday. See if you don't.'

"She was sly. She was daunting, daring, charming, *evil*. And attractive? I sat in the audience saying, 'I'll make a deal with *that* devil any day.' "

He drew in a deep breath and exhaled. "My God, we were all afraid to *breathe*, because it seemed as though any little thing might ruin the magic. And as Marguerite cries *'Tu me fais horreur'* and falls away from Faust to rise to Heaven, as Faust kneels to pray, as Mephistopheles bows to the sword of the archangel, we could feel her anger and frustration and fear when she sang, 'I am judged, I am condemned.' "

He was quiet again. "That's why I had to sign on. Just to talk to Bear. Then I was lucky enough to find you."

Denny had a tone of voice that went with her frown when she concentrated; Jason heard it then. "But we didn't even know Bear was here," she said, "until we landed." The tone intensified. "How did *you* know Bear'd be here, and come to this ship?"

__ 9 _____

JASON _____

DAYS PASSED, WARM, then hot; and then the beginning of the weekend, dawning with a blast of heat that erased the final traces of a breeze from the night before. A low mist obscured the sere hills and the shallow basin of the sea, though the sky was generally clear. The amphitheater was gradually filling, and she saw with distaste that the crowd would be, if these first few were an indication, cheerful and noisy. It was depressing. Lys was third on the program, and Rat fourth. She'd wanted the crew to stay aboard the *Argo*, but Bear had flatly said no; she was going to see what happened. Jason was in Dhimitri's private box. Bear and Denny, M'orru, and Kenot were below, in the stadium seats.

High cirrus clouds scattered shadows across the floor of the Arena. Dhimitri Papandreou was with her, watching the people arrive. "We have very little entertainment here," he said in his aged brandy baritone. "The people enjoy what they can."

"The people are here to enjoy a public whipping," she said. A fly bumbled into her face and she brushed it aside.

A sound broke over the amphitheater, a pleased roar. A young girl, only just pubescent, was being brought to the stocks. But the audience reaction was not for her but for the flagellator, who was obviously a favorite. The woman walked the length of the stage and back in a catlike prowl, lithe and menacing, and the audience responded with gleeful shouts

145

and suggestions. But she was all business once the girl was in the harness. Jason looked, and looked away.

A muscle twitched on Papandreou's cheek. A smile? No. "You needn't go through with this, Captain," he said.

The girl didn't do at all well; she fainted after the first three strokes, and the crowd booed. They booed, too, both the second felon and his flagellator. Somehow it had never occurred to Jason that flagellators would have fans.

Dhimitri was watching her with real distress. "Our people have grown used to the penitent boxes over the years, Captain, but they could be very dangerous for anyone who is new to them. My private box is cool; you can watch the proceedings quite clearly from here." He cleared his throat. "You benefit no one by this."

Jason nodded toward a row of small wooden structures, like confessionals, lining the Arena, discreetly cordoned. "Are those your private booths, *kyrie?*"

"*Kyria*, yes. But I wish you'd reconsider." His voice was strained, distressed; a furrow creased his unlined forehead. "The booths are mainly for our religious penitents."

"Will you let them go?" she asked. "I'll pay any fine you choose."

"*Kyria*, I cannot."

The announcer called out. "Elizabeth Lyskopoulis. Breaking and entering and grand theft. Fifteen lashes. Kyria Melina Tsakirides, flagellator." A great roar rose up from the crowd. Tsakirides was another favorite.

Lys was brought forward between two tall guards, who carried her to the block and strapped her into the padded frame with ceremony and dispatch. The previous convict was carried away, stumbling and only half conscious. Papandreou brushed away a fly. Unconsciously he reached for the square of cream-colored silk in his breast pocket and polished his hand briefly. "At least have a doctor in attendance, Captain Horiuchi. Jason." She opened her mouth to object. "We provide a physician for the flagellants, Captain. Surely that isn't too much to ask? Please."

She nodded curtly. "Have her wait outside then." The sun was almost overhead now, reflecting off the water with painful brilliance. The mass of people was shifting impatiently, rippling in waves. Dhimitri gestured to someone in the crowd, and a moment later a young woman hurried up, carrying a small black bag. Jason opened the door of one of the booths and allowed the woman to affix the malleable helmet, studded on the inside with a myriad of small silver points. "We do have connections for the Net, if you would prefer," she said dubiously, "but if this is your first time I wouldn't recommend it. You'll feel everything sufficiently well through the helmet, *kyria.*"

"The helmet will be fine, doctor. The door closes the circuit? Then if you'll excuse me."

When she'd been a child, Jason had hurt herself badly. Osamu had refused to let her have any medication. He explained patiently that pain was the body's way of setting limits, and unless she could feel her own pain she would be unable to judge when she'd pushed herself too far, and might therefore injure herself further. For Osamu it was a gentle lecture, and he repeated it again and again until she no longer complained to him when she hurt. So perhaps it was a victory for him. The incident, and the lectures, had long been forgotten, but Jason remembered them in the aftermath of pain between the third and fourth strokes of the whip. The woman was an expert, and perhaps that was why the crowd applauded. If Lys was grateful, it was because no sensation radiated into her lower torso. Jason, sharing her agony, was only dimly aware of the padded walls of the confessional booth.

Jason damned herself for her quixotry, and when her mind cleared a little she decided to stop, to give up and offer Lys what comfort she could later. The whip fell again and drove even thoughts of stopping from her mind.

She'd gotten a grain of sand in her eye once, and couldn't get it out. It had scratched her cornea. For a week she couldn't move her head because when she did it felt as though someone had taken sandpaper to her eye. It felt worse than anything she'd ever known before, and for a while she tried not to blink because it hurt so badly. But then the natural moisture of her eye dried, and she had to blink anyway, and that was worse still.

When she'd been six she'd broken her leg and when she'd awakened she'd seen the bone sticking out, white like the porcelain in her bathtub at home, with bright red blood pooled around it—she'd torn an artery. Osamu hadn't complained about her cries of pain that time. They may have kept him awake, because he'd ordered her given sedatives routinely.

It was odd how easily she lost count. She was certain more than once that each stroke was the last, and each time she was wrong.

There was a time when she'd first escaped Osamu's control, and was fresh from winning her first proxy fight. She hadn't realized how the tension was affecting her until one day she'd been unable to stand. It was a muscle spasm, they told her later. It would ease with time. They gave her muscle relaxants, which didn't help, and massages, which sometimes did. But one day, when she *had* to work, it had taken her several minutes to prop herself against a wall, and nearly an hour to work herself, inch by inch, into an upright position. It was infuriating to be unable to do simple things. Sometimes, when she moved too suddenly, it helped to yell.

She didn't have the solicitous attention of the court's warders. When she passed out finally she wasn't brought back to consciousness for the crowd's pleasure but instead fell forward, hitting her head against the padded wall and so signaling Dhimitri's private doctor. So in the end, despite her quixotry, she didn't share in the full fifteen strokes, nor did she hear the master of ceremonies call out, "Santos Sanjuli. Breaking and entering, and grand theft. Fifteen lashes." Kyria Tsakirides was replaced. Perhaps she was tired from her exertions. In any event, Jason missed the drama at the end of Lys's sentence, when the master of ceremonies, apparently ignorant, insisted that she get up and walk off the stage. It seemed to be a familiar routine, for his tone was unctuous and a part of the crowd laughed appreciatively. The same people were disappointed moments later when he read his cue card, realized his mistake, and became more honestly courteous, calling for Lys's wheelchair and helping her into it afterward. She was not quite conscious, and had to be wheeled away by a bored attendant.

But Dhimitri's doctor was efficient, and Jason was revived sufficiently to watch with dull eyes as Rat was strapped into the frame. He disappointed the crowd at first because of his stoic calm, though each stroke caused him to cry out. But he pleased the crowd after all, because with the seventh stroke, as artfully timed as the first six, he made no sound at all. The flagellator made as if to strike again, but paused and instead gestured to a medical attendant. Rat was quickly examined, brought down from the frame, and carried out of sight, while the crowd seemed collectively to hold its breath. Another felon was announced, strapped in place, and whipped without incident; but his penitence was anticlimactic, and he was not given the attention he might otherwise have deserved.

In moments a tall, elderly man dressed in a black cassock walked falteringly onto the stage, combing his hands through his thick gray beard. The crowd exhaled rapturously. He blinked away rheum and stared through eyes that bulged disconcertingly from their sockets. Then, after a brief invocation, he began to pray for the soul of the departed (he checked his card) Santos Sanjuli, not a citizen of New Crete, who had most unfortunately lost his life while receiving instruction in the path of righteousness.

His dithyramb was interrupted briefly by a scattered welter of applause from Alecko's box, but his sonorous intonation was still drifting on when Jason rose, wincing. "I want Dhimitri," Jason said. "Where is he?"

The doctor was a tiny woman, but determined, and she tried with gentle pressure to ease Jason back to the cot. "He's in his box, of course. You may see him shortly, but for now you must rest."

"Bullshit," Jason said. "I'll see him now."

The doctor became surprisingly forceful. "You may know a great deal about the Net you use, but you don't know anything about these booths!" She waved her hand. "If you had been in connection with your friend down there when he died, you might have died with him. You've been traumatized, and you should lie still."

Jason forced herself erect. "I'll see him now," she repeated. She started up the stairs, lost her balance through weakness, and almost fell; but sheer determination kept her upright.

Dhimitri seemed subdued. At Jason's insistence he summoned a magistrate and explained that he was releasing Lys to Jason's custody.

The magistrate was puffing with the exertion of climbing from the judicial box suspended high above the stadium. He wheezed for a moment, catching his breath, and then faced Jason. "No. Her name must first be posted publicly, so that people who believe they have a legitimate complaint against the woman will be given the opportunity to bring their complaints forward. During this period she must remain on New Crete; thereafter she may be taken away at any time."

"I want Kyrie Sanjuli's remains also. If not now, I want them delivered to my ship by this evening."

The magistrate puffed himself up self-importantly. "But that's impossible. You cannot take a body through space. It's illegal. And unchristian." He said the second as if it were decisive.

Dhimitri reluctantly agreed. "I'm sorry, Jason. I cannot permit that."

Jason's expression was unreadable as she turned and walked away. A throng of people were leaving their seats to head for the concession stands. The exciting first climax of the day had apparently made many people hungry. Jason pushed through angrily, trying to reach the emergency gate through which the ambulance would arrive. Partway there she was blocked by Alecko Papandreou. "I am so sorry," and he held out a hand in assumed sympathy.

She hesitated, then grasped his hand firmly. Let him think whatever he wanted. A roving CDC camera spotted them then, identified them as Important People, and captured them in flat. It was not set up for three-D, nor for sound recording; very little of note ever happened at public flagellations, and the CDC therefore seldom sent its expensive equipment there. But with Alecko's chiseled features and Jason's wide smile they made an attractive couple, and that evening's Core broadcast ran the picture during their "People" section under the chatty heading "Old Friends Meet at New Crete Fête." The news of Rat's death wasn't aired until a later broadcast.

They returned Lys's Petrovsky frame, though someone, through curiosity or malice, had disassembled it in such a way that it was irreparable. Jason was quiet on the ride back to the ship, letting her hand rest lightly on Lys's shoulders as she lay prone on the gurney. Lys was almost unaware of her own surroundings.

Bear came up to fuss with the stretcher. She refused to

allow the ambulance attendants to help. Denny was quiet, M'orru was crying, and Kenot shocked Jason by coming up, speechless initially (for the first time since Jason had known him), but finally saying, "He was a good man, Jason. He knew his job well, and he did it." For Kenot that was the equivalent of an hour-long eulogy.

Bear watched him walk away. "I appreciate that," she said. "Kenot said that partially for me, I think. I loved the little bastard, you know." She wiped at her eyes with her forearm. "I'll make arrangements for an ambulance to bring Lys back to the ship."

Between them, Bear and Jason brought Lys to her cabin and laid her carefully on her bed. As Jason pulled closed the door, she found the crew around her in a semicircle. "What the hell are you all looking at? Get to your stations. We're leaving as soon as we get clearance."

Capella said, "I thought you had to stay for the public posting, in anticipation of complaints."

"Where'd you learn that, Capella? Never mind. I don't want to hear it. If you have something to tell me, it can wait until we get to the Core."

The crew scattered to their stations. There were terminals at each station on the bridge, but many more were placed throughout the ship. Denny, Bear, Lynch, and Capella dropped into their seats on the bridge, while M'orru went off to her garden and Kenot left for the engine room. On short trips both stayed with the rest of the crew; but M'orru was more comfortable with her plants, and claimed she was more able to relax among the greenery, while Kenot simply preferred to be alone.

But clearance was withheld. "I'm sorry, *Argo*. There is a hold order on your ship. A field marshal will be over soon to seal your engine room; please stand by."

"Control, this is the *Argo*. I'll be lifting ship in five minutes. The field had better be clear by then, because I'm not waiting." She shut off the radio and swiveled to check the rest of the crew. "Everyone's ready? Good." She looked up at a sound; Lys had rolled her chair onto the steel clamps and was spiraling down the ladder to the deck. "Lys. Go back to bed. We're lifting shortly."

"I know." Lys's movements were cautious, but she managed to roll the chair up the ramp. "I won't be left out now, I want to *know* we've left. Please, Jason."

"I don't have time to argue. Strap it. We'll talk about it later."

Lys moved to her station, locked the chair into position with the clamps she'd built herself, and slipped her silvertip into place. Jason said sharply, "Edit out your Touch connection, Lys. I can't concentrate." Lys's pain, and her own, reacted synergistically so that other sensations were blotted out. Lys opened her board without comment and cut out cutaneous nerve receptors from the data fed into Jason's system. Jason's pain abated. "Thanks, Lys. Everyone, climb into the Net. We're ready to sail."

There was an aching tension that made itself felt in her shoulders and the back of her neck. She was aware of time passing now, with Capella's metronomic sense, and felt the ship around her, stirring and subsiding, almost sentient, certainly an extension of herself. Through the spinal socket she felt the fine distinctions of Sight, Sound, Touch, Taste, and Smell, all relayed to her and through her as the nerve center —the brain—of the *Argo*.

The tension in her back and shoulders increased. Expectantly now, she waited, and knew the time was . . .

Now. She triggered the drive and felt the sudden, disquieting feeling of translation.

She imagined the protest from the tower. At least another fine would be waiting for her when she reached the next CDC port, and probably an official note of protest and censure. They were sailing into the hot afternoon air of New Crete, past the atmosphere blanket, through colors that fled into the ultraviolet, rising above the exosphere into relatively free space. The radio gave out a constant angry buzz, proof that the port authorities were still trying to contact her. But she ignored it. She wasn't used to running, but if she had to run she'd run like a fox, and that meant not stopping to see what was behind her until she could stop in safety.

Safety was the Einstein–Rosen Bridge, still hours away. She had the ship to herself, alone in her web of heightened senses. It was a time to recuperate, to lick her wounds and think, and she took advantage of it. Later there would be time to ask advice from Lys and from Bear, to plan for the future, to consider Alecko's startling assumption of authority—for Dhimitri had been ineffectual, and that had never been true before.

The steady throb of the ship recalled the days when she, Bear, and Rat had done heel-and-toe watches on her first ship, but then a bitter taste brought her mind back to the present: M'orru, reminding her that the engines were burning hot. She adjusted the fuel mixture to compensate, and then rapidly swept through the systems to make sure everything else was all right. The air was sweet, swept clear by the breezes she could both feel and hear—and See, as she lowered her visual threshold into infrared. Lynch opened his eyes briefly then, and for a moment she could See herself seeing herself, a queer doubled perception; but then he closed them again, and to all intents and purposes dropped off to sleep.

As he did, she felt a tentative touch, like someone pulling the strands of the Net, testing their strength. It quickly passed, and she wondered if she'd imagined it. But suddenly she felt a crushing pain, the equivalent of a cerebral vascular accident —a "stroke"—and in that instant she lost all sensation of connection, to her ship or to her crew, and all awareness of the passage of time. She felt cut off, isolated: alone. She couldn't Feel Denny, nor Hear Bear. She was like a single point in a sea, adrift.

She heard Capella, not through the Net. "Captain? Where are you? I can't feel you with me anymore. And I don't know how long we've been out of contact." She imagined she heard a touch of hysteria in his voice, but she didn't answer because she couldn't.

But now that she was awake again, and could concentrate through a haze of pain, she knew she recognized what she'd felt. She'd felt it before, in the mind of a horse mad with fear. "Alecko?"

She Heard his laugh. "You left New Crete illegally, Jason Horiuchi. You've broken our laws. I'm afraid I'll have to bring you in for trial." The pain in her head had subsided to a dull ache. It began again more sharply. She screamed.

"Captain, what's the matter?"

Lynch. A hell of a time for him to wake up. His voice was concerned, but she didn't know what to tell him. And in a moment she didn't have the time.

From Denny she felt fire, then freezing cold.

Through Bear she heard a deep rumble which rose and rose until it was a high shriek which left her ears aching painfully.

The ship was a living organism, with Jason as its head, its nervous system, and the rest of the crew senses and systems and organs, all capable of being hurt. "Now your Second," Alecko said cheerfully.

"Well, that's hardly fair," he said after a moment. "She's not fully in your Net. We'll have to fix that." And then she felt claws raking down her back, tearing the skin. Lys screamed. "Ah, that's better," Alecko said.

Much of Jason's mind was occupied with pain, but a part kept on in grim evaluation. He hasn't touched Lynch, she thought, nor M'orru or Kenot. What sets those three apart?

Jason felt each touch as a galvanic twitch, like a frog's leg laid open by a lab student's knife. Bear growled, a high whining note that was uncomfortably foreign. It was a brief, teasing touch, leaving Jason with tinnitus and Bear crying in pain. Then he passed on. Denny twitched and screamed. Lys was caught and held in the second *after* the falling whip. Jason could feel again the pads on her groin and the salt-laden sweat as it rolled into an open wound. I'll have to remember to tell Alecko what a good job he's doing, she thought inanely. I'll have to—

In her garden, M'orru's angular, coltish grace was broken by tetanic contractions. Her left calf spasmed as she fell; her left leg, flailing, kicked aside the support of a heavy repotting table. She lost consciousness when the falling steel severed her spine.

Jason didn't. She heard Alecko say, "Well, that's a shame," as casually as if he'd dropped a drachma down a sewer. Jason couldn't stand; her legs wouldn't support her. She may be alive, you bastard, she wanted to say; she may need help. But she couldn't stand.

He attacked Denny with predatory, hateful pleasure. And he laughed again. "This is part of my vermin patrol." Denny's opinions might be half-formed, her enthusiasms firmly held yet brief, but her tactile delight was adult; and now she felt her nerves catching fire like a short circuit frying electrical wiring. Her groping fingers curled around the arms of her work station, feeling nothing. If the Net had been cloth she would have shredded it then, reaching out for sensation and finding none.

"Captain?"

Without Touch, she couldn't feel the integrity of the ship; without Taste, she couldn't balance the fuel mix. The air, at least, still Smelled sweet: Kenot, the goddamn cynical bastard, must have come through okay. Her ears were ringing, but she could still Hear. And she could still See. Her Sight, in fact, was in front of her, Lynch looking at her with an expression of concern.

"Captain, what's wrong?"

"I'm dying, boy. Can't you see?" She almost laughed. You came close, Alecko, but you haven't beaten me yet. See, I can still make a play on words.

She wished her ears would stop ringing, and then hoped fervently that they wouldn't, because of what it might mean if they did. She opened her eyes and watched Lynch. The queer doubled perception then was more startling than she could have imagined, to see herself seeing herself seeing herself seeing herself. He was partially in and partially out of the Net now, and his vision was not the crystal clarity of Seeing, but the blurred reality of his own imperfect eyesight. She blinked and closed her eyes. He didn't. She could still see herself, an out-of-focus ivory spot in the center of his vision. She muttered, "Look at something else, Lynch; we're still linked."

She opened her eyes; he looked hurt, but he turned his face away. She could still see through his eyes, and what she saw was the blurred figure of Capella, crying, cradling Denny in his arms.

Then Bear squealed. If Jason were inside a church bell she might hear that sound when it rang. While it happened, she heard nothing else; then it stopped. She shook her head to clear it, but couldn't hear the sound it made, nor the background noises of the ship. Where she should have heard the thrumming of the ventilators, moving air around the ship, and the creak of the metal decks breathing, and the sibilant hiss of the coolant that shielded the pile, she heard only silence.

First M'orru; then Denny; now Bear. First M'orru. Then

Denny. Now Bear. She repeated it like a litany. She couldn't Taste, or Feel, or Hear. But she could still See, still Smell; and Lys could Hear and Taste for her until they could sign on more crew. Capella could help out, too. He was a musician, and would Hear at least adequately, and perhaps he could Touch as well. Three-fifths crippled, she thought, but I'm still moving.

For the third time, Lynch asked, "What's the matter, Captain?"

For the first time she answered. "I can't tell you. *I don't know!*"

Lynch was standing just past the range of her vision. If Jason strained, she could see him as a shadow out of the corner of her eye. The feeling was frustrating.

And then the wavering edge of her vision dropped away and she was seeing a net, but not the spectral vision she was used to, with each physical object standing out brilliantly as in a false-color photograph, revealing mass and makeup, hot spots and cool, and variations of hue and saturation. She saw instead a real net, enclosing space. There was no color but only a stark black-and-white image, hard-edged and uncompromising. It was impossible to look at it and not wonder if this was how Lynch saw his own world.

But on each strand of Lynch's net, wrapped like cocoons, were tendrils of gray thread, like spider silk.

Alecko had pulled on the Net like someone testing its strength; Lynch bulled through like someone tearing aside cobwebs. And as each strand tore, Alecko screamed.

"Who *are* you?" he cried out finally. "Where are you broadcasting from?" The intensity of Alecko's voice was so strong that Jason heard him thinly through her strange linkage with Lynch, who stood with his head cocked to one side as though listening. He continued methodically tearing. The illusion of powdery dust in the air was so strong that Jason was tempted to cough. "I'm Lynch. On the *Argo*. Who are you?"

"You *can't* be! I know everyone on that ship."

"Well, you don't know me." He continued to cut through cobwebs with a single-mindedness bordering on obsession.

"You're hurting me!" Alecko cried, astonished.

Lynch said, "I meant to. Leave me alone. This is hard work."

Alecko's voice, strained, hostile, said, "Do something, damn you! That's what I'm paying you for. Do something—"

And the final few threads snapped, and Lynch stumbled and fell.

10

JASON

THEY COULD LEAVE now, limp back home to Metacenter. Jason toyed with idea. The wormhole was near and translation would be relatively easy:

If she (Capella or Bear) could sense the Duration of the pulse

And (Denny) could Feel it,

And (Lynch) could See the writhing convolutions of deadly energy,

And (Kenot) could Smell the rotting, vegetative smell of approaching translation . . .

Bile filled Jason's mouth, but (M'orru was dead) she couldn't Taste it, and (Denny again) she could barely feel its acrid burning.

No, she wouldn't return to Metacenter just yet.

She unstrapped the bands at her waist and chest and removed her silvertip. Lynch was watching her. "What in God's name did you do?" she asked.

"I don't know," he said.

"Then make a guess: what do you *think* you did?"

He recoiled. "You don't have to shout at me. I thought I was helping you."

After a moment he was able to sit up. He clasped his hands around his knees and thought for a minute before answering.

159

"It was something you said, Captain, on that first flight. Something about the way the brain sees things the way *it* wants to, instead of the way you think it should. You all called it a Net, but I always saw space the way I'd seen it in pictures. When you said, 'That's ultraviolet light' or 'That's infrared light,' I didn't see anything different from the pictures I grew up with.

"But then I thought, Maybe it really *is* a Net. And it was. You saw it the same way I did? After that it was easy. There's a warehouse in the Arkaikon—nobody uses it much—and when I was a kid someone dared me to break in. So I did. It was dark, and the first time something sticky hit my face I was scared to death. I didn't even think about it. I just started tearing things up. That's what I did just now."

"Well, you did fine, Lynch, however you did it." She looked around and found his glasses, knocked into a corner at some time during the flight. "Here, take these."

Capella was holding Denny and crying. Denny, on the other hand, was beginning to struggle in his hands. "I'm all *right*, Capella! Damn it, let me go."

Jason said, "Let her be." She checked Lynch, whose vital signs were stable, then crossed to Lys. Her pulse was good, slow but steady.

"Denny, would you go to your cabin, please. You may be hurt more badly than you think. I may need your help later, and I'd like you to get some rest if you can.

"That goes for all of you. If you're hurt, or think you may be, stay out of the way. Rest. We're short-handed now. I don't want things to get worse. If they can." She bowed her head. Her fists clenched and unclenched. "M'orru's dead." (She'd never before had someone die while she was in the Net. She felt as though surgery had cut away part of her. There was a hole where M'orru had been, and it hurt to touch it.) "Maybe Kenot. We'll have to check, and clean up. Capella, what time is it?"

"I don't know!" His voice was bitter. "Just leave me alone, Captain, can't you?"

She stared at him. Alecko had tried to call on someone for help. It might have been Capella; it could easily have been Capella. She wouldn't pursue that thought just yet. "For now," she said after a pause. "Bear. Are *you* all right?"

She got no answer and tried again. The second time Bear

was looking toward her. She seemed to be in shock. "I can't hear you, Jason," she said too loudly. "My head hurts. Who's running the ship?"

"We're drifting," Jason said. She had to repeat it twice before Bear said she understood.

Jason could trace the path of M'orru's galvanic struggles by the trail of wreckage. The tiled floor glistened from overturned hydroponic solutions, and bins of vegetables lay scattered.

She wondered who Dhimitri would get to run his business after she was finished with his son.

M'orru's spine was severed; that had ended her struggles. Kenot had her head in his lap, but he stood when Jason entered. Between them, Lynch and Kenot levered the metal table (it was slick with blood and kept slipping) back onto its base.

When it was done, Kenot stepped back. "If I stay with you I'll get killed." He stated it simply: a fact. "I'm signing off once we land. You'll have to find someone else to keep your engines running. I sent out résumés the day Lys was arrested, because I knew you were heading for trouble. I've got a berth on the *Iraklion,* shipping out at the end of the week."

Jason said, "That's a Papandreou ship."

He nodded. "They pay money, Captain. That's all I'm concerned with. Hobbies are fine, but they don't pay the rent." He tried unsuccessfully to keep from looking down at M'orru's body. "She didn't want to die; you can see it." He knelt and touched her cheek with what seemed—for Kenot—to be a peculiarly gentle and sensitive touch. Standing, he brushed dust from his pants leg, and rubbed ineffectively at something more than dust. "I'll be at my station if you need me."

— 11

JASON

BEAR ASKED, TOO loudly, "What do we do now?"

Jason stopped midway across the bridge, heading for her cabin. "We go back to New Crete."

"What?" Lys rolled up, nudging the toes of Jason's boots. "You're crazy! We can make it to Metacenter. Hell, we can make it to Earth, if we have to. *Why go back?*"

Jason said calmly, "Because I'm going to kill that son of a bitch."

_ 12 _____

LYNCH _____

DENNY STOOD QUIETLY. Lynch didn't move while she watched, but sat in the chair, knees against his chest, nearly fetal. He'd been crying. His smeared glasses were on the table beside him. For once she didn't try to make things better; she was too aware, for once, that she had made things worse. Instead she padded down the ladder and across the bridge to the starmap, her own favorite escape when she was depressed.

The journey back after Alecko's attack had been wretched, dull, slow, and excruciatingly boring. Jason and Lys had huddled together throughout most of the trip, talking, talking, talking. Meanwhile Bear had stayed in her cabin, recuperating; her hearing, it seemed, was completely lost. When she'd come out she'd been cheerful, trying to raise Jason's spirits, and Lys's, and Denny's own; but her eyes were swollen and red, and she often seemed to be straining to hear. And always, after a time, she'd stop what she was doing and stare into the distance without seeing anything, and a few minutes later she'd be back in her cabin with the door closed.

Denny had paid little attention, because she was worried about her own troubles, which included a persistent form of paresthesia which was inhibiting her ability to function. She found herself unable to grasp and hold the simplest objects, needing help even with her meals. She couldn't even tell without looking whether her hands were open or closed. Every time she reached for a fork it felt as though she were touching

165

it through six inches of cotton batting. It wasn't lessening any even now, and Denny couldn't control her fear that the condition was permanent.

Capella was no help. She'd sent him away one night after he'd refused to accept her explanation that, though *he* was enjoying himself as much as he ever did, she felt nothing at all. He hadn't bothered to hide his own evident pleasure, which had increased her feelings of frustration. Thereafter he'd spent his time in the galley, banging utensils around and generally acting like a spoiled child. That was where he had been when Lynch had come in once for something to eat. The two of them had ended up fighting and it had taken Jason to stop it.

She realized—now—that she shouldn't have automatically taken Capella's side. But he had been her lover, she did feel sorry for him, and she knew Lynch hardly at all. Now Jason was angry at her, too, for interrupting when she'd had Capella pinned to the wall with one hand at his belt, another at his collar, holding him with his feet a meter off the deck.

Involuntarily, she giggled. He'd looked so foolish there, with Jason almost a foot and a half shorter, holding him up with no apparent effort. She was stronger than she looked. But she'd told Jason anyway it was Lynch's fault, that Capella had been minding his own business, that Lynch wouldn't leave him alone. It was *almost* true, so it wasn't really a lie. But Lynch had looked hurt; and Capella, that goddamn skinny, tall asshole, hadn't even had the grace to be grateful.

Afterward Lynch and Capella had maintained an uneasy truce, each keeping to a cabin by himself, checking first to make sure the other was away before emerging. Kenot, by mutual consent, had already set up housekeeping in the engine room, carrying down a cot and a hotplate, coming out only when Jason had a question or when he wanted fresh food from M'orru's larder. And without Capella to keep her company, or Bear to talk with, Denny hadn't felt much like leaving her cabin either. By default the bridge had become a quiet refuge where Jason and Lys spent most of their time.

And the *Argo* had limped back to port. Early on, just after Alecko's attack on the ship, Jason and Lys had radioed a series of instructions to Jason's lawyer, but that was the last translight transmission they'd made, and there had been nothing since but the maddening, slow, sublight journey back to New Crete, a full AU under conventional power.

Denny had been curious about that transmission and had tried to listen in without success. Apparently Jason had wanted to tie up Alecko Papandreou's time while the *Argo* was returning so that she would have a free hand later for whatever she was planning, but they had neither invited Denny's opinion nor answered her questions when she'd asked.

Denny hugged herself, wishing she could feel her hands. She knew by the indentations on her arms that she'd have bruises later. She didn't care; some sensation, at least, got through. She didn't want to be hurt any more, but if her isolation increased any further she'd rather die. It was an uncomfortable thought from which she shied away, but it had recurred throughout the voyage back to New Crete.

Despite her growing dissatisfaction with him she wished Capella were here, but he'd gone out, she didn't know where. She couldn't yet admit she was relieved. Some of the things he'd said about Bear had gone right past her, she couldn't understand why he'd been so excited about the opera and all, and she'd been feeling left out.

Like Lynch, she thought.

She went to the keyboard, logged on, and called up the starmap, which came to overwhelming life in the plasma pool beside Jason's chair. Each leaf of the map was no more than a millimicron in thickness, and staring into it was like staring into the universe, vivid and intense, the colors so bright they were hypnotic. You could scroll through, cell by cell, which gave the impression that you were rushing headlong through galaxies, shimmering and coiling around you, the light of stars quickening and dying as you approached and passed by. Certainly it was valuable as a navigational tool; but, like many things Jason owned, it was an art object as well, one in which you could easily lose yourself.

Denny lost herself. Once the starmap was keyed, it responded to whoever sat in either the Captain's or the Second's chair, waiting for prompts through the silvertips. She started from her home, quickly heading out through 30 Doradus (because of the brilliant splash of red that she met there), and on out through the Megellanics. She wouldn't admit it if asked, because she thought people would make fun of her, but she was frequently homesick. Tykel was a new world, much newer than New Crete, and her leaving had been largely a matter of luck; Tykel didn't have the resources to command regular visits from Core ships. When she'd left she'd vowed never to return, but she'd been back. Once. It hurt to discover she could not go back to live; her horizons were no longer narrow enough.

She was a little startled to find Lynch at her elbow, staring into the depths, his glasses, though still streaked, cleaned somewhat and his breath coming in exalted pants. "What is it?" His voice was reverent.

She thought, Hey, maybe I've done something right. "It's an astrolabe. Haven't you ever seen one?"

He shook his head without taking his eyes off the screen. "It's beautiful."

Her hair fell into her eyes as she leaned forward and she pushed it back. After a moment she got up. "You can guide it if you want. Come on, sit here." He nodded without taking his eyes from the screen and edged into the chair. She pulled loose her silvertip and the screen went blank, to yaw drunkenly when she slipped Lynch's probe into place. When he held onto the arms his knuckles were white. "It's a simple circuit, just like your messenger system was, and it's sensitive to your movements. When you move your eyes, it'll move with you. Do you know any star systems?"

"Some. Not many."

She should cut her hair short, like Lys. She brushed a limp strand back with one hand and said, "Well, just think about the ones you know and focus on one. Ask the computer for a star and it'll try to find it. I try to remember the catalog numbers, but the map's programmed to respond to most of the popular names for things, too. Not all of them, though; a lot of star systems look different the farther you move from the Core. The Emperor's Crown isn't visible from where I was born, and the Great Bear has another star and is called the Crouching Rat. See, the map doesn't know that, because the Bear is still the Bear at the Core." She paused. "When you want to scan slower or faster, or move from side to side, or go back to your starting point, just think about it and the map will do the rest. Sometimes it's easier if you say what you want out loud. It helps you to focus on what you want."

Because he was already keyed in, the screen lurched

drunkenly when he nodded. More cautiously, he moved his head slowly up and down and side to side, watching the changes. He quickly found the 30 Doradus gate and swept through. For a few seconds the control room seemed to pulse with crimson reflections; they watched together in silence.

He thought next of the sky around Moulinos, viewed on a clear night, and the map obediently swung through a panoply of stars, too quickly to identify any one. A star blazed in the upper left quadrant, and its light washed away lesser stars farther away. Lynch looked at it, awed. "Is that the sun?"

His shoulder was touching hers. Without knowing it, she put her arm around him to hold him closer. He moved away. Neither really noticed. "Yes. I guess Jason still had the approach corridor programmed in, because that's what we're seeing. It's pretty spectacular, isn't it?"

He didn't need to reply, because his rapt attention was of itself an answer. She knew what she was going to do next, but argued with herself anyway because she'd need the arguments sometime soon when Jason asked her to explain. On the one hand, modular holograms ate energy like no one's business. On the other hand, Jason wanted the crew to get along with Lynch, and this would be one hell of a way to win his confidence. Leaning over with one hand on the boy's shoulder, she reached for the mini-keyboard inset into the arm of the Captain's chair. The keys were too small for her fingers, and she fumbled once or twice before she got the right command file.

Lynch felt the floor drop away.

No: he could still feel the chair beneath him, and Denny had to be standing on the deck; but it *should* have dropped away because what he saw was three hundred sixty degrees of space, magnificent but daunting. Below, stars blazed, dimmed but not eclipsed by the sun of New Crete. When he breathed it was a sigh, and it seemed almost to hurt. "Oh, God."

Denny's smile was broad. "Yeah!" She tugged on his arm. "You can stand up now; it doesn't react to movement when it's set on panoramic. It'll stay locked until you change it."

He stood and looked down at his feet. The universe spread below him, served under glass. If he concentrated he could still see all the equipment in the control room, because each chair and table shimmered slightly around its periphery, but looking closely at anything but the stars around him was the last thing he wanted to do. He breathed deeply again and again, and felt his eyes watering once more. He didn't care.

Denny stood behind him. She said, "If I had a ship like this I'd stay in here for hours and just watch the stars go by."

After a moment he said, "I would, too." Another few seconds and he said, "Thank you."

Once Lynch's only reading had been what was in the orphanage library. There had been a lot of ancient Greeks. He'd read Hesiod and Haviaris, Odysseus Elytis and Xenophanes. Now he searched the heavens for Sol, the old sun, the *real* sun, looking for the light that had inspired them. Velvet space was punctuated with bright lights trailing phosphorescent spumes. Slow, methodical light showed the stars as they had been centuries before; as Lynch scanned, near stars grew brighter and far stars faded, and the light of millennia splashed and pooled beneath him and around him. His focus narrowed, and narrowed again, until he hung in perspective near Roche's limit, looking at a gibbous Earth below him. The blue-green planet was beautiful. Without taking his eyes from it he groped for the chair behind him, found its arm with the tips of his fingers, and sat, staring at it with shining eyes.

But Earth disappeared and the cabin lights came on abruptly, too bright. He blinked in the sudden glare and saw Capella leaning over Lys's console, his fingers still resting on the controls. "You just wasted a hell of a lot of money. The *captain's* money." He took his hand from the controls and straightened, crossing his arms over his chest. His expression was the deep, brooding sullenness that he'd worn so long now it seemed habitual.

"Capella, he wouldn't even have known about the map if I hadn't shown it to him. It was *my* idea." Denny looked at him, bewildered. "You're not being fair."

Capella ignored her. He walked up to the boy so Lynch had either to look away or look up at him. "The captain hired you. She may want you here, I don't. And I'm going to make it as hard for you as I can."

To his credit, Lynch didn't back away. He looked up instead. "She hired you, too. And only a day earlier then me. You can't hurt me and you can't drive me out. I'm a member of the crew and I'm going to stay." And then, because he couldn't stay any longer without showing how much he had been hurt by Capella's attack, he ducked his head and dodged away, slipping past Denny's upraised arm without touching her. He would have gotten his coat, but that would have meant staying on board longer and maybe running into Denny or Capella again, or into another member of the crew. So he headed for the lock instead; and outside he used the ladder instead of waiting for the lift, just as he walked away from the port instead of waiting for one of the shuttles which in this early evening were still running regularly a few minutes apart. Waiting for a lift meant someone might see him, and waiting for a shuttle suggested he had some place to go.

He was a messenger, he knew Moulinos better than all but a few of the residents, and now he simply wandered. Though he'd lived in or near the city as long as he could remember, he had no friends, at least none he could talk to now.

His wandering took him to the Arkaikon, the gaudy strip of old city that was an embarrassment and a secret pleasure to a lot of people in Moulinos. One block wide, several blocks long, it existed in a netherworld between several discrete areas of the city. Below it was the commerce district. The main road west led to a shopping district and, farther out, to the older mansions of Moulinos, on hillsides overlooking the sea. North was the warrened cliff of the Old Town, where hundreds of thousands of people lived in apartments clinging like mollusks to the granite spine. Earthquakes had sheared clear the cliffside twice in the history of the city, but the stuccoed houses had been rebuilt each time, with smaller rooms and more of them for the swelling numbers of people.

His old apartment was buried in that warren. He could go home, stay there until Jason came for him—if she did. But the thought of staying there alone, waiting, while the hours stretched and Jason Horiuchi *didn't* come made him physically ill. His stomach ached with tension, and walking hadn't eased it any. He looked into his wallet to see if he had any money left, but it was empty. Then he remembered shoving some of the advance Jason had given him into the pocket of his jeans, and he reached deep to see if it was still there. Wadded tightly into a ball at the bottom was some paper that felt like money. He pulled it out and found a handful of low-denomination drachma notes, grimy and wet with sweat. He tried to flatten them out without success, so he smoothed them as much as possible and stuck them in his wallet. It wasn't much, but it would buy him at least a few meals.

He hadn't consciously planned it but he wound up where he always did when he was lonely and upset. The first time it had taken him hours to work up his nerve, and he still looked around each time to see who was watching. He looked around now; as usual, no one showed any interest in him. He tried not to look avidly at the list of features; it didn't matter, he'd play them all anyway once he got in the booth. But that, too, was a habit, and he studied the holos with absorption and self-loathing.

In the holo booth he could be anything: man, woman, both at once. He could indulge in any sexual act he wanted, with anyone, *as* anyone. If only it were so easy in life.

Eventually the machine ran out of time and the kaleidoscopic sexual images stopped. Lynch sat shivering with reaction until a rapid pounding on the door of the booth awakened him with a start. "Time's up," a peremptory voice shouted. "Put more money in or get out."

He opened the door to leave, but it took a few moments to orient himself. His head ached, and he rubbed his forehead with the fingers of his right hand, massaging his temple with the ball of a thumb. Less desperate now, he took the time to read the vivid poster hanging from the side of the video booth. It promised a "shocking, exciting, and educational adventure! Learn secrets of sexuality heretofore known only to tireless researchers like Krafft-Ebing and Kinsey! Discover a primitive world of passion and lust! The finest in *adult* entertainment!" In smaller type, the poster claimed, "Our performers have been especially trained to duplicate the wide range of human sexual experience. Whether used as an educational tool or as a means to increase your own ability for sexual expression, 'Sex Around the World' is guaranteed to be a vivid journey of discovery. Choose from the following acts of combinations, and launch yourself on a sex trip that's Out of This World." Halfway down the list (it was a long list) he grinned, but it was pure rictus. When he'd first visited the peep shows he'd wanted experience and he'd gotten it, after a fashion.

He'd heard that the better shows, out on the Timpani, hired performers who enjoyed their jobs, and their enjoyment was communicated to their audience. That was what you paid for. But no money was wasted on style in the Strip. He'd spent two hours under the sexual persona of performers who (it

seemed) would rather have been doing anything else. He felt
sad and hurt and, as always, sickened by the experience.

His knees were weak, and he suddenly leaned back, sup-
porting himself against the side of a booth. He took several
deep breaths. The smell of semen and urine suddenly as-
saulted him, a strong bleachy odor that hit him in the pit of the
stomach and refused to let go. He retched, but he'd had little
to eat and nothing came up. Back braced against the sex
booth, he gave in and cried, racking sobs that hurt his chest
and released some of the pent tension of the day.

The other customers, with the ease of long practice, suddenly stopped seeing him; he was left alone as people flowed
around and past him, without catching his attention or giving
theirs.

Eventually he felt well enough to stand. He brushed ineffectually at spots of dust and dirt on his clothes. With an
attempt at dignity he walked through the corridors of booths to
a dark, filthy, and foul-smelling washroom. Broken fixtures
hung from the walls, painted black to discourage graffitists.

In the blackened nitrate of a cracked mirror he saw something translucent dried on the right lens of his spectacles.
Without thinking, he took them off, started to breathe on the
lens to clean it, abruptly changed his mind at a sudden
thought, and instead ran the lenses under hot water (offering a
grateful prayer that at least the water worked) from the washstand tap, polishing the glass vigorously. Even then he found
himself touching the lens distastefully. He told himself he was
being an idiot, and polished the lens more vigorously.

When finally his glasses were clean enough to wear, he put
them on carefully, scrubbed his hands again for good measure,
combed his hair—wishing again that he had hair like Capella's or a tight nap like Lys's—and straightened his clothes
as best he could. Then, in a fever of embarrassment, he realized he needed to urinate. There were no vacant booths. He
stepped to a urinal, but nothing happened. His embarrassment
grew. Finally, avoiding what he thought were the stares of
everyone else present, he pressed the side of the urinal, releasing a small rusty flood. In the slight sound of rushing
water, he was able to squeeze out a few drops. The relief was
enough to relax his spasm, his stream began to flow easily,
and he offered up a silent prayer of thanks.

He washed his hands again mechanically, obsessively,

scraping the fingernails of one hand with the nails of the other, working the coarse, granular soap into the ridges and whorls. When he eventually looked down he saw with surprise that his hands were reddened and raw. His throat felt sore; it hurt to swallow. He swallowed. The nitered mirror blurred and danced before his eyes and he realized to his shame that he was crying.

He left the dim arcade and stood blinking in the bright afternoon sun. Someone had spilled a pail of water in the street and the pink bricks were stained red and steaming as the heat ate the moisture. He watched as his eyes adjusted to the light, as the minor pool dwindled and died.

A voice at his ear said confidentially, "We've got girls waiting for you, sport. Naked. No cover." Lynch jumped. A street barker, dressed incongruously in an old-fashioned tuxedo, was eyeing him with curiosity.

"Uh, no thanks," he said politely.

The barker lowered his voice to a penetrating stage whisper. "Let me tell you now, the bartender plays around, too, if women aren't to your liking."

Lynch almost cringed, but instead shouted, "No! Now can't you leave me alone?"

The barker grinned, not offended, not even surprised. "Sure. But if you don't want to be stopped, you'd better move along." With practiced ease he ignored Lynch and turned his attention to two young men walking arm and arm. "Sirs! We have a young boy on stage who has to be seen to be believed! Now, I won't tell you how young, but . . ."

Lynch fled before he heard more.

The broad avenue splintered into a series of smaller streets, each paved with the ever-present, irregular pink brick. Lynch didn't much care where he ended up, so he turned off into the smallest street, little more than an alley, and followed it as it wound unevenly and erratically past a series of tiny shops. At any other time he would have been fascinated; each shop was unique. In one were bright toys, knickknacks of wood and plastic, tiny horses with minuscule bridles, segmented wooden caterpillars that clacked when you pulled them by their bright primary-color cords. In another was a collection of musical instruments, from tiny harps no bigger than his little finger to mammoth brass wind instruments. A third had a thousand postcards in the window, while a fourth had clothes whose colors were so vivid they hurt the eye. And those were just four of a score or more, each with its own collection of attractions. But he could think of only two things, and the thoughts kept chasing each other through his head: He could never return to the ship, not now. And he was losing his one chance, his one real chance, to see.

His glasses were fogged by a coating of dried salt, but vision existed somewhere below his consciousness and he kept walking.

He'd have to stop soon. He had very little money—enough, maybe, for three or four meals and a shower. That would give him energy, and keep him awake so he could keep walking. His thoughts followed his faltering steps. The captain would be missing him soon, and he'd be missing his chance to. See, his chance to. See. He'd be missing his. His steps faltered. His vision blurred still more.

He collided with an old man, drunk, in a filthy brown overcoat and a stained knit cap pulled low over his eyes. "I know you," the old man said. "I seen you walking with my captain just the other day. You going to ship on th'*Argo?* 'S a beautiful ship. Saw it. Captain Horiuchi, she runs 'er." He reached out a grubby hand. "Say, you got a drachma for an ol' shipmate? 'D I tell you—"

"Leave me *alone,*" Lynch shouted, and almost lost his own balance because his shove had knocked the other off his feet. Lynch backed away and then started to run.

Behind him the old man laughed raucously. "You just tell your captain old Robinson said hello, an' we'll call it square. Robinson. You remember that."

Lynch walked away, shuddering. Was that what old crewmen turned out like? But now, Bear was that old, wasn't she, and she was fine. He climbed roads that turned to hills that turned rugged, that narrowed and widened again. Sometimes the paths were several meters wide; sometimes he had to edge sidewise to pass without touching walls. Once, without realizing, he stopped for several minutes to stare at a brilliant wheel of color: a stained glass window set into a courtyard wall facing the afternoon sun. The stuccoed wall (a long passageway, really, in shadow, cool in the afternoon heat, whose center blazed with that miraculous rainbow) was filigreed with light. It was a gift of New Crete, of Moulinos, available for those willing to walk out of their way. The guidebooks wrote about the pastel walls of the city, and talked about the climb to Oros Dikti ("Breathtaking grandeur, with a sweeping view of the New Gulf of Messara"—"Neo Kolpos Messara," they usually added in very bad Greek—"with one moderately good tavern"), but they seldom encouraged tourists to walk from the Strip through the area known locally as Splagchnon ton Moulinos. Only an angel or a fool would try.

One fool stood entranced, swaying, exhausted. (At night, sometimes, he would take off his glasses and walk through the city streets, watching each traffic light and neon sign—harsh-edged while in focus—dissolve into fairy globes of color surrounded by coronae and nimbi, grown friendly and inviting. With his glasses on again, because even friendly lights grow terrible with threat after a while, the harsh edge of the city would return.) But someone came through the tunnel, muttered, *"Sygnomi,"* and strode on by.

Lynch shook himself like a wet dog on a rainy day and continued his aimless, wretched walk. The captain. The captain would. Would be missing. Be missing him. Soon. He'd be. Be missing. Missing his chance to. See, his chance to. See. He'd be missing his.

I should stop and eat, he thought and stopped instead at a tavern midway up a steep hill, where the sun (now setting, with ochre strands like broken and dried yolks spread greasily across the sky) reached only through narrow rectangular windows set high up the low walls, lighting browned tarry timbers now blackened with age. It was dim, dirty, and oppressive. It was exactly what he wanted.

He ordered a drink, feeling competent for the first time that day; his self-composure was slightly shaken when the bartender, who looked like a barrel on which someone had stuck, as an afterthought, short arms, stubby legs, and a swart, flat-nosed face (and then had forgotten a neck), suggested that he needed to order a particular *type* of drink: "We have lots of alcohol here, friend, and I don't like to guess."

Lynch surprised himself; he said, "Give me something cheap and strong." He usually drank beer; that was what he'd been drinking the night he was arrested.

The bartender nodded. "Right," he said and took a squat

heavy tumbler from below the bar, filled it two-thirds full with
a clear liquid, and shoved the glass across the bar. "Thirty
lepta," he said.

Lynch passed over a bill, accepted change, and sipped the
drink. It was heavy and sweet and tasted strongly of licorice.
The flavor erupted into his nose with stinging force. "Jesus
God," he said, surprising himself again; but the bartender
didn't seem to notice. "What the hell *is* that?"

The bartender's face was expressionless. "Ouzo. You
wanted something cheap. Give it a chance; it'll grow on you."
He nodded as if in dismissal and began to polish the bar with a
rag that might once have been white. Lynch, recognizing from
long experience that dismissive gesture, took his glass and
walked to the end of the bar through a scatter of irregular
chairs surrounding insubstantial and inelegant round tables. At
the back of the bar a narrow ladderlike staircase ran downstairs to what seemed to be a dismal cellar while another staircase, slightly less steep, ascended in narrow double-backs to a
low-ceilinged floor above.

The upstairs was nearly deserted, with three people in the
corner groping each other drunkenly and making conversa-
tional points in slurred undertones, while at another table a
young woman sat with a newspaper spread before her, ostentatiously making notations in the margins, then reading them
aloud, shaking her head, crossing out material, and writing
again. She could have easily hung a sign at her side reading
"Poet at work."

Lynch took a seat at the far end of the room, beside one of
the rectangular windows, within reach of one of the ceiling
beams and overlooking the bar. He glanced down. The bartender raised two fingers to his forehead in a grave salute;
startled, Lynch waved back tentatively, then turned back to his
drink. He took another cautious sip and let the sweet liquor
burn in his throat before he swallowed. Through the window,
on the street below, he saw nine kids reel down the alley,
passing between them a trapezoidal brown bottle with a long
narrow neck.

They drank. They swayed.

One, grinning, reached up under the bulky sweater of another and grabbed a handful of what he found there. The other
looked down—frowning? No—but she made no effort to
move, or to move his hands.

After a while they drifted apart and nothing else happened. (Lynch was . . . disappointed, and probed at the disappointment like a tongue at a sore tooth.)

One of the nine took a drink, grinning through her gapped teeth; another, suddenly violent, reached out and shoved. Two staggered from the push, fell against each other, laughed, and collapsed onto the sidewalk. Then eight laughed.

One didn't. She watched the others with a sullen face and tucked the ends of a bulky sweater into the waistband of her pants, cinching tight a broad leather belt. And *then* she laughed and, grabbing the bottle, drained it.

Nine stood, swaying; the wine was gone and, soon, so were they, reeling up the alley and the street and the broader avenue until they were all out of sight.

Kids, he thought. And envied them. And thought: I should go back to the ship. I should let them laugh, and laugh with them. (I should tell them to fuck off; I should tell them they can't jerk me around like that. But they could, and he wouldn't.)

Someone else, very drunk, was tying a scarf like a leash around the neck of a sick, scared, and very thin puppy, too tightly: an old man, muttering to himself and shaking clublike locks of graying black hair. Under the harsh street lights his ebony face seemed laced with cyan. "I know how you feel, pup," Lynch whispered, his face pressed tightly against the cool filthy glass. Did the dog whine? He couldn't hear.

"Do you want another of those?" Lynch looked up, confused. A thin, tense face, sallow, eyes obscured with heavy makeup, lips flattened into a look of perpetual disapproval: a waiter.

"Please," Lynch said, holding up his glass, noticing with surprise that it was empty. I wonder when that happened, he thought. To avoid another interruption, he took some of his remaining drachmas and fanned them across the surface of the tiny round table, then turned back to the window.

Two boys came up and tried to talk; the man, drunk, shook his head. Beaded hair swayed like a skirt in the wind. Angrily he tugged the scarf's end. The puppy tottered to its feet, tentatively wagged a stubby tail, and walked along shaking its head. The tight cloth was too short to reach the street unless the dog's owner remembered.

Lynch watched him forget.

He sipped his glass of ouzo, hiccupped, and thought, with surprising satisfaction, I'm drunk. I should go back to the ship. He took another sip.

The old man came back down the alley, dog along, now not alone; another man in an old padded green jacket came too, stumbling, running one hand through rusted steel-wool hair and holding a new cushion, very large, one end trailing the ground, bumping along with the redhead's staggering progress.

They're going to sleep together outside, in that old shell of a building next door, Lynch thought. They're drunks; they don't think there's anything wrong about sleeping out in the open. He felt superior and envious.

And then he didn't think about much of anything, because he was suddenly, violently ill. He had no warning, and no time to do more than try to avoid his shirt or his shoes. Afterward he looked at the detritus with dull surprise, wondering if people really drank to feel like this and, if so, why. The nattering buzz he heard resolved itself into a waitress, who seemed to disappear as soon as Lynch brought her into focus. But then she metamorphosed into the squat ugly bartender. That was really quite interesting, and Lynch giggled uncontrollably as he tried to guess why anyone would *want* to make that particular change.

The giggles lasted until he was hauled roughly to his feet and frog-marched down the narrow stairs, through the bar, and out into the street. The hand on his neck had twisted the collar of his shirt so that he was choking, and his terror penetrated his alcoholic fog slightly so that he heard the bartender clearly when the man shoved his face close to the rough cement walk in front of the bar.

"Look. What do you see there?" The voice was a rough growl.

Lynch squirmed and looked. "Buncha names," he said as clearly as he could.

"Right." The bartender released his hold and Lynch fell forward, gasping. "Those are the people who've been permanently thrown out of this bar. You don't want your name on the list." More gently then, he lifted Lynch to his feet, held his shoulder until he regained his balance, and said, "Go home. Go for a walk. Sleep it off. But do us both a favor and don't come back until you're sober and can drink to drink, and not to get drunk." He left and Lynch was standing alone in the street.

The streetlights blurred. He was crying and his eyes wouldn't focus properly. Because it was downhill he walked on Diairo, a road which cut at a slant through the Old Town to the waterfront. He walked because he had nothing else to do, and still couldn't face returning to the ship, but the restless sound of the water slapping against the piers and the dismal empty stalls of the marketplace at night echoed and augmented his melancholy mood. The sea seemed to whisper that he was unlovely and unloved, and that he would always remain that way.

He walked slowly, with many pauses, stopping to clear his eyes or his sinuses, or simply to pick himself up when he stumbled, which he did frequently. The air was thick with the smell of salt water, creosote, and old wood, and the piers held pitfalls in the dark, from coiled cable to invisible lines of tent stays stretched taut across what he thought were open pathways. It was over one such that he fell a final time and lay, and began crying in earnest, unable and unwilling to get up again.

If self pity could reach a peak and then descend, he was at his nadir now. He could move, if he wanted. He could stand, if he wanted. But there seemed little point. I'll just lie here and die, he thought. They'll shovel me off the end of the pier in the morning with the rest of the garbage.

He closed his eyes then, enjoying in a perverse way the rough pier rubbing up against his cheek, so he felt rather than saw someone stop and stand above him, and heard a calming, quiet voice: "You sound as though you could use a sympathetic ear. May I join you?"

__ 13 _____

LYS, BEAR, JASON _____

Lys said, "I think we should all be present for this discussion."

Jason explained patiently: "Denny's ill, Kenot's gone, Bear can't hear." She spread her hands. "We're all present."

"Capella?" Lys asked suspiciously. "Lynch?"

"Lynch is gone, I don't know where," Jason said. "Capella . . ." She frowned. "I think Alecko was trying to talk to someone on this ship, before Lynch cut him off. And I can't think who else it might have been."

"Kenot?" Lys suggested hopefully.

"No. I know how you feel about him, but he wouldn't have done anything to hurt M'orru."

"What happened to M'orru was accidental," Lys said, and then hesitated. "No, you're right. Whatever I think about him, he's loyal; he might do any number of things, but he'd never betray you while he's on your payroll. I still think Bear should be here. She's been with you, off and on, longer than I have."

Jason shrugged. "You're right; but it wouldn't do much good if she can't hear what we're saying."

Lys got an odd, intense look on her face. "She can read, can't she? I think I've got something that will help. Call her in, and we'll see."

Jason rose. "When I die prematurely, my epitaph will read 'She humored her employees.' Capella?" She leaned out the door until she had his attention. "Send Bear up here, please."

* * *

Lys had rescued her notepad and cleared its memory. She took out another chip and slid it into the waiting slot. Bear was watching over her shoulder. "I've never used it in this configuration, myself," Lys said, "but it may help you."

Her words flowed like oil across the screen.

Bear looked interested. "I thought you had to write on it with a stylus. Will it—Yes!"

The screen echoed her in Century Old style, a staid typeface that Lys thought suited her; but for Bear it was a poor choice. "I think with a pen in my hand better than I do with a tape recorder," Lys said. "The notepad can do both." She hesitated. "Did you know you're almost shouting? I didn't think so. Let me try something."

Bear read the moving words, tracing one finger across the screen. When it stopped scrolling, she handed the pad to Lys, who rapidly readjusted it, then held the screen so Bear could see it, and spoke slowly. "I've hooked up a graphics program. It'll use different type sizes and styles, to let you know if you're speaking too loudly or too quietly. It should help you modulate your voice. I hope."

The screen seemed tiny in Bear's big hands, but she held it gently. "Thank you, Lys." She whispered it. The words showed up in eight-point type, suitable for footnotes. "Thank you, Lys"; she tried again. Forty-eight-point headline type loomed on the screen. A third time she said, "Thank you," and was rewarded with fourteen-point, readable but not overwhelming.

Lys took the screen again. "One other thing. Sometimes we may talk too fast, and the screen will wrap before you've had a chance to read it; or you'll want to save a particular message. If so, there's a 'save screen' function control. You can save one screen at a time, or write everything to memory."

She recapitulated her short conversation with Jason, and the three began again. Bear looked troubled, then angry, when Jason related her suspicion about Capella. "I hope you're wrong," she said as Jason's comments finished scrolling. "I like him. But if you're right, and I find out, you'd best simply stand out of my way." She turned to Lys. "We're going back. I agree with Jason. There's unfinished business. For you there's the possibility of additional fraudulent charges; I wouldn't put it past Alecko Papandreou." She shrugged. "But that possibility exists whether or not you return to New Crete, and if Jason's successful, the problem ceases to exist. I say we go back now—he may not expect us."

"And I made it possible for you to participate in this conversation," Lys said. "That's why I'll never be a captain; I don't learn from my mistakes." She rolled to Jason's terminal, so that she had her back to Jason and Bear both. After a minute she turned. "Then we go back. Hadn't we better start now?"

"What's the time, Lys," Jason said idly and waited.

"Four-fifteen," Capella muttered automatically.

"Ah," Jason said. "Did you catch that, Bear?"

Bear had Lys's notebook in her hand. She saved the screen first, freezing those three small phrases. She lifted Capella easily, with one huge paw at his throat. One thumb was on his windpipe and pressing. He was struggling and throwing Bear off balance. So she grabbed a handful of his belt and pants and twisted. He didn't have much air, but he used it to make a muffled protest. "Shut up," Bear growled, and added, "*I may be permanently deaf because of you!* You want to start something? Go ahead—I'd love an excuse."

Jason was holding Lys's notepad in her hand, tapping the screen thoughtfully. "So your time sense came back, Capella," she said. "That was quick." She fingered her jaw, thinking. "We'll double-check with Dr. Kalb this afternoon. But I think we've found Alecko's entry into the *Argo*. Am I wrong, Capella?"

"Yes." It rasped. He rubbed his throat and tried again. "Yes! I don't even know him! I was looking at the clock when you asked; I automatically read the time and said it aloud."

She shook her head. "Not good enough. There's no time prompt on my screens. I don't need them when I'm in the Net." She turned to Bear. "He's all yours."

Later Bear said, "I'm through."

"Where is he?"

"My cabin." Lys rolled up. "We can lock it."

"How's he doing?"

Bear grunted. "He can stand. He could even walk out of here now. But he'd be in a lot of pain if he did. Nothing's permanently injured, though, and no bruises will show." Her teeth gleamed. "I'm a professional."

"Good. Did you learn anything new?"

Lys said, "Nothing you didn't anticipate. He's got a military override, which is how Alecko broke through. I think you might be able to reverse the direction, if you had enough power behind you."

"Power won't be a problem," Jason said. And smiled.

_ 14 _____

JASON _____

VERNON KALB FINISHED his examination of Bear, set down his
tools, and crossed to a small sink. He held his hands high,
waiting for the proximity tap to recognize his presence, while
he summarized his findings.

"Ms. Vouris." The sensor hadn't yet noticed him, and he
still held his arms up in an unconscious pose of benediction.
"Out of curiosity, how old are you?"

There was a slight lag while she waited for the screen to
stop spooling. "Chronological age? About seventy-five."

The basin began to fill; steam rose. Kalb dipped his arms to
the elbow, took several leaves of soap, and began scrubbing
vigorously, raising his voice over the rush of water. "I thought
so. There's a significant retardation of senescence, one of the
benefits of your Net. You're older than I am, but much
younger physically. I've noticed it before, with people who
spend a great deal of their lives on the deep-rapport level. I
don't recall that there's been a clinical study done; the findings
would be interesting, if so.

"You may not be aware: rumors call you people immortal.
Too many of your old friends age and see you unchanged year
after year—the contrast between your age and theirs seems
more marked than it really is—and they begin to wonder.

"I confess once I was strongly attracted to having the implants myself. I believed the rumors, you see. But I'm a coward, and I'll only know the experience vicariously, through

185

your descriptions. The thought of lying in a stupor while some second party uses my skills is absolutely terrifying! Now ask me why I'm a Bonded Network Neurosurgeon . . ."

He pulled free a half-dozen paper towels and frowned in irritation. "Ms. Lyskopoulis, you're an engineer. Perhaps you can explain why no one's ever developed a decent towel holder. They're either placed so water runs up my sleeve or down onto the next towel."

"Never mind. Ms. Vouris, for you I have only bad news. The eighth nerve is completely destroyed. Rebuilding would be a long, costly process, with no guarantee of success. And it cannot be done on New Crete. You might find a surgeon at Metacenter who could help you. I doubt it. I believe your hearing loss is permanent. I'm sorry."

Bear said nothing, but she had been intently watching the screen, and as his last sentence scrolled she closed her eyes for a moment. When she opened them again she watched Capella, who was sitting across the large room, flanked by Jason and Lys. His face was the color of wet sand, he was sweating, and he seemed to have shrunk in on himself, so that he looked very young and frightened. He slumped forward, his hands clasped in his lap, and stared at Kalb with dull apprehension.

More briskly, Kalb spoke to Denny. "Ms.—Dendrite?"

Denny was subdued. Ever since Lynch had run off she'd been quiet. She had walked in as Bear cold-cocked Capella. It was while she was dragging him away, like a sack of wheat, that Lys explained that Capella was probably in collaboration with Alecko Papandreou.

Denny had been more puzzled than hurt then. She'd had only to listen to Capella's rambling conversations, both before and after the attack in space, to know that he would never have intentionally injured Bear, and certainly that he would never have interfered with her ability to sing, which he worshiped with an unhealthy passion. On the other hand, if she were wrong and Capella was responsible in some way for what had happened to her, she'd have Jason and Bear hold him down while she made a few incisions in the *other* thing he was so passionately fond of. Lys, watching her, had accurately guessed her train of thought. "You may have to stand in line," she said. "Jason liked him; Bear, too. I didn't, but I thought it was just that he reminded me of M'orru."

Denny had been stubborn, because she hadn't wanted to

believe Capella could fuck her over so badly. "But you don't have any proof, do you," she said, hoping it was true.

Jason had been gentle, for which Denny was grateful. "Lys keeps a log for me of every flight," she said. "I played the keystrokes back, because I knew Lys had removed herself partially from the Net early on, before Alecko's attack. Her cutaneous responses were restored in both afferent and efferent modes, and the commands came from Capella's terminal."

The doctor said impatiently, "Ms. Dendrite?"

"I'm sorry, Dr. Kalb," she said. "I was thinking of something else. You can call me Denny, sir."

"Denny, then. There's not much I can tell you. I've never encountered anything quite like it. It's as though someone laid a damper on your neural responses. The effect may wear off; it may not. I'm sorry I can't offer you more reassurance.

"Ms. Lyskopoulis." Lys looked up. "You're very lucky. Whatever happened to the rest of the crew seems to have passed you by. Or perhaps you've recovered by now, I don't know. I'll hazard a guess, which is quite unprofessional and more mystical than I normally choose to get, that the pain from your recent flagellation insulated you in some sense from the worst of the onslaught. I don't really mean to suggest that you should be grateful you were whipped, but it may have helped.

"Now we come to the most interesting case—this young man." He patted Capella's shoulder. Both Jason and Bear edged nearer. He sat hunched in his seat, well aware, and unhappily so, of their looming presence. "You were quite right, Captain. See here." He dimmed the lights so that the image on his monitor dominated the room. With a light pencil he stroked it across the levels of neural circuitry. "This is the standard implant. You'll see that the dye shows a complete pathway." He shifted the pencil. "But here is a mechanical circuit, a message circuit like that of your other young man— Lynch, was that his name?—and here's a command override circuit; as you said, the kind used in the military."

Jason stood. "May I talk with you privately for a moment, Doctor?"

He blinked. "Certainly Captain. We can use my office." She followed him into the next room, and waited only until he closed the door. "Could you modify his implant so I could control any such third party?"

"If you had enough power, Captain, and gave no warning, you could do so now. It's not like a radio circuit, for which you'd have to know the correct frequency. I suspect the damage done to your crew occurred only because it was a surprise attack from an unexpected direction, one you hadn't known existed. Even with that advantage, you see, your casualties were remarkably mild. One woman died, but it was not *directly* the result of the intervention. Rather, it was brought about by a grand mal seizure, and any number of things can trigger such an effect."

"Are you saying that what happened to my crew was *accidental?*"

Kalb shook his head. "No, but it seems to me that the attack on your crew was actually quite weak." While he talked he picked up a file folder, opened it without really seeing it, set it down, picked up a pen set, clicked the button on the pencil twice, reached for the skull of a small lizard, dropped it, and picked up an onyx cube which he tossed idly from hand to hand. "I know it feels much different to you, but a strong attack would have been much like a short circuit frying the wiring on an automobile. It would have been rapid and dramatic, as when a car catches fire, or anticlimactic, as when the power surge takes place so quickly that it carbonizes the wiring entirely. In that case your only clue that something's wrong is when you turn the key and nothing happens. I use a homely example, Captain, but I hope it illustrates my point.

"I would say that whoever did this was very far away from you at the time of the event. Don't tell me who it was, Captain, or even whom you suspect. I watch the news and I have a good idea. I don't want to place myself in any greater jeopardy than I have to. If you are correct, this man has attempted murder, and if I were to believe your story, I would have to report it to the authorities." He stopped tossing the cube and looked at Jason evenly. "I would rather not do that.

"Had he been nearer," Kalb continued, "your troubles would have been worse, and had he been in physical contact with one or more of you, you would all be dead now, and not asking me for advice."

"I'm glad, then, that it was a weak contact." Her lips thinned, throwing her cheekbones into prominence. "Believe me, I wouldn't want to endure anything stronger."

__ 15 _____

ALECKO, DHIMITRI, JASON _____

AT THE FIELD Denny, Lys, and Bear set about locking Capella into solitary while Jason negotiated with A. J. Pandey for additional storage time.

Lys was at her terminal when Jason returned. "I may not have to throw away my fortune beating Alecko, Lys." Jason took off her coat and threw it over the back of her chair. "Before I have the chance, A. J. Pandey will take it all away, under the god of Good Business."

"Denny's gone out, but she'll be in contact. I let her go; I thought she needed time to cool off."

Bear sauntered in and saluted with full military snap. Whatever she'd done to Capella had released much of her tension. "All secure, Captain." She carried Lys's notepad at her side, as though she might consult it for the orders of the day. "The last time I had to put someone in lock-up for you, Jason, you weren't yet captain, and it was for his own good." She dusted her hands. "As a matter of fact, you were still a sergeant, and I'd just made buck private." She sat down heavily at the Third's station and swiveled idly in the chair. "I wanted to catch you in the wardroom after lights-out some night and beat the crap out of you. I never managed, and by the time you relaxed your guard I figured out that you weren't so bad after all."

"I didn't know until today that you'd ever served in the Army, Jason," Lys said. "Your sordid past is revealed!"

Jason sighed. "It's best forgotten, Lys."

Bear continued to swing in a half circle, back and forth. "No it isn't. I learned a lot from you, Jason, and I haven't forgotten.

"So. What's our next step?"

"You mean you don't want to trade war stories? Tell Lys how I' left my happy home, to wallow with you mud puppies?" Her tone was mocking, then serious: "We've served Alecko with a restraining order, to keep his hands off the *Argo*. Wolde's to submit a motion to quash Alecko's lawsuit and vacate the criminal warrants, and he's trying to convince the presiding judge to issue a bench warrant calling for Alecko's arrest on charges of murder, attempted murder, and felonious assault. In addition to the criminal charges, Wolde's also preparing a civil suit charging Alecko, Dhimitri, the Museion ton Papandreou and all its staff, *and* Papandreou et Cie with persecution, intimidation, intentional and negligent infliction of emotional distress, unlawful detainer, restraint of trade, and God knows what else. I've encouraged Wolde to be creative. Let Alecko *try* to claim that I'm a well-known criminal! There isn't a shred of evidence, and he'll look as though he's protecting his own ass."

"You're bloodthirsty, Captain," Lys commented.

"I'm *angry,* damn it!" She paced. "I had Wolde set up a meeting with Dhimitri. If the judge is amenable—he should be, I pay him enough—Dhimitri will be ordered to attend. I think he'll want to anyway, out of curiosity, to see what I'm up to. Am I going too fast for you, Bear?" She paused while her final words scrolled. Bear held up her hand, thumb and forefinger circled: OK.

"Good." She rested her hands lightly on Lys's shoulders. "We'll allege that your conviction and Rat's were obtained by Alecko's perjured testimony, that the notary's testimony is likewise open to question, and that a visit to the museum will add corroborative detail regarding your appeal. I'll release the pleadings to the press before Alecko can file for a protective order placing the proceedings under seal. That will place them under some additional pressure, but, more importantly, it will make the museum a legitimate target of discovery. Hell, I might as well have Wolde file interrogatories, too, and requests for production of documents. Who knows, I might be able to get the real blueprints, if I can describe them with sufficient particularity."

"You're talking like a lawyer," Lys said, not without admiration.

Bear held out the notepad, her expression carefully innocent. She'd reprogrammed the pad so that it had recorded Jason's speech in Old English lettering which covered the screen in a staid, stately sprawl. At the bottom, Lys's comment was a much more conventional Bookman Bold.

Jason was surprised by the violence of her own reaction. She tore the pad away from Bear's hand and erased it with the edge of her thumb. "A friend of yours is dead. Mine, too. This isn't a time for jokes."

Bear looked at her without expression, her arms resting at her sides. Jason involuntarily stepped back. Bear nodded and held out one hand. Jason handed her the notepad without a word.

Bear read the three short sentences and nodded again. Then, still impassive, she smashed the pad against the metal of the wall. She let the pieces drop to the floor. At the door she turned. "I have to joke once in a while, Jason," she said —too loudly—"or it hurts too damn much. Good night."

Lys said, "Never mind. I can make her another."

16

LYS, JASON

JASON FLIPPED HER knife in the air, catching it by the blade. It reminded her of Vernon Kalb, and she set it down. But in a moment she'd picked it up once more and was fidgeting, opening and closing the blade with casual flicks of her wrist.

Lys said, "Relax, Jason."

"I'm getting impatient, that's all." She tossed the knife again, realized she was doing so, and jammed it into her pocket. "Also, this is too much like my early days, when I had to sell myself and every plan I made to Horiuchi's board of directors."

"They're all friends of yours, Jason. What you're experiencing is so common, it's even got a name. It's called 'stage fright.' Hold on a moment, please, while I synchronize." Lys chuckled; she was in enormously good spirits. "Six crays, and for this afternoon they're mine, all mine. Just look at that configuration profile!" She tightened her hands on the wheels of her chair and pulled in opposite directions, spinning to face Jason. "If all they've seen is the marionette you animated, we'll give them a show which will *really* impress them."

The bridge of the *Argo* was crowded. Jason moved to the cleared area center stage while Lys rolled to her terminal, from which she could monitor all six crays. She had broken her screen into a complex series of windows through which she could view the data at any of the other terminals—or, if she chose, at all of them.

"Hello, everyone," Jason said. "I'm glad you could come." Benali of the *Scapegoat* looked, as usual, both harried and irritated. Watteau sat primly in her chair, apparently inattentive, but Jason knew from experience that Watteau would miss no detail of the performance. Sattar Das and Natalie Tereshkova were deep in conversation; Jason hadn't known they knew each other.

Simon of *Pan* lounged in his chair in an attitude of bored indifference. "I was more interested in meeting again that boy you brought to my ship. Where is he?"

Jason purposefully hadn't invited Simon, but he'd heard about the meeting and insisted on coming. "We don't need him for the demonstration," she said, "so he isn't here."

Simon remained vulpine even while yawning. He patted his mouth delicately and suggested, "He's run away. That's encouraging. Perhaps I'll find him."

She didn't respond to his prodding. "I showed you all a brief piece of animation a few days ago," she said. "Now you'll see what a cray can do in the hands of an expert. We'll start with a simple walk-through; the more complex material will follow later."

At Lys's signal Jason began to walk slowly around the open area. Halfway through the circuit she halted, motionless, and watched with curiosity as another body seemed to flow from her bones.

Jason faced an Asian woman dressed in black from her serviceable leather boots to the linsey-woolsey fabric of her shirt. She bowed. The hologram walked a few paces away, turned and echoed her bow. "My God! Is that really what I look like?"

Lys didn't turn from her terminal. "Captain Watteau, that was Jason's voice, synthesized through your computer. Is it convincing?"

Watteau ran a hand through her hair, sweeping its pre-Raphaelite wave over the back of her chair. Her eyes opened wide in an expression of innocence. "How am I to know? I was but a youth newly with it when Jason Horiuchi sailed on the *Lin*. I did not become her captain until much, much later. But, yes, it sounds like the Horiuchi of Horiuchi, Pte."

Lys leaned away from her terminal to give the spectators a

chance to look. "If you look here, you can see that the simulacrum is apparently breathing, 'her' pulse is normal, 'her'
blood pressure is good, 'her' temperature is ninety-eight point
two. Slightly below the average, but normal for Captain Horiuchi."

Tereshkova said, "Your simulacrum has a temperature?"

"Heat is a measurable wave form, Captain Tereshkova.
Hence we can reproduce it as a hologrammatic transmission."
Lys spoke formally, then laughed. "Actually, I didn't know I
could until I did it. As far as any observer can tell, our fraudulent Jason is alive." She turned back to her terminal. "Notice,
please, that the model and Jason both have the same basal
metabolic rate. We've given the computers enough information so that they can extrapolate from the data at their command any number of potential changes to Jason's metabolic
rate, up to and including fight-or-flight levels of adrenalin."
She patted her cray affectionately.

Das of the *Mahayana* slapped Jason's back. "You see? I
said you'd show us something new!"

Jason walked around the animated figure. "It really is very
good, Lys." She added to the rest, "I had some worries about
the animation, but I reasoned that a computer that could create
and maintain a starmap could maintain an adequate hologrammatic illusion, if properly programmed. With Lys, I knew it
would be."

Lys had left the hologram standing motionless, one hand
held waist high, another raised in benediction, like a priest or
a Balinese dancer. Now she tapped two keys on her terminal
and spoke, *sotto voce,* into the microphone by her side.
"Don't let her fool you," the hologram said. "I'm the real
Jason Horiuchi."

"We've worked hard to cover every conceivable situation."
Lys was speaking in her own voice again, while the hologram
resumed its somewhat eerie rigidity. "Jason and I spent several
tiresome hours asking and answering every question we could
think of, about Jason, her life, her family, the family Papandreou—anything that would serve to make the mannequin
more believable. This particular cray configuration can extrapolate from Jason's known style in order to react to any number
of possible scenarios. For example, the hologram could carry
on several conversations simultaneously, with several different
people, and correctly respond to each individual's unique per-

ception of Jason Horiuchi. We hope. That's partly why Jason decided we needed several computers, to adjust to a possib!e multiplex environment. An extremely multiplex environment," she amended.

Simon said, with lazy malice, "I doubt you could fool us. We all know Captain Horiuchi quite well. The slightest false note would be apparent."

"You may be right, Captain Simon. But you know it's a hologram. You might not be so quick to notice a discrepancy if you were to meet our creation on your own ship, unsuspecting. Most animated holograms can be spotted because each image is sharp and clear, while the eye actually tracks something in motion as a series of pictures slightly out of focus, because of the lines of movement. Our hologram is correct down to the smallest detail." She spoke with pardonable pride. "If you examined any single cell of our program, you would see movement lines, fully modeled in dimension. We give you the emperor's new clothes in reverse; the clothes are there, but the emperor is gone. Are you ready for the next phase, Captain?"

Jason leaned on the back of her Captain's chair, facing her audience. "We choreographed this last night. See what you think." She moved to the center of the ring and bowed gravely to her hologram, who bowed back. Without warning she snapped a kick at the hologram's "shoulder," a move that was blocked as her ankle was apparently held between two crossed wrists. Jason broke the hold, and the next few minutes witnessed a wild melee of rough-and-tumble street fighting that looked, generally, lethal. Lys, with an eye for detail, had primed the computer so that each blow sounded with a meaty and sickening force.

After a moment, the blows were real; Bear had entered, surrounded by a computer-generated pocket of empty air. Jason had been waiting for the substitution, but was unable to spot it when it occurred. She had grown complacent—because, after all, the blows weren't real—until a very substantial leg sweep knocked her to the floor. She recovered, but her timing was off because she had to compensate for Bear's greater bulk, hidden within an envelope her own size. It provided another level of challenge and Jason took full advantage, pushing herself to her limit.

It lasted only a few minutes, but it seemed longer. At a

signal from Lys, Jason got ready, and at a second signal she stopped, motionless, and watched with interest while the hologram emerged again from her shell. Now Bear, as "Jason," was fighting "Jason," an empty shell, and no one had noticed the substitution.

She threaded her way between Tereshkova and Das, stroking his thigh lightly as she passed and looking back, amused, at his startled, speculative expression. Her earlier tension was lost in the pleasure of hoodwinking an audience, as she'd done years ago on the *Lin*. Watteau considered herself an illusionist? Let her see what a real master could do!

In her cabin she donned her dress uniform, straightening the sunburst precisely over her left breast. She'd deliberately worn drab clothing earlier so the shock would be more intense. Now she pulled free from the simple clasp holding her hair and began threading it quickly through an intricate tapestry woven of silver and silver-black freshwater pearls, irregular and lustrous. Finally she donned the highly polished calf-length boots and walked carefully back to the main deck, striving now for silence.

She sat carefully in her captain's chair, making sure it neither moved nor made any sound. Lys was just finishing the question-and-answer session. "Jason" held up her hand. "I'm tired of being Jason," she said. "I'm going to be Bear again for a while." While the audience was still murmuring in confusion, Jason spoke from behind them.

"Do you still think you could decide between me and the hologram, Captain Simon?"

__ 17 __

JASON AND THE OWNERS __

SIMON HAD GONE. The others moved into the galley to discuss the performance and Jason's plans. Watteau sipped coffee, and her large eyes stared at Jason, naïflike, over the rim of her cup. "I saw you on the news last night. I was much amused by your claim that the *Argo* was a diplomatic vessel of the United Governments of Old Earth, and that Alecko and Dhimitri Papandreou individually, and as agents of Papandreou et Cie, had therefore attacked Terran sovereignty."

"She's got the papers to prove it," Lys said and Jason added, "I've been Terran ambassador now for several years." She brought out a crisp white sheet of heavy rag bond paper, folded in thirds on its long edge and bearing an impressive gold sigil in the lower right corner. Das asked to see it and she gave it to him. "No one has ever asked me to do anything, and no one has asked me what I've done. Sometimes I throw parties, and in the past I've attended inaugurations and coronations, if they weren't too far out of my way."

Das refolded the document and handed it back. "I should address you as 'Your Grace'?"

Jason restored it to her pack. "'Majesty' is sufficient." But she was growing restless. "I'll need to leave soon, to meet with Dhimitri Papandreou."

"You need to find Lynch, too," Lys said quietly.

"Yes. And Lynch." Jason was pensive.

Captain Benali had been quiet, occupied with moody

thoughts of his own. At some point soon his depressions would deepen into schizophrenic withdrawal, but he was still capable of forcing his attention to his surroundings. "You're going to meet him today?"

"This early afternoon, yes."

"So soon," he muttered. "And so you will need our equipment today, and be done by tonight? Do you need our—*my*—assistance as well?"

Jason shook her head, not disagreeing so much as to clarify. "I don't *need* your help, no; but I value your opinions, and you're welcome to offer suggestions as well. More importantly, I thought you deserved to evaluate for yourselves my chances of success. I am involving you, after all."

"So soon," Benali muttered again, and pushed his chair back from the table. "No, Captain. I appreciate your offer, but I must go home to my children. They worry about me." He rose. "You must get along without me." He looked around with a vague, apprehensive stare and stumbled slightly as he walked away.

Jason escorted him to the threshold. When she returned, Tereshkova was talking to Bear, who was moodily adjusting and readjusting a new notepad that Lys had built for her. "And what will you do now, Ms. Vouris? I hear you may retire." Bear had adjusted the notepad until Tereshkova's type style was an anglicized version of a Cyrillic alphabet. Bear's own conversation was currently displayed in a medieval uncial style.

"I've retired several times before," Bear said, "and never liked it much. But for now I think I'll stay here." She didn't look up; her eyes were fixed with determination on the notepad. "Jason and I are getting on each other's nerves; there's really no place for me in the Net now. And there's a place I'd like to visit, on the western shore of Mykonos, a stone chapel in the Levka Vourna. Most of New Crete is NGR, New Greek Reformed, but the monks at the Monastery of St. Stephen are Roman Catholic. They've preserved the Latin hymns, the old Gregorian chants, and have returned to an earlier, traditional Mass. I'll appreciate the pageantry, even if I can't hear it."

Watteau said, "But won't you have anyone with you?" She didn't quite look at Jason.

Watteau's typeface was a spidery, calligraphic script which Bear read to the end before she answered. Talking with Bear was now like having a radio conversation with someone on another planet, involving frustrating long silences for everyone concerned. "No. Oh, I tried to convince Jason we could put aside our differences," Bear said lightly, "but she said no, as she's done for the last fifty years. It's hopeless. I'll die an old maid."

Das accidentally inhaled a mouthful of coffee. "You've got lovers pining away, like Camille, in every city you've ever visited," he said cynically. "'Oh, Bear. Cough. *Please* don't go! Cough. I *need* you. Cough.' Ouch. Damn it, Bear, I'm not hardened like your captain here; if you're going to jab me, do so with a lighter touch."

Jason stopped pacing. "I'm sorry," she said. "I have to go."

The public transit terminal was not far away from Lynch's apartment. She felt Lynch, tenuously at first, then more surely. He was home, then; good. More, he wasn't alone. She felt (as she had occasionally with M'orru and Kenot, more often with Denny and her lovers) the touch of another, relayed through the Net. So shy, virginal young Lynch wasn't quite so innocent as he had appeared! She recalled his quivering intensity, the feeling as though he were looking over her shoulder, and the odd double vision as she and he both saw through his eyes, and her own. She put in her silvertip to let Lys know that she'd found the boy.

She rested halfway up the stairs to Lynch's apartment. Now that she knew where he was, there was no hurry; and if he'd found a lover she wouldn't interrupt. She checked her watch. She needn't meet with Dhimitri for another two hours. She sat on a landing, enjoying vicariously the feeling of fingers on her thigh, her sternum, her groin; lightly grazing, hardly touching: quite erotic.

At a broad landing, a brisk breeze brought the stale fishy odor of barnacles and salt, with the slight undercurrent of creosote. The smell combined with the feelings she was sharing with Lynch, to unlock the startling, vivid memories of a walk along Ocean Beach on an overcast day when she was eight and curious. Gulls wheeled and seals cried, and, farther up the beach, interlocking couples lay on blankets, on sand. One such had given her a dollar to go away. She'd spent it visiting the camera obscura, the last such camera in the world.

She felt her skin flush with arousal, and to diminish the feeling (so that, when she talked to Lynch later, she *could* talk), she began to climb again. Her legs would be in much better shape were she to climb stairs like these every day. It was a wonder that skinny little Lynch didn't have flanks like a horse.

If she was to be a voyeur, she reflected, then this was the best way. She stared out at the bay with half-closed eyes, hardly seeing it. Lynch/(she) was held closely, his/(her) back warmed by the touch of skin; fingers massaged his/(her) neck, easing tension; one hand stroked his/(her) abdomen, another rubbed a cool dry palm in a circular motion over his/(her) right nipple. One hand held his/(her?) testicles loosely, and—

—there were *four* hands. Jason couldn't later recall climbing the rest of the stairs, not the equally steep, more cramped staircase to Lynch's apartment. She did recall snapping the lock with a single well-placed kick; that was satisfying. More satisfying still was the look on Alecko's face as he came out of the bed, naked, reaching for his clothes.

Lynch blinked owlishly; his glasses were on a bedside table. "Captain?" he said questioningly.

Alecko was regaining composure. "Good evening, Captain Horiuchi. Jason. I hope you have a reason for breaking in on us like this."

"You might say so," she said and stepped toward him. He backed away. His movement catalyzed; she didn't notice that she held the knife until she'd drawn the sharp edge down his chest diagonally, so that a thin line of red grew from his left nipple down almost to the groin and began to leak.

He held a hand to his chest. "You cut me," he said in shock. "I'll be scarred."

Jason said, "Don't be a fool. It's just a scratch." And then she stepped back. "I shouldn't have been able to do that." She snapped the blade shut. Several memories surfaced quickly, kaleidoscopically. Alecko, in a bar: "I'll show you a bit of what he's like . . ." and "It's easier if I'm in contact with you." Robinson in the rain: "I asked him for change on the street. He ignored me until I grabbed his arm. He noticed me then, by God!" Denny, in the museum: "Oh, it was sexual all right, at first," and Alecko's peculiar intensity thereafter, trying to stay in touch with Denny, trying to maintain physical contact.

Then Kalb: "Had he been nearer, your troubles would have been worse, and had he been in physical contact with one or more of you, you would all be dead now." Her naivete infuriated her. "You're not a telepath," she said. "You son of a bitch, you lied about that, too." Her pupils, widening in the dark room, widened further until the iris nearly disappeared.

"I never said I was," Alecko answered. He looked ill, only partially because he reacted badly to the sight of his own blood.

Another memory: Alecko standing, swaying slightly, his face pale, just after his rapport with Jason and Bear. He looked much the same now. She felt the edge of the knife, pleasantly sharp against the ball of her thumb. He'd been in rapport with Lynch then.

"Lynch was one of the only people you couldn't affect on board ship: Lynch and Kenot and M'orru. M'orru died, but that felt accidental to me, a fringe benefit." She said it bitterly. "It might hurt less if you'd killed her deliberately.

"I wondered what set those three apart. I think I know. It's that you hadn't met them. M'orru's dead now, and Kenot's moved on; but you still needed Lynch, didn't you? You couldn't get close to him any other way, I suppose, so you decided to seduce him."

Lynch said, "It's not like that, Captain."

She looked at the boy. He was still naked on the bed. He looked small, thin, and very young. "You don't know what you're saying, Lynch." She nodded her head toward Alecko. "He killed two friends of mine, and badly hurt three others, one permanently. He would have killed you if he could have managed it."

He looked up at her. "When Rat and M'orru died you shut me out and spent your time with Bear and the rest. I saved the ship, and all you'd say was, that's nice, Lynch, we're talking now, come back later. So I left. I wanted you to come and find me, but you didn't. Instead *he* showed up." Lynch gestured with his thumb. "He paid attention to me. He sat with me. He listened to me talk. He didn't even say anything when I threw up on his clothes. He just held me. Later he said, 'I can always get new clothes, Lynch.' Just like that. Captain, maybe you're right about him"—he indicated Alecko again.

"But he listened. You didn't." He paused, embarrassed. "And when we were—you know—in bed together, I felt him, through the Net. It didn't feel like the same man who attacked the ship. I think you were wrong, Captain Horiuchi." He took off his glasses, breathed on each lens briefly and rubbed them between thumb and forefinger on the blanket to clean them. Deliberately he put them on again, adjusting the gold wire earpieces carefully. "I may be back to the ship later. I signed a contract, and whatever happens, I am grateful to you. For now..." He turned to look at Alecko again and smiled tentatively, then turned back to Jason. "For now, I wish you'd leave, Captain."

She looked from Lynch to Alecko. He was in the corner holding his ribs. The cut had stopped bleeding—it hadn't been deep, after all—but he had a patchwork of red down his side. Some blood had clotted in his pubic hair. He looked awkward and discomfited, and his gaze moved back and forth from Jason to Lynch.

She nodded curtly and left.

__ 18 _____

DHIMITRI _____

DHIMITRI WAS AT his city apartments. "You're early," he said.
A tic pulled at the lower lid of his right eye and his corneas
were reddened, swollen. Good. She hoped he'd lost a lot of
sleep. "Alecko won't be with us this afternoon, Captain. He
has other business to attend to." Then, with a faint trace of
humor: "O Kyrios Dawit has been keeping us rather busy. Our
lawyers have looked over all his papers and have advised us
that personal appearances were appropriate."

"Good. That's his job." She glanced at her watch. "Shall
we go?"

His linen coat looked as though he'd slept in it. There was
more bothering Dhimitri Papandreou than a few meaningless
court appearances; and they were meaningless, she knew, simply a way of jockeying for position, of keeping the Papan-
dreous busy while she maneuvered.

"No," he said. "No, not quite yet. Captain. Jason. My son
is expecting you to burglarize the museum today, while you
are with me. As much as possible, he is personally monitoring
the security today. He would derive a great deal of pleasure
from catching you, perhaps enough to overcome his common
sense and cause him to manufacture evidence."

"As he did with my crew?"

He waved a hand testily, dismissing her. "Don't talk nonsense. That's a fiction for the judiciary, and you know it. I
admire your audacity, but save it for the cameras."

Her lips thinned in a faint smile. "You'll see me by your side, Dhimitri, every step of the way."

His tone was dry. "Somehow you don't reassure me. Well, I've done my best. Yes, Yiorgio?"

Jason hadn't heard the man come in. Now she stared in surprise. He was an older man, yes, and his gray hair formed a tight nap on his skull. His eyes were blue and his skin was brick red; but though he was stocky he was not fat.

Dhimitri followed her gaze. "You've never met my secretary, have you? Yiorgio Celik. He's been a help to Papandreou et Cie for years, though he never ventures off New Crete. He thinks it's bad luck. Don't you, Yiorgio?"

"Not bad luck, Kyrie Papandreou; but there is nothing off this planet that I need or want." He bowed. "Kyria Horiuchi, of course. *Hehro poli*. I've heard of you."

"Alecko Papandreou has . . . mentioned you," Jason replied, "but somehow I pictured someone very different."

"The younger Kyrie Papandreou does not like me, I'm afraid," Celik said. "He believes my esteem for his father stems from greed." His voice was a light tenor, attractive and warm. "The museum called to say they're ready for your visit. They ask if you want the galleries closed or whether they may remain open. A number of people have made reservations for today, *kyrie*."

Dhimitri glanced at Jason. She said, "Oh, leave them open, by all means."

"Keep them open, Yiorgio. We'll put our best foot forward for the celebration. Tonight's the official opening of the festivities," he explained. "There will be a fireworks display at compline, to signal the start of the Tricentennial. If we hurry, we can complete your tour in time to join the party at the museum."

Dhimitri drove easily, with enjoyment. Because he knew the road well, he had time to point out things to Jason even around hairpin turns which would have been frightening with a less skilled driver. As, she recalled, they had been with Denny.

He stopped at a rise and gestured out over the wide expanse. She followed him until they stood on the edge of the bowl, looking over. Olive trees and open fields; it was familiar. She and Denny had stopped here on their way back from the museum.

"There you see the salvation of this planet," he said with satisfaction. "With such small independent farms, and factories, New Crete's long-term survival is more easily assured."

"You'd have a much greater return if you placed the land in the hands of combines."

He sighed. "I suppose it must seem a contradiction. As a man of business I want the maximum return possible. But this also is my home. I want New Crete to become self-sufficient."

"And conglomerates wouldn't serve that goal."

"No." He lit a cigarette. "Smaller units encourage a broader base of necessary and desired services." He smoked in silence for a moment. "I have managed to convince a few people that I am a benevolent dictator, and a few others that I am truly planning for the future. The rest simply think I'm a lunatic. Perhaps that's why Alecko is so successful encroaching on my power."

A faint buzzing in her ear: not the Net circuit, but her private phone. The crack of her jaw clicked the switch. «Lys, Jason. You should be near the museum by now, so I'm switching on the hologram. If Papandreou doesn't notice, we've passed the first test.»

Dhimitri held the door for her, then started the car. "Do you remember internal combustion engines?" she asked.

"Not very well. I'm a little young for that."

"I do." Jason leaned back in the comfortable seat and listened for the sound of the motor. "They were dirty, smelly, inefficient, and expensive, and the reciprocating engine was about the silliest excuse for a motive force imaginable; yet I miss them." She examined her arm, resting on the door of the convertible. It seemed normal, the twill fabric of her sleeve rippling convincingly in the wind. She glanced at the speedometer, which hovered near 90. Her hands were tingling, anticipating.

Lys said, «We're tracking you beautifully, using the Papandreou satellites, no less. Good luck, and I'll talk to you again once you've entered the Net.» The line went dead.

Jason expected Dhimitri to turn. "You won't get away with it," he'd say, or "That setup doesn't fool me and it won't fool Alecko," or even "What the devil are you doing? Stop fidgeting!" But he continued to drive silently, one hand on the wheel, occasionally glancing over at her without surprise or even much interest. As she pulled her silvertip free from beneath her jacket, she could still see "her" arm resting casually on the low door of the car, and when she moved her head she could see peripheral traces of the hologram. She inserted the probe. («That's got it, Jason,» Lys said.) There were actually two separate holograms being broadcast, at enormous expense, one to show her present where she wasn't, and a mask to hide her presence. She could see the visible hologram, and the effect was disconcerting.

"Is something the matter? You seem abstracted." Papandreou was looking at her curiously.

"Sorry. I was drifting a little, I suppose." It was startling to hear her own voice replying. From now on she would remain quiet, while all "her" responses were given by Lys or by the computer.

«I tagged the switch-over to your silvertip insertion. One set of vital signs, no overlap, perfect transition. Lys out.»

"This trip was to be a vacation for me," "Jason" said, "a chance to see my brother and his children. It hasn't quite turned out that way."

"I can sympathize." Dhimitri's voice was mild. "I do sympathize. I always plan to take time off, next week or next month; and somehow the time never materializes. Do you know the twentieth century poet Walt Kelly?"

"I don't think so." Damn. Jason did. She hoped it wasn't a matter of record anywhere, in case Alecko, like Lys, was monitoring this drive.

"I forgot—your period is earlier, isn't it? You and Wolde Dawit both. Chaucer, Twain, Wodehouse, and the like. You should look up Kelly, though. I have the Galactica collection of his works. I've looked for the illustrated edition, but it's hard to find." The car whipped around another switchback. "There's one poem that summarizes my occasional attitude toward the company. 'Something, something, something, this life is for squirls; I'm off to the corner, to whistle at girls.' I wish I could quote the whole thing for you. Now, I don't know what a 'squirl' is, but I submit that the only true, meaningful life would be to stand on Kelly's street corner, admiring the people who attract you. But somehow I never quite get around to it." He sounded crestfallen. "We're here."

A uniformed attendant trotted out. "Good afternoon, Kyrie Papandreou, *kyria.* We've been expecting you." The attendant drove the car away.

"There are some advantages to owning a museum," Papandreou remarked.

"I suppose so. But I'd rank private parking attendants fairly low on the list. Let's go in." Do I really sound as pompous as that? Jason marveled.

They were in the massive entryway, walking through milling crowds—tour groups, waiting to be shown through the museum. Several gravitated toward Dhimitri, whose mane of white hair and well-cut suit leant him a doyenish air. He took Jason's arm. "If you don't want to head a parade of gawkers, we'd best look purposeful for a moment."

She allowed him to direct her path, thinking, I'll have to maintain my distance. If he reaches for the hologram after we've split up, the charade will be over. As if in response, the hologram said coldly, "Don't touch me again, Dhimitri. I've learned from Alecko; it's bad for the health to get close to the Papandreou family."

"I am not my son, *kyria*," he said stiffly, but thereafter maintained his distance. "Is there anything particular you wish to see?"

"The jewel gallery, of course, and Catherine's ruby. But first I'd like to see the antiquities. I didn't have time to study the 'Artemision' before." Jason stood still and let the hologram flow from her, following Dhimitri.

«Get ready, Jason. Denny's going to Hear for you, Jason,» Lys said, «and Bear's going to Feel. I've edited out everything but Denny's eighth nerve input, and left all but the eighth nerve material for Bear. And I'll be blocking the subsonics in a moment.»

Dhimitri looked gratified. "My son told me you liked the piece. So do I. There is so much spirit there, and such energy. That it has lasted two and a half millennia gives me hope for the human race." They stood silently watching, Jason waiting for a signal.

«I'm glad the computer's handling most of this, Jason! Right now I'm "seeing" through your eyes and through the hologram *and* through my own eyes. I don't know how you tolerate it; it gives me vertigo. On three, then. One. Two. Three.»

She reached forward. Her hand touched corroded bronze. Second test passed: the museum computer, workhorse that it was, was now overloaded. The crays had taken an average day's ingo/outgo, had extrapolated from it, and were now overriding the museum's computer with their own version of what was currently happening. Scanning lasers and other more lethal devices were still activated and operating; but if they were discharged, the computer would never know, the video hookups wouldn't show it, and, for the official record, nothing would have happened. The museum's computer was fairly fast for its type, but it handled data in a strictly linear fashion, sequentially as it occurred, and it needed to resolve each current problem before it went on to the next.

The crays wouldn't give it the time. Jason envisioned it as a short-order cook, swamped on the first day of a new job, and almost felt sorry for the pathetic, inanimate, underpowered device.

Dhimitri and her hologram had walked on, and were paused before an Elgin marble. Jason hurried to join them and was almost run down by a family of seven, moving hurriedly away from the anger and grief radiating from the Tikelian artifacts she'd seen on her previous visit; she'd forgotten, momentarily, that no one could see her.

She had to hurry to catch Dhimitri and "Jason." Lys said, suddenly urgent, «Stay away from the doppelgängers! They're on a different frequency than the rest of the museum's equipment, and apparently our broadcast interferes with their mechanism.» Cautiously Jason moved to the center of the room, avoiding the "windows" through which Alecko's strange tableaux could be seen.

Dhimitri paused to introduce "Jason" to a member of the museum staff, who held out a hand in greeting. Oh, damn, Jason thought, and stepped into position within the hologram like an actor toeing the mark. Jason had her silvertip in, the hologram did not. Lys couldn't shut off the image or the discrepancy might be noted. The hologram appeared to hesitate before reaching out "her" hand, and in that instant the match was made.

«We should have anticipated that,» Lys said. «We'll both have to be more careful.»

Jason held out her own hand. "Nice to meet you. You're fortunate to work in such beautiful surroundings."

The woman murmured politely and lost interest. She had a question, minor, which took only a moment to resolve. Dhimitri watched her walk away. "There you see one of the reasons why I seldom visit during gallery hours. If I had not been here, that woman would have answered her own question. But it is easier to ask me than to think, and so she took the path of least resistance. Many do, so that when I am here my time is consumed by petty little details, and work is done more slowly because people stop what they are doing to find me, to ask their questions. Really, the Papandreou runs more smoothly when I'm not present." He added in afterthought: "She's one of the few people I've recognized here today."

They stepped aside to let a tour group pass. They were wearing mufti in such a way as to make it obvious that they were more used to military dress. Apparently Alecko didn't trust his security system as much as he had indicated, and had provided a backup. Dhimitri, she was amused to note, was watching her as closely as Alecko had. It was terrible, the suspicion with which people viewed her. Now came the hard part: she could only wait.

"It's as beautiful as I remembered it." She gazed into the case, captivated by fire on velvet. Several other people were crowding close, and she was bumped more than once.

«If you can, lean closer,» Lys said. «I want to give the cray as much detail as I can, for the projection.»

Her vision suddenly blurred, and became preternaturally clear. «Lynch just joined us,» Lys said drily. «Maybe Master Alecko hurt his poor little ego; at least he came running home to mama. He understands that he's not to interfere, and that at the first hint of trouble I'll cut him out of the Net. I thought he might be helpful.»

Jason nodded. It was too late to do anything about Lynch now. She stepped closer, until the edge of the touch-me-not began to irritate. (Lys, with some justification, was not blocking the fields unless it was necessary.) Whoever had laid out the case knew design; the other gems complemented the ruby's blaze, but none came close to its beauty. There was only one star under that glass; the rest were window dressing.

"Please be careful, *kyria*. I would not like you hurt accidentally. The rest of you people, too. You can look all you want, but please keep your distance. If you want a closer look, we have microphotographic holograms in the viewing room." There was no flicker of light, no sound—indeed, nothing at all to signal that a masquerade had begun. But on the lower right side of the cabinet Jason now saw an almost insignificant nick, shining slightly brighter than the rest of the casing.

The crowd around her thinned. Jason stood still, and her hologrammatic image moved away through a gap in the crowd.

"She" followed Dhimitri, and the first band of people drifted away, too, listening either to the museum's discreet lecture or to Dhimitri himself, whose talk was in grand counterpoint to the museum's dry, just-the-facts approach. Another group now stood gazing placidly at an overlay which stood between them and the real jewel cabinet.

Dhimitri and "Jason" left the room, and a knot of people, in the wake of someone who seemed to know where he was going, followed along. Except for a few stragglers lost in the cavernous room, the jewel gallery was empty. Jason had been anticipating and now felt a slight tug on the Net, followed by a stronger pull. It came through Capella; but Capella was in a sensory deprivation chamber, isolated, unable to sense anything but the steady passage of time.

The alien presence, puzzled, withdrew, but remained hovering on the edge of her perception. It was faint, almost non-existent, and might easily have been drawn out of her imagination and memory.

Lynch felt it more strongly still. «*He's* the one who attacked the ship!» he said. He sounded relieved. «It isn't Alecko, then. I know what *he* feels like.»

The lock on the case was strong but simple; she had opened harder locks by the time she was ten. Touch-me-not fields and scanner rays: all very nice, but they gave a false sense of security.

Alecko opened a gallery door and walked quickly in. He muttered, "Excuse me," and shouldered an elderly couple aside. Something was wrong, but he didn't know what it was, and he paused with his hand on the top of the glass case, not four feet from Jason, looking around the room, uncertain what he was looking for. He pulled against the lid to check the lock. He ran his hand around the rim of the case. He looked up into Jason's eyes, (or so it seemed; for a moment Jason forgot that she couldn't be seen) and his expression was troubled. Finally he said, "Ladies and gentlemen, attention please." (At school in Tierra del Fuego, there'd been a guard dog, friendly but suspicious of strangers. Occasionally, for no reason Jason could ever see, he'd lift himself off the porch, walk stiff-legged down the flagstone path, and stand, sniffing the air and swinging his head from side to side, watching. That was how Alecko looked now.) "For security reasons, this gallery must be momentarily closed. It will be open again in half an hour. Please leave now, and thank you for your patience."

«We can wait until he leaves, too,» Lys suggested hopefully. Jason wouldn't risk speaking while Alecko was in the room, but she shook her head: no.

Alecko checked the case again, looked toward the hallway through which Dhimitri and "Jason" had exited, made a tentative start in that direction, and halted. "I know you're here, Jason; I can feel you," he said to the empty room. His expression grew petulant. He wasn't used to doubting the evidence of his senses.

Jason took out a small tool kit and waited. «You're close to your maximum heart rate, Jason,» Lys warned. «Don't burn off calories you may need later.» Jason selected a tiny probe, slipped on her gloves, thin enough to work through, and waited.

Alecko stepped away toward the corridor. Jason began timing herself, invoking Capella's skill. He was sixty seconds away; that gave her a minute to get into the case, and to get out again.

Ten seconds. She probed the lock and gently twisted. Alecko stood by the door, undecided. Fifteen seconds. Jason felt the first tumbler give and reversed direction, probing for the second. Twenty-five seconds. The second tumbler fell into place. Now the third; the fourth; fifth; and final. Thirty-five seconds.

He started back, walking rapidly, half running. Forty seconds, and she had the lid open. Forty-two. He was at her side, feeling something wrong, seeing nothing. He hesitated.

She didn't. Fifty seconds and she closed the lid, inserted her probe, and twisted, and twisted out of the way as Alecko stepped up to run a worried hand over the casing. She hunkered down by his feet, back against the glass of the cabinet, breathing shallowly. His hand, missing her by inches, paused at the lock. He leaned forward, palms on the metal rim, and peered in.

Jason fingered the velvet-wrapped package in her pocket. I could cut him now, she thought. He'd never see me. She set a hand down for balance instead and rose noiselessly to her feet. Dhimitri and her hologram would be on the lawn, waiting for the fireworks. She hoped the discussion would be foolish and inane so that she could in good conscience laugh without looking like an idiot. She felt like racing, but she walked instead, making no noise on the marble floors.

She checked her watch. Time was running out rapidly; even the crays could only manage to block the museum's computer convincingly for a short period of time. An hour was the upper limit; she'd used half that already.

A door, open earlier, was closing as she approached it. She recognized a pressure change; the building was being sealed. She risked one word. «Lys?»

«Alecko gave orders to shut down the building,» she said. «It's taken Dhimitri by surprise; they're arguing about it now. I can't talk much. Alecko is suspicious of "you," and he's following a little too closely for comfort. The crays are doing a good job of keeping you out of reach, but I want to monitor the conversation, in case of error. Lys out.»

Poor planning on Lys's part; that was one of the reasons she wasn't in command. But Jason couldn't protest because, though Lys's conversation through the Net could not be heard by Alecko because it directly stimulated the nerves, there was a possibility that Jason's might be; she subvocalized to make her conversation more clear.

The easy route to the garden was blocked, and time was running out. Jason headed in a generally northerly direction, remembering patterns of ramps and stairs from her previous visits and from her more recent study of Lys's blueprints.

She rounded a corner and almost ran into a troop of soldiers—Alecko's mercenaries, no doubt—who had linked arms to sweep the corridor. She moved back to let them pass, but a detachment of the group broke off and moved arm-in-arm through the hallway where she was standing.

Two were standing slightly farther apart than the rest; she dropped to a squatting position and let their linked arms pass over her head. (She could Feel their closeness.) They didn't quite brush her side with their legs.

She could (Denny now) Hear more troops approaching. The corridor was a dead end, the branches she'd tried locked. «Model,» she said, and hoped Lys was listening. She needed to orient herself. One of Lys's projections would help.

«Had it waiting.» Lys. «We'll talk later.» She saw a glass skeleton of the jewel gallery and adjacent rooms and halls suspended in her vision. Locked exits were shown in neon red on the model, and there were a lot of them.

The only open space was Alecko's doppelgänger gallery, so situated that it could not be closed off from the rest of the museum. She'd have to pass by the Tikelian sound sculptures, and the effect would be magnified in the Net. Already she was wearying of the supernally clear impressions she was getting, the stimulation from the museum artifacts. There was less to react to in space; it wasn't nearly so tiring.

Jason saw the rays of a scanner: Lynch, in the Net. It was a portable, not part of the standard museum security, and so not offset by the disinformation broadcast by the crays. Bear's awareness (less acute than Denny's, but still adequate) let her trace a weaving path through the beams. If one came in contact, it would be lethal; they were programmed for organics. No wonder she couldn't hear any troops in the immediate area.

The sound sculptures had an unexpected effect, because their weariness and sorrow triggered Bear's subdued and so-far inhibited mourning. Her grief was overwhelming, the sensation was so strong that it reverberated back through the Net, infecting both Denny and Lynch.

Bear's conviction that Alecko was responsible for her deafness was strong, and Lynch absorbed its impact directly; he began suddenly to doubt his own conviction that Alecko was innocent—a conviction that was based, after all, almost purely on his wish that he was right.

Good, Jason thought, I can use that; and she left the sound gallery and moved into the moving picture show.

A dog, running, reeled and fell as she entered. She moved past and it staggered to its feet and resumed its joyful gamboling; but now it was slightly out of sequence, and anyone who was familiar with the exhibit—for example, Alecko—would notice.

It was too late to be concerned. Time was passing. Her (Capella) hour was almost up. More troops entered, crouching behind shields held overlapped, like (and the image pleased her) ancient Roman soldiers. They weren't going to let her pass between them this time; Alecko must have noticed the hole in their defense and ordered it plugged. She assumed the shields came from the museum stores; if so, it was a particularly effective touch.

Amazing, she thought. Alecko doesn't even know—yet—that I've actually stolen the damn stone, and he's already spent more than its price on the open market trying to stop me. She (Bear) gauged her distance from the end of the hall to the wall of soldiers. Plenty of room to build up momentum. She backed away, ran forward lightly, and rolled into a forward flip, bouncing over the crouched line.

She was almost outside. One door, locked, was between her and the garden. She hoped it wasn't on the alarm system or, if it was, that Lys was paying attention and would compensate. It didn't really matter, because she intended to be outside in the next few minutes if she had to break a window.

. . . She arrived in the garden in time to watch Alecko trace a dainty and unintended minuet across the broad lawns as he stalked the hologram. «He knows something's wrong,» Lys commented, «but he can't figure out what it is.»

He was an empath and could feel that, somehow, the figure of Jason beside Dhimitri was only a shell. He circled closer, and closer still, and reached out to grab "Jason's" arm.

Jason removed her silvertip and slipped into the hologram envelope, and Lys cut the transmission.

She spun quickly, knocked Alecko's arm loose with one hand, and jabbed the stiffened fingers of her other hand into his stomach. His face crumpled in confusion. He had *known* there was no one there, just as he had *known* that Jason was in the museum after "she" had left with Dhimitri; but both times, it seemed, he had been wrong. He relied heavily on his feelings, which were generally more accurate than other people's physical evidence, and the punch in the gut had jolted him more mentally than physically.

"My pardon, *kyria,*" he said eventually. "You seemed distant, almost as though you weren't there. My curiosity got the better of me. I apologize again."

Dhimitri abruptly remembered the duties of a host. "Alecko, Captain Horiuchi is my guest. If you cannot restrain your hostility, you must leave."

Alecko said, "Of course, father," contemptuously. He left.

Dhimitri sighed. "And I am intending to turn my company over to him."

Jason said, "Yes. Even smart men may be stupid at times. Excuse me. I have to call my ship." She replaced her silvertip while Dhimitri watched with interest.

"It must be convenient to be in such constant contact with your people."

"It is, but as you said yourself, it requires submitting to 'mutilating surgery.' Of course, no Papandreou would deign to suffer through that."

Dhimitri watched her with dignified, sad eyes. "You're being extraordinarily offensive, Captain."

"Good. I mean to be." Where was Lys? Why hadn't she reported?

But then she did, sounding shaken. «Your timing was good, Jason. As soon as he left just now, Alecko attempted to attack you through Capella. Capella had a seizure. Apparently Alecko tried to awaken him. He didn't realize, or didn't care, that it wasn't possible. Capella's badly hurt.»

Jason's face whitened with the effort to control her anger. "Dhimitri, your son just attacked my crew. Again. Someone else"—she wouldn't call Capella a crew member—"has been hurt, and may die. Your son is becoming criminally dangerous. Will you stop him now—or shall I?"

Dhimitri rubbed a forearm wearily across his brow. "Jason, you're allowing your opinion of my son to create phantoms, so that every misfortune you suffer you blame on Alecko. Two of your crew members are arrested for theft; it's my son's fault. One of them later dies during corporal punishment; Alecko's responsible. A member of your crew has a seizure while *you* are trying to escape our jurisdiction; again, you blame Alecko! Can't you see that you're obsessed? That two of the incidents you cite are your fault, or your crew's, and that the third may legitimately have been an accident? Go home, Captain! Rest for a while. See a therapist, if you must. Later you will see this all in perspective."

Alecko returned. "The museum has been burglarized, father, while you two were touring." He turned. "Kyria Horiuchi, I would like your permission to search your person."

"Refused, Kyrie Papandreou."

He smiled wolfishly. "I insist." She saw a few of the museum guards assembling, not ostentatiously, behind him, and assumed there must be others behind her as well.

"She was with me all along, Alecko," Dhimitri said reproachfully. "Surely you can't suspect me of complicity, and I can assure you she took nothing while she was by my side."

"She stole something from my museum, father. I'm going to get it back."

"*Your* museum?" Dhimitri's tone sharpened. "You forget yourself."

"Father," he said, "*it's mine.*" He swung his arms wide, indicating the guards. "They came to *me* with information, father. Not you. You'd sit in your chair, breaking wind, worrying about giving offense, while looters walked off with all your goods."

"Dhimitri," Jason said, "have him call off his dogs."

He looked at her helplessly. "He's right. They're his dogs. I cannot."

"Good. Then I will."

Alecko looked up, astonished. "Are you *threatening* me, Captain? Here? You must be insane."

"As Terran ambassador, my powers are fairly broad. I'm considered a peace officer in the field. M'orru Fabris was a Terran citizen. I'm arresting you for her murder."

He chuckled. Lynch recoiled. She could feel his reaction; he had recognized in Alecko what he'd been trying to avoid. Good, she thought. Stay angry, Lynch. I can use that, too.

"M'orru Fabris died on your ship," said Alecko, "alone in a room, from an accident precipitated by a seizure disorder. As my father said. I was an AU distant then, in another ship. I could hardly be held responsible for her death, could I, Captain?"

She turned to Dhimitri. "Your son is insane."

Dhimitri bowed his head. "He is still," he said, "my son."

She prodded Capella (he was now little more than a shell, and dying; but he would last long enough for what she wanted) and watched Alecko react. She pushed harder, sending nerve inpulses skittering along the line, and Alecko jumped as though he'd been burned.

"That hurt, Captain," he said thoughtfully. She felt her own nerves catch fire, as had happened on board the *Argo*. But she was ready for his counterattack. As Kalb had suggested, it wasn't, after all, that strong. Now she was prepared; and she'd been using the Net *much* longer than Alecko.

Lynch had said something, quoting Bear. Seeing metaphorically; yes. Well, *metaphorically,* she wanted to see what she was doing to Alecko. She visualized his nervous system, laid out like one of Lys's models, lit up like neon, with the neurons controlling each of his senses a different color. The nerves along the myocardium—the structure surrounding the heart, part of the heart itself—flashed bright crimson.

Lovely, she thought, and squeezed.

When Alecko could breath again, and his chest had stopped hurting so badly, she said conversationally, using the Net so there'd be no record of what she said, «You told me what you were going to do when you called on my ship. I noticed your politeness then, and said I'd pay you back in kind. I'll start now. Your left arms are numb, Alecko, from the elbows down.»

His security forces started forward. "Halt," she said in a tone of voice she'd once used to command an army, and they stopped. Some of them glanced at each other nervously. "Retreat and regroup," she said, and some did.

Alecko said, "No!" His voice was shrill, not at all urbane, not at all civilized. "Stop her! The first to kill her can name his reward!"

Dhimitri was sweating. "You don't know what you're saying, Alecko! Look around you! There are people here who are listening to you, and they'll remember." He turned. "Captain, for God's sake, don't listen to him. You men. Please disperse! This is a private matter; it doesn't concern you, and you will not be needed."

Several of the soldiers started forward again; one, less alert than the others, ignored Dhimitri's warning. Or perhaps he simply had more faith in Papandreou power than the rest. He started forward, leveling his rifle.

She was still linked; Lys had kept the Net active when Jason disconnected. Time, and distance: she disabled him easily. "Next," she asked.

Something Proximate: she fell to the flagstones as a shot cut across the patio. These rifles had laser sights; she couldn't afford to ignore them.

Alecko, clutching his left side with his good right arm, tried to run. She stimulated the muscles surrounding his spine so that they cramped, so that each step would cause excruciating pain. «That's what it felt like to Rat just before he died,» she said. «I can demonstrate further, if you'd like.» He stood still.

«Do you remember what you did to Bear Vouris, Alecko?» she continued. «I described the feeling to a doctor. He called it 'odynacusis'—a big word which means 'painful hearing.' This is what it feels like.»

Alecko screamed. Jason looked at him without sympathy; without, actually, much emotion at all. Her anger was too consuming to permit anything but this methodical dismantling of Alecko's being. «I hired a boy, Lynch Lysikomos. You took him to bed. Do you know what he's afraid of, Alecko? I suppose now you do; that's why you seduced him, isn't it? He's afraid of going blind. That won't happen to him now, but let's see how you like it.» There were fewer lights on the schema now; another neon tracery blanked out.

Her ears began to ring, but only faintly; her sight blurred, but only briefly; her skin, slightly, began to itch; a faint odor of cinnamon filled her nostrils; and she tasted, momentarily, brine: Alecko, trying to respond in kind. She had felt Bear and Lynch and Denny recoil from their positions within the Net; and then each had relaxed, relieved.

Dhimitri couldn't hear what she was saying; he could only see the result. "He's my only son, Jason."

"But I'm not doing anything, Dhimitri. I'm not a telepath; I have no paranormal powers. I'm not even an empath, like Alecko. I can only affect people in my own Net—and you assured me no one in your family has had the surgery."

Possibly some center of Alecko's brain was too primitive to know it was beaten. He still stood, swaying raggedly, like a weathervane in the wind.

"Please." Dhimitri refused to look at her. "Please, Captain. Jason. Don't kill him. Whatever he may have done, he is . . . still . . . my only son."

Jason turned to Dhimitri, then back to the tottering figure. She stepped forward and brushed away the hair from his collar, and found what she knew would be there: a silvertip probe, mounted flat so it could be concealed beneath his collar. Whether it was from vanity or secretiveness she couldn't now say. She pushed the tottering figure. He staggered then, and fell. "You want him? He's yours."

Jason heard, off in the distance, a sputter of sound, and saw a flare on the horizon. Dhimitri stood over Alecko. He looked like a very old man. "The Tricentennial," he said. "Our time to—to *celebrate*. I had completely forgotten."

EPILOGUE

BEAR RUFFLED THE fur on her arm, covered in a loose silk blouse, and stretched and said, "The abbot asked me, somewhat diffidently, if I would mind wearing slightly more clothing when I come to services." She looked at her watch. "It's time for second vespers. Will you join me in the chapel? You, too, Denny; you'll appreciate what I'm going to show you."

She walked slightly ahead of Jason and Denny, to lead them, but deliberately for another reason as well. "One of the only good things about losing my hearing is that you can't interrupt me if I can't see you. You have to listen to me rattle on. Down these steps. Careful; it rained last night and they're slippery. Here we are." She whispered. "Quiet, now. The service will start soon."

The chapel was built in the form of a huge stone cross, with a mammoth stained glass window facing east over the altar, and another facing west, now ablaze with light from the evening sun. This was not the main cathedral, where tourists came to listen to the High Mass, but a smaller, more intimate church, and its austere pine-wood pews were filled now with robed monks at worship. Bear led them through the nave to the northern transept. She whispered again. "Lean against the stone, Jason. You too, Denny. The choir's about to begin."

The High Mass in Latin carries a heavy weight of tradition behind it. Accepted, rejected, banned, and reinstated over the years, Latin remained the major language of the Roman Catholic Church, whether in fact or clandestinely, during the Church's frequent attempts to be the church of Everyman. The first high notes of *Veni Creator Spiritus* rolled ponderously through the small chapel. The music washed like a tide over Jason, and for the moment other things seemed unimportant. She looked at Bear, whose eyes were closed and who was leaning into the wall, her back, arms, and the palms of her hands pressing against the gray stone. Denny, too, was pressing herself against the wall, rapt. Curiously, Jason did the same.

She had already felt the vibration through the soles of her boots; now it rumbled through her, deep bass shaking her bones. The longer the choir sang, the stronger grew the vibration, until the entire chapel was a single resonating chamber.

When it was over she exhaled. Breathing might have spoiled the spell. Bear's broad face was for the moment completely relaxed, at peace.

Later Bear said, "It's never been easy to lose something you treasure, and music was a big part of my life. Someone told me once that his hearing had sharpened, and that made up for his going blind; and I knew he was lying. But had I been able to listen to the choir when I first came here, Jason, I wouldn't have leaned against the transept wall, depressed, and I wouldn't have learned what I did in that chapel."

Jason was quiet. "I came up here to apologize," she said.

Bear nodded. "I know. You want to take everyone's failures as your own, Jason. You want to accept the blame for Lys's injuries, and mine, and for the deaths of Rat and M'orru. Well, you can't. We all chose to sail with you; we knew the risks.

"If you won't let us take responsibility for our own mistakes, Jason, we don't get to claim our successes, either." She fell silent as she negotiated a slippery, moss-covered slope. "I'm staying here, Jason; the abbot has offered me one of the visitors' cottages for as long as I want it. We've had bad times, you and I, and sometimes you make me angry; but I love you, and I hope you come back to see me." She held out her hand. "Good-bye."

"Good-bye, Bear." What else could she say? She held out her own hand. "I will come back. And good luck."

Denny was quiet, satisfied initially to look out the window of the bus at the changing barren landscape. But as the bus neared Moulinos, she said, "Bear was real hard on you, huh?"

"Not really." The ruby made a substantial lump in her pocket, uncomfortably pressing against her side. Lys had suggested she lock it in the ship's safe, but Jason preferred to carry it. And, she thought ruefully, she still had the hologrammatic pendants in the *other* pocket; she hadn't found the opportunity yet to give them to Lys. "Every once in a while I need to be reminded I'm not perfect."

Denny giggled. "Anyone who's sailed with you knows that, Jason." And: "What are we going to do now?"

She had rested her head on the back of the bus seat, lost in thought. Now she woke again. "Now? I don't know."

Denny watched the scenery pensively, and gnawed at a ragged thumbnail. "I never helped kill anyone before," she said. "I liked it at first. It was exciting. It scares me a little now." She turned in her seat until she was facing Jason. "Will Mr. Papandreou really let you walk away like this?"

Jason answered, knowing it wasn't an answer, knowing more questions would come. "Yes."

The bus slowed, and stopped. They got out at the terminal. Near Lynch's old apartment; near Kalb's office. Near Dhimitri's city residence, for that matter, and by the time Jason realized it, she was already drifting in that direction.

Denny was like a kitten puzzled by a strange closed box. *"Why?* I thought he loved Alecko. As much as anyone could, I mean."

"He did, Denny. And he'll try to strike back at me, some day. But for the moment, his board of directors won't let him."

Denny's puzzled look increased. "Why not?"

"It would bring him bad publicity, which could cost Papandreou et Cie money. There's no direct evidence linking me to Alecko's death. Dhimitri understands the principle."

"Alecko's dead, Captain! Isn't that more important to Mr. Papandreou than his company?"

"Certainly. But he's in control of Papandreou et Cie again; he can afford to wait, to attack me when I least expect it."

"It's just a game to you, isn't it?" Denny asked, honestly wondering.

Jason said seriously, "It is now. It wasn't when I was fighting Alecko. I'm sorry Dhimitri was hurt, but I'm not sorry Alecko's dead." She was eagerly anticipating extended, violent, potentially lethal and always unexpected future confrontations with Dhimitri. He was a more subtle fighter than Alecko had been; while he lived, he would make life interesting for her.

Dhimitri had replaced his burgundy curtains with black velvet, which were drawn tightly over the windows so no light escaped, and he'd hired professional mourners whose dolorous murmurings were nevertheless cut through sharply by a shrill, ceaseless chant: *"Khristos einai o Theos mou!* Christ is my God! Give alms for the love of the Lord!"

She saw him now, aged infirm, leaning between crutches against the wall. Denny stared. "Jesus Christ. How come he's still alive?"

"Fanatic devotion." And then she looked more closely. "No; maybe I'd say instead a unique skill for survival. How are you, Robinson?"

He grinned, exposing stained teeth. "Not bad, Captain Horiuchi. I wondered if you'd still recognize me."

"I almost didn't," she said. "So you're a professional. I thought you were just a dedicated amateur."

He pulled at his loincloth. "I've got my permit and everything. Of course, I had to lie about my name and my religion. Excuse me." A couple was passing. "I love the Lord," he shouted so fiercely it was startling. *"Khristos einai o Theos mou!* Have you no spare change for God's love?"

Jason looked up at Dhimitri's windows, heavily curtained. Had she been in the Net, she couldn't have felt the burden in her pocket more strongly. She looked at Dhimitri's window again and drew a thumbnail down her jaw, thinking.

And smiled. She spoke in the dhemotiki, the street speech of New Crete. "Old man, for the love of the lord, I give thee this," and added in English, "Take it, Robinson. It's yours."

She handed him the wrapped package.

He took it, still chanting. Then he glanced down and his rhythm faltered.

But she was already walking away.

ACE
SCIENCE FICTION
SPECIALS

Under the brilliant editorship of Terry Carr, the award-winning <u>Ace Science Fiction Specials</u> were <u>the</u> imprint for literate, quality sf.

Now, once again under the leadership of Terry Carr, <u>The New Ace SF Specials</u> have been created to seek out the talents and titles that will lead science fiction into the 21st Century.

— THE WILD SHORE Kim Stanley Robinson	08874-7/$3.50	
— GREEN EYES Lucius Shepard	30274-2/$2.95	
— NEUROMANCER William Gibson	56959-5/$2.95	
— PALIMPSESTS Carter Scholz and Glenn Harcourt	65065-1/$2.95	
— THEM BONES Howard Waldrop	80557-4/$2.95	
— IN THE DRIFT Michael Swanwick	35869-1/$2.95	
— THE HERCULES TEXT Jack McDevitt	37367-4/$3.50	
— THE NET Loren J. MacGregor	56941-2/$2.95	